And T

"The ones beh   !"
Camellion call

Automatically, he and Ray Merrit pushed back the sliding doors of the van, jumped out, spun around, and opened fire on the amazed AVO in the middle of the block. He cried out and fell sideways, his left side ripped and slashed by slugs. The man next to him, the AVO commander, stopped a bullet in his left shoulder bone, and tried to draw his pistol from the holster on his belt. His hand got as far as the flap. . . . He died in a splatter of bone chips when a slug shattered the front of his skull.

"Come on! Let's get the hell out of here!" yelled Merrit.

"The job is not done. Patience is the reward of all virtue," the Death Merchant said.

"Quite true, Mr. Camellion, but proverbs are the final sayings of dead men!"

And then came the earth-shaking explosion. . . .

The Death Merchant Series:

#23

DEATH MERCHANT
THE BUDAPEST ACTION
by Joseph Rosenberger

PINNACLE BOOKS   NEW YORK CITY

THE DEATH MERCHANT #23:
THE BUDAPEST ACTION

Copyright © 1977 by Pinnacle Books, Inc.

All rights reserved, including the right to reproduce this book or portions thereof in any form.

An original Pinnacle Books edition, published for the first time anywhere.

ISBN: 0-523-40-078-5

First printing, July 1977

Cover illustration by Dean Cate

Printed in the United States of America

PINNACLE BOOKS, INC.
275 Madison Avenue
New York, N.Y. 10016

Dedicated to Laszlo Lengyel—in appreciation for his having opened the Hungarian Special File

> "*Arise, Hungarians, the Fatherland calls you!*
> *The time is now! Now or never!*
> *Live oppressed—or live in freedom.*
> *That is the question to be decided!*
> *By the God of all Hungarians, we swear, we swear*
> *That we will nevermore be under the yoke.*"
>
> —Sandor Petofi (1823–1849)

CHAPTER ONE

Although the building was air-conditioned, the lightweight clothing of Richard Joseph Camellion and Thomas Lakatos was soaked with perspiration. But this was not only because they were burglarizing the Scientific Race-Protecting Institute. The Hungarian July night was unusually warm, the temperature almost 83 degrees. Physical exertion also played a major role.

The Institute was only a short distance from Kossuth Square in Pest, on the left bank of the Danube, which separated Buda from Pest by curving through the center of the Hungarian capital. The neo-Gothic building, built in two large sections of seven stories each and connected in the middle by a smaller section of five stories, on top of which was a tall clock tower, was surrounded by a twenty-foot-high decorative barrier, or wall, constructed of large glazed bricks of various shades and hues. The front gate was guarded day and night by green-uniformed members of the dreaded *Allamvedelmi Osztaly:* the State Security Authority, or, as the Hungarian secret police was more commonly referred to—the AVO. The two guard-houses inside the complex, one on each side of the attractive heavy-mesh gate, had also been designed to blend in with the tree-shaded parklike area between Rakocziut Utca and the Institute, which faced Rakocziut Street. Each guardhouse was built of green and brown bricks, the sloping roofs camouflaged to resemble leaves.

The breakin would not have been possible without the help of the *Kettos Kereszt Szovetseg:* the Society of the Double Cross—the name not derived from any form of treachery, but from the double-armed Cross of Lorraine, which the Hungarian underground organization used as its emblem. Not only was the anti-Communist group giving the Death Merchant all the assistance he needed, but

1

some of its cells in Budapest had even managed to obtain a set of the blueprints of the Institute building, as well as a schedule of the AVO guards and a schematic of the alarm system.

The various doors and windows were securely locked, each one protected by a photoelectric cell. Should any door or window be forced open, the circuit would break and an alarm would sound in the main control center on the first floor of the building's connecting section. The corridors were protected by high-frequency radar beams, but these detectors would not present any difficulty for the Death Merchant and Thomas Lakatos. Since the AVO made hourly rounds in the halls, the radar would be turned off.

At 11:30 P.M., Camellion and Lakatos—each man carrying a Hungarian Zel submachine gun in a small suitcase—had approached the Institute from the east, both realizing that if the guard schedule were not correct, the caper might fall apart before it even got started. At 10:48—no guard would be patrolling by the east wall for another forty-five minutes—the Death Merchant had tossed a special type grappling hook to the top of the wall. Connected to the hook was a knotted rope, which the two men had used to pull themselves to the top of the wall, then down again to the ground on the other side. A quick flip of the rope and Camellion had freed the hook.

Getting inside the building had been almost as easy. Camellion had used a glass cutter to trace out a large circle on the pane of the bottom window. He had then put adhesive tape over the circular section of glass, fastening each end of the tape to the larger section of the window before gently tapping the round piece free and pulling it carefully to the outside.

Working very quickly, the Death Merchant had taken a small Solenoid-Inductor Intensifier from his pocket, had reached through the opening in the glass, and had attached the intensifier to the right metal frame by means of the device's magnet. Under ordinary circumstances, the lower window would have to be raised to trigger the photoelectric alarm, but now it could be raised with safety,

2

the Solenoid-Inductor Intensifier making it impossible for the PE union-beam to break its cycle.

Putting his arm through the round opening in the glass, Camellion had reached up, unlocked the latch, and then, withdrawing his arm, had pushed upward on the bottom window. Quickly, he and Lakatos had crawled through the opening into the hall of the first floor. Rapidly but gently Camellion had closed the window, grateful that it was at the end of the darkened corridor where it would not be noticed by a guard, unless the man walked to the end of the hall and flashed a light over the window. The odds were that no guard would. Why bother to walk all the way to the end of the hall and check a window he had inspected and found secure earlier in the evening?

Camellion and Lakatos, moving through the hall lit with only a few dim guard lights, had gone to a rest room, assembled their submachine guns, and slung the weapons across their backs by means of leather straps. Camellion and Lakatos next pulled Diekmann P-66 .22 Magnum automatics from shoulder holsters and screwed noise suppressors onto the ends of the short barrels. They had to assume that they had been given an accurate schedule of the guards' rounds and that the corridors of the building would be free of patrolling AVO for the next half hour.

There would be only one AVO security officer in the east-end building: the guard at the desk in front of the bank of four elevators on the third floor. He was stationed there because the first office to the east of the elevators belonged to Dr. Imre Meleter, the chief biochemist of the government's Scientific Race-Protecting Society, and the mastermind in charge of the project being carried out in top secret at Karolyi Castle high in the Bakony Mountains of northwestern Hungary. Dr. Meleter was the inventor of the hideous NK-hk-4.

The goal was Dr. Meleter's office, or more specifically, his safe, which contained the report file of the progress being made toward the completion of the NK-hk-4 hallucinatory gas experiments. The Society of the Double Cross was positive that the safe in the office was at least fifty years old. The report was in that safe. That is why Thomas Lakatos had come with the Death Merchant. Not

3

only was Lakatos the backup, but it would be his task to find the correct file, once the Death Merchant had opened the safe. Camellion could not read Hungarian.

At least fifty years old! To the Death Merchant this meant that the lock on the vault was a simple cam-and-fly combination arrangement. Manipulation would be strictly a mechanical procedure. About twenty minutes was all Camellion would need to open the box. Another ten minutes to photograph the pages of the report, and then Camellion and Lakatos would quietly leave the building by retracing their route of entry.

Like two shadows, the deadly Dieckmann pistols in their hands, Camellion and Lakatos had crept from the rest room to the stairway fifty feet down the hall. Within a very short time, the two men were on the third floor, the Death Merchant crouched against the wall across from the top of the stairs, Lakatos right behind him. The AVO guard was around the corner in the corridor, twenty feet to their right. They could hear the man clearing his throat occasionally and now and then turning the pages of the newspaper he was reading.

Thomas Lakatos leaned closer to Camellion and whispered nervously, "The time is passing very quickly."

In reply, Camellion reached into the Swiss army-type shoulder bag resting against his left hip and pulled out a weapon that resembled a CO2 Pellet Pistol. But this pistol didn't fire BBs. It fired toxin-tipped darts—either to kill or to put to sleep—silently and accurately up to 250 feet. Moreover, the dart was so tiny—the width of a human hair and a quarter of an inch long—that it was almost undetectable.

The Death Merchant leaned around the corner, said *"Elnezest kerek!"* in a normal voice, and raised the dart gun.

In response to the Death Merchant's "Excuse me," the AVO man swung around, startled, his eyes widening with surprise. There was a low pop as Camellion pulled the trigger and the tiny dart struck the guard's right cheek. The guard tried to rise, closed his eyes, and slumped forward, sliding from the wooden chair, the Thiasulfaziazine

4

on the tip of the dart taking effect instantly. The drug had not killed the man, but it would keep him unconscious for several hours. Simulating a heart attack, the drug would quicken his breathing and make his pulse irregular. All attempts to revive him would be useless.

Camellion and Lakatos rushed to the desk. Richard picked up the unconscious AVO guard, placed him on the chair, brushed the almost invisible dart from the man's cheek, and permitted the body to lean gently forward so that the man's head rested on the desk, his arms hanging limply at his sides.

Camellion and Lakatos hurried to the door of Dr. Meleter's office, and Richard went to work on the door's Yale lock with a number 4 lock pick. The door and the office itself were another risk; yet Camellion was forced by circumstances to assume that the Society of the Double Cross was right and that Dr. Meleter's office was not protected by an alarm system.

If the SDC is wrong, I'll have to use some of the goodies in my shoulder bag. Even so, we still might not get out of here alive.

The lock clicked open. The Death Merchant wrapped his hand around the knob, turned it, and pushed open the door. He and Lakatos moved into the office, Camellion closed the door, and instantly began looking for the telltale signs of an alarm system. None was in evidence—no beam eyes of photoelectric cells or bulbs of audio or motion detectors.

"Watch the door," Camellion said to Lakatos, who followed him through the glass partition into the rear office, the section which was strictly the domain of Dr. Meleter.

Camellion and Lakatos paused when they were several feet past the partition, and Richard moved the beam of his penlight over the side walls of Dr. Meleter's office. What he found gave him a feeling similar to being told that he had only six months to live. For several long moments, Richard just stared at the walnut-paneled walls, his attention absorbed in the two horizontal strips, one on each wall. Waist high, the walnut strips protruded perhaps an inch from the walls. The Death Merchant had seen this type of decor many times before, and the strips had

5

always concealed plates transmitting a magnetic field throughout the room. When a foreign body disturbed the field, a signal was given at a central security station.

Directing his beam toward the rear of the office, Camellion received another shock. The vault, far from being at least fifty years old, was a modern 8′ x 5′ spin-wheel, slug-locked, structure-supported steel container. To open the vault would have required diamond-tipped drills or an electric torch and hours and hours of work. It was also bluntly obvious that the vault and magnetic field alarm had just been installed. Dr. Meleter's desk had been shoved against one wall, and pieces of walnut paneling of various lengths and widths were stacked in front of the vault. The work could have very well been done that same day.

"This is all wrong," whispered Lakatos, staring at the vault. "It looks brand new. Can you open it?"

"It is, and I can't," Camellion replied. He switched off the penlight and returned it to his inside coat pocket. "We're leaving. I think we've been spotted by detectors behind the paneling."

Lakatos cursed in Hungarian and moved alongside the Death Merchant, who turned and swung back through the partition. They were almost to the middle of the darkened outer office when the door to the hall was pushed gently open and an AVO man stepped cautiously into the opening, a 9mm NV-Budapesti pistol in his hand. The surprised Hungarian had time only to turn his head and shout a short warning before Camellion placed a long-nosed .22M projectile in his head.

"They're inside the office!" someone in the hall shouted in Hungarian. "Take them alive!"

Green-clad AVOs rushed through the doorway, oblivious to the security agent whom the Death Merchant had just killed. The man's body had fallen in the hall, close to the door, but the corpse didn't hinder the AVOs in their efforts to get to Camellion and Lakatos. The cadaver didn't hinder the Death Merchant either. Once more his Dieckmann pistol went *ZZZZTTtttt*, the .22M hollow point striking the first AVO just below the third button of

6

his shirt. The man snorted, grabbed his middle, and went down on one knee.

The pudgy Thomas Lakatos fired his silenced Dieckmann Destroyer, the .22M bullet grand-slamming into the target's stomach. Crying out in agony, the security slob grabbed his belly, staggered backward, and went out of action. By then it was too late for either Camellion or Lakatos to trigger off more shots. The AVO guards, determined to capture the two intruders alive, swarmed all over them.

Lakatos tried to poke the muzzle of his Dieckmann into the angry face of a tall AVO, but the man ducked and attempted to grab Lakatos' right wrist but Lakatos kicked him squarely in the groin, spun to the right, and ducked the barrel of an NV-Budapesti automatic aimed at the side of his head. The AVO, who had swung the weapon, wasn't fast enough to sidestep the .22 Magnum hollowpoint which Lakatos pasted in his belly. Nor was Lakatos able to dodge the two other guards, who rushed at him from the front. One man grabbed the wrist of his gun hand, the other aiming a fist at his square jaw.

The Death Merchant was not without his problems. One AVO made the fatal mistake of aiming at the Death Merchant's chest with a right-legged front kick, while two other AVOs rushed at Camellion from either side. Camellion blocked the kick with his right forearm, turned counter-clockwise with blinding speed, and, with his left leg, knocked the amazed man face downward with a sweep-kick, heel-smashing him in the side of the neck the moment he hit the floor.

The end of the Death Merchant's foot was still buried in the dying man's neck when Camellion felt two brawny arms dart around him from behind and fold tightly over his chest, pinning down his arms, locking them to his sides. Wanting to kick himself because he had not wasted his previous attacker with the Dieckmann Destroyer, Camellion found he had more trouble than just the man who momentarily had him pinned with a back bearhug. The other guard was coming in at him from the left, his big fist raised and aimed at Camellion's chin.

At 5'11" and 176 pounds, Richard Camellion was not

a big man; yet he was not only an expert's expert in hand-to-hand combat, but every muscle in his body was in superb condition, as efficient as coiled steel.

Camellion spun around, taking with him the man applying the bearhug. The man behind tightened his hold, determined to hang on. The Dieckmann Destroyer slipped from his right hand and fell to the floor. The second AVO, as determined as his comrade, ran around in front of the Death Merchant, just as Richard heaved himself upward a foot off the floor. Coming back down, he used his right foot to step with all his might on the right instep of the man behind him. There was a crunching sound as the astragalus and scaphoid bones shattered. The AVO howled in agony, the sudden, intense pain forcing him to release Camellion.

The Death Merchant, taking a deep breath, didn't have time to reach down and pick up the Dieckmann, not with the fist of the AVO in front hissing in toward his forehead. This time the man's hand was encased in steel knuckles.

The AVO stopped grinning when he found his intended blow neatly blocked by Camellion's left hand and arm. The next thing the AVO knew, his scrotum exploded with a pain he hadn't dreamed possible. He had only a dimming glimpse of Camellion's foot leaving his groin before the world turned a deep black and his consciousness left him.

Camellion returned his right foot to the floor, shifted to the left, and at the same time raised his left arm under the left arm of the tortured AVO who had been behind him. Bravely the man tried to fight back by striking out with a right-handed sword-ridge chop. The Death Merchant blocked the blow with his right forearm a hair of a moment before his left fist delivered a center punch to the AVO's solar plexus. The AVO gunman grunted in pain and it seemed that his eyes might pop out of his head. Camellion had more in store for the man. When the half-conscious man doubled over, the Death Merchant brought up his left knee, which connected solidly with the AVO's chin, and smashed his right elbow down on the back of

8

the goon's neck. More dead than alive, the AVO dropped, three of his vertebrae fractured.

Seven feet away, Thomas Lakatos had managed to duck the fist thrown at his chin and had slammed the AVO clutching his wrist with a front stab kick, the terrible blow to the belly forcing the AVO to his knees and causing him to moan in agony and to vomit uncontrollably.

The AVO who had thrown the right tried again. Once more Lakatos dodged, but this time he wasn't quite fast enough. The fist barely connected with Lakatos' chin, just enough to scrape the half-dozen layers of cosmetics that the Death Merchant had used in disguising him to look like no one even faintly resembling one Thomas Lajos Lakatos.

Lakatos threw a left uppercut, missed, and blocked another punch tossed by the AVO with his right forearm. The battle ended when the Death Merchant came up behind the AVO and chopped him across the back of the neck with a sword-ridge hand. The guard dropped like an anvil coated with lead, his eyes rolling back in his head.

"We'll have to fight our way out," Camellion said ominously. Turning, he scooped up the Dieckmann Destroyer, shoved it into his shoulder holster, and removed the Zel submachine gun from his back.

Lakatos removed his own Zel and pulled back on the cocking knob.

"I don't understand it," he said, an expression of disbelief on his face. "Even if there is an alarm system in Dr. Meleter's office, the AVO couldn't have gotten here as fast as they did. But they did!"

The Death Merchant stepped over an unconscious AVO, one hand dipping into the bag on his hip. "The tipoff must have come from the desk in front of the elevators. Probably the guard was supposed to phone in. When he didn't, the AVOs came to investigate, found him, and were just about to check the office when we spotted them."

"Our plan is bankrupt. The way things are going, our chances of reaching Frantisek are practically nil." Lakatos, who was very nervous, watched the Death Merchant

9

move closer to the door. The Hungarian moved alongside Camellion, who pulled a P-T grenade from the bag, got down on one knee by the door, and licked his lower lip.

"Our escape plan isn't bankrupt, not by a long shot," Camellion said, "although I must admit it's on the fourth mortgage and six months behind in payments. Our only chance now is to use the stairs. Get ready with one of your smoke grenades."

Camellion leaned forward, stuck his head out the door, and took a quick look up and down the corridor. Two groups of AVOs were creeping down the hall, one from each direction, the closest knot of men, to Camellion's right, not more than fifty feet away, the second group, eighty feet away, still at the end of the hall. When the AVOs to the right saw Camellion, two of the men raised their Kiraly submachine guns, but Camellion ducked back too quickly for them to fire. They didn't stop their forward movement. For a moment they slowed down; then they increased their speed.

"They're walking right into it!" Camellion said almost happily. He pulled the pin from the phosphorus-thermite grenade and pitched it forcefully through the doorway, throwing it to the right.

The Death Merchant put down his submachine gun at the same moment that the P-T grenade exploded with a loud hiss. Like a great snow-white flower suddenly opening, the incendiary splashed its intensely burning petals of phosphorus and thermite all over the men of the advancing AVO contingent. The dozen AVO men, totally helpless against the billion drops of liquid fire, screamed hideously.

Within seconds the phosphorus and the thermite were burning through their uniforms and eating into their flesh, seeking their very bones. The dying AVOs could have been a troop of howling monkeys turned loose in a banana store as they screamed and rolled on the floor— only monkeys wouldn't have burned. The flesh of the monkeys wouldn't have dripped from their bones.

"Give me your smoke grenade," Camellion said, holding out his right hand without looking at Lakatos and reaching into his hip bag for another P-T grenade with his left.

Lakatos placed the smoke grenade in Camellion's hand. Richard pulled the tab with his teeth, flipped the canister through the door to his left, said, "One, two, three," then pulled the ring on the P-T grenade and tossed it to his left. He picked up his Zel chatterbox and glanced at a wide-eyed Thomas Lakatos, who was only twenty-seven years old and had never been a part of such instant, effective slaughter.

"Stay behind me," Camellion said. "Keep low and fire short bursts to the right."

The loud shrieking to the right had stopped, replaced by some screaming to the left, from those AVOs who had been caught in the splash of fire, which was melting them into eternity.

"Now!" Camellion said sharply.

The Death Merchant jumped out of the doorway into the hall, the Zel submachine gun, its muzzle pointed to the left, roaring and jumping in his hands, a stream of 7.62mm projectiles tearing through the thick black cloud of smoke and boring into the screaming AVOs, some of whom had become blazing torches, blazing to the extent that the cartridges in their belt pouches were beginning to explode.

Although terrified, Lakatos was right behind the Death Merchant. He muttered prayers in Hungarian, his finger light on the trigger as he hosed the area to the right with short bursts, although he felt it was simply a waste of ammunition. Nothing moved. There were only the corpses of the burning AVOs, the pop-pop-popping of exploding pouch cartridges, and the stink of well-cooked flesh. But Lakatos was too frightened to vomit.

The Death Merchant, way out in front, caught a quick flash of the guard at the desk in front of the bank of elevators. The man still lay face downward, his arms at his side. Another AVO, coughing from the trioxide-chlorosulfonic screening smoke, crouched at the end of the desk facing the stairs. Catching sight of Camellion, the man did his best to lift his Soviet-made Makarov automatic and send a nine-millimeter bullet at Camellion. His finger

11

didn't even get to press the trigger. The Death Merchant scattered his skull and brain with four Zel projectiles.

Camellion pushed himself against the wall paralled to the top of the stairs that angled downward to the second floor. Next to the stairs was the flight leading to the fourth floor. Richard pulled the nearly exhausted magazine from the Zel, shoved a full clip into the Hungarian submachine gun, and placed a cartridge in the firing chamber. Lakatos, behind Camellion next to the wall, also reloaded. The young Hungarian was so nervous he looked as if he might suddenly disappear, leaving only his clothes in a rumpled pile on the hallway floor.

A siren started to scream from the direction of the front gate.

The Death Merchant leaned around the corner of the wall and raked both sets of stairs with the full clip of high-velocity cartridges, the numerous ricochets blending in with the monotonous wail of the alarm siren. He pulled out the empty magazine, dropped it to the floor, and reloaded the hot weapon, for a moment recalling the series of events that had culminated in placing him in this extremely dangerous position in which his only salvation—and Lakatos'—was flight.

Nine days earlier, Camellion and Raymond Merrit, a CIA street man, had entered the People's Republic of Hungary, their West German passports and Hungarian visas identifying them as citizens of the West German Federal Republic and members—brothers—of the Catholic monastic order of Benedictines. Camellion, as Brother Helmut Krim, and Merrit, as Brother Hugo Schmid, had supposedly left their monastery near Cologne and had come to Hungary to make the pilgrimage to the shrine of Our Lady of Bakony, which was reputed to be a kind of Lourdes in miniature, complete with miracles, such as the healing of the sick. If nothing else, the yearly July pilgrimage to the shrine in the Bakony Mountains was a great tourist attraction, drawing religious people from all over the world. Tourists meant money. This was one reason why the Hungarian Communist government had not closed the four-hundred-year-old shrine. The other reason was that freedom of religion was supposed to exist in Hungary. It did, but at a price. All religions enjoyed equal standing, the churches, Catholic (the largest denomination), Protestant, and Jewish, separate from the state, yet receiving government subsidies. In turn, the government had the right to appoint its own nominees to any ecclesiastical post not filled within a stipulated period. All ecclesiastical appointments had to have state approval, and all the clergy had to take an oath of allegiance to the state. However, most men of the cloth felt that they were not bound by the oath. One could not swear falsely in any agreement with hell. One's duty to God came first.

The Death Merchant was not counting on divine intercession to help him and "Brother Hugo Schmid" get to Karolyi Castle, which was only five miles north of the shrine. It was at Karolyi (*hawk* in Hungarian) Castle that—if the intelligence report was true—a fantastic weapon was being developed: NK-hk-4, an hallucinatory gas that didn't kill, but kept its victims deranged for as long as two weeks, reducing them to the level of idiots. Colorless, tasteless, and odorless, NK-hk-4's value lay in its power and its worth as a weapon of war. One liter (1.06 quarts) would suffice to immobilize a city the size of New York. The possibilities were more than fantastic: they were mind-boggling. An aircraft could spray the gas over the city. Within a few hours at the most, millions of people would be staggering around like drunks, unable to think, slobbering, crawling on their hands and knees, having lost even their individual identities.

The second terrible potential of NK-hk-4 was that it wouldn't damage the hardware of the city attacked. Not a single building would be affected. Some accidental fires would be started by the deranged populace, but in general the city would remain intact, its public utilities and other vital functions undamaged. In contrast, the explosion of a thermonuclear device would leave tremendous devestation, a radioactive wasteland of no value to anyone.

The Central Intelligence Agency could not afford to ignore the direct threat to the United States. The puzzle was why the development of the gas was being carried out in Hungary. Why not the Soviet Union? Or was the gas strictly a Hungarian project? If so, did the Soviets know

13

about the gas? The company had to have answers, and Richard Camellion was the man elected to get them. His assignment was to obtain the NK-hk-4 formula and destroy the laboratory at Karolyi Castle.

There was another little chore that the company wanted the Death Merchant to perform: take direct action against Dr. Imre Meleter so that he wouldn't be able to duplicate the formula.

At the moment, the Death Merchant was of the opinion that he would be extraordinarily lucky if he and Lakatos stayed alive long enough to get out of the building. He'd consider it a near-miracle if they succeeded in getting back to the priests' home at St. Matthias Church in the Rozsabomb (Rosehill) section, on the other side of the Danube. In keeping with their cover, Camellion and Merrit were staying at St. Matthias Church, which was run by the Benedictines. All seven of the priests had taken an oath of allegiance to the Hungarian government. Four of the Benedictines were members of the Society of the Double Cross. One of the priests, Fr. Dominic Redlich, had been at the church for only three months. He had been appointed by the government's Department of Religious Affairs, and the other priest suspected that he was an AVO informer.

The Death Merchant took a deep breath. "Let's try for the second floor," he said to Lakatos. "If we can get to the outside, we'll have a chance."

Camellion moved from the wall and rushed to the top of the stairs that led to the second floor. Machine gun ready, he started to creep down the stairs, his eyes moving from left to right, then stabbing into the semidarkness ahead of him. Panting, Lakatos stopped as Camellion paused at the bottom of the stairs and looked around the small area. Because the stairs were located in an inset, Camellion could not see the length of hallway. It didn't matter; there wasn't time.

He and Lakatos hurried to the final flight of stairs. Twenty-five feet below was the ground floor—*and there have to be AVOs on all sides of the building. Damn!*

Expecting a savage blast of gunfire any second, the two

14

men moved down the stairs, crouched so low they looked deformed. They were almost to the bottom of the stairs, which made an S-curve and opened into the lobby of the building, when Camellion heard feet moving over the marble floor, the telltale sounds coming from the left, from the direction of the AVO Central Security Center. Accompanying the sounds of shoe leather on marble were the jerking beams of numerous flashlights, the horizontal columns of light cutting the darkness ahead.

"Let's use our hand grenades," whispered Lakatos, who had also detected the approaching AVOs and knew that the enemy hadn't yet seen him and Richard Camellion, because the lights over the stairs were not turned on.

The Death Merchant began to creep toward the bottom of the stairs.

"We'll need one hand grenade for the front door and the rest for the back gate," he said, turning in the direction of the jerking and dancing yellow beams, which by now were no more than a hundred feet away. Afraid that the agitated young Hungarian might disobey and blow the show, Camellion added roughly. "We've only three grenades each. Do as I tell you—unless you want to walk on the carpet of heaven or sit on the hot furniture of hell!"

Camellion was about to thrust the barrel of his Zel through the ornamental iron railing on the left side of the stairs as one of the beams of light raked briefly across his face.

"Get down!" he hissed at Lakatos. He jumped up and threw himself forward, firing to the left in a wide, sweeping motion as he fell to the hard floor, his first few cartridges exploding a few moments before several of the AVOs, catching sight of him, raised their Zel submachine guns and fired long bursts. Some of the AVOs' copper-gilded slugs struck the ornamental designs of the railing and zinged off with loud, drawn-out whines. Other bullets passed through the embellishments of the left railing, burned through the air over the stairs, and either went past, or ricocheted from, the filigree work of the right railing. None of the slugs came close to Camellion or Lakatos, who had dropped to his back on the stairs.

The Death Merchant's first blast killed four of the

15

AVOs and mortally wounded three more. The dead and the dying, some of the AVOs crying out in fear and pain, crashed to the floor. Those who hadn't been hit had only a split second to drop the muzzles of their submachine guns toward Camellion and pull the triggers. But during that lag-time, Camellion fired another curvilineal blast, and Lakatos—his speed surprising Camellion—triggered off a long, raking burst. Only one AVO managed to pull the trigger, and his slugs sizzled a foot over Camellion. Then he, too, was grunting and falling into eternity with the remaining three AVOs.

"Let's move!" Camellion shouted, and got to his feet, the smell of burnt cordite strong in his nostrils. He waited until Lakatos caught up with him, then began running down the long hall, going to the left. He reloaded his Zel as he ran, thinking of how the sound of his and Lakatos' feet on the marble continued to echo, reminding him of an empty, half-darkened tomb.

Fifty feet ahead was the front entrance.

Outside was more death.

CHAPTER TWO

One wounded AVO man tried to rear up, open the flap of his holster, and reach his Budapesti pistol—a useless effort which a three-slug burst from the Death Merchant's machine gun caused to fail. The AVO flopped back and dropped into infinity.

Camellion stopped twenty feet in front of the tall double doors that opened to the outside of the building and looked up and down the darkened lobby and the hallway which, beginning on each side of the lobby, traversed the length of the Scientific Race-Protecting Institute building. Except for tiny night lights on the walls, the long corridor was deserted, as empty as the lobby that contained only marble pillars, a statue of Lajos Kossuth ("the George Washington of Hungary") and a huge red, white, and green Hungarian flag on the rear wall. Underneath the

16

flag, in three-dimensional Gothic letters made of black marble, were the words *ISTAN ALDD MEG A MAGYART*—"God Bless the Hungarian."

This is one hell of a way to spend the middle of the summer, Camellion told himself, and moved over to the bronze statue of Lajos Kossuth, in front of whose base stood Thomas Lakatos, looking twice as uncomfortable as a schoolboy passing a graveyard at midnight.

"Watch the hallway, but do it from behind a pillar out of the line of fire from the front doors," Camellion ordered, "and give me the rest of your smoke canisters and your hand grenades."

His right hand going to his kit bag, Lakatos' eyes glistened and his voice quivered. "What are you going to do, Camellion?"

"I'm not going to throw firecrackers to get us out of here!" Camellion said simply, opening his hip bag with one hand to receive the smoke canisters and hand grenades. "Do what I tell you, and when I tell you to follow me, do it. Now get behind one of the pillars."

The Death Merchant, his swiss army bag bulging with smoke canisters, six hand grenades, and three P-T burn bombs, ran to the doors, looked behind him to make sure that Lakatos was not in the line of fire from outside, then lifted his Zel and shattered the two locks with a dozen 7.62 millimeter slugs, the series of rapid explosions echoing up and down the empty lobby.

He pushed open one of the doors and jumped to his right, expecting a burst of gunfire from the outside. But nothing happened. The AVOs were playing it cool.

The windows in the front of the lobby were wide and went from floor to ceiling. The Death Merchant ran to the third window to the right of the doors, took a position to one side of the window, and looked out into the night bathed in warm moonlight. Not a single AVO was in sight. Camellion wasn't fooled. There had to be secret police stationed behind the trees, waiting. He looked down the long road toward the gate, yet was unable to see the guardhouses because of the intervening trees.

There was still hope, however. Parked in front of the steps were several Geza automobiles and two Hungarian

17

versions of a military medium cross-country personnel car. AVO vehicles—two white arrows crossed above and below the Hungarian flag were painted on the front doors. Odds were that the personnel cars wouldn't need a key to turn over the ignition. *All I'll have to do is press the start-button.*

The siren at the front gate continued its mournful wailing.

The Death Merchant hurried back to the side of the door he had pushed open, then turned and motioned to Lakatos, who was watching him. The young Hungarian trotted over to Richard, who handed him a demolition grenade.

"Listen carefully; here is what I want you to do," Camellion said. "Go to the very last window in front, shoot out the bottom, and throw the hand grenade as far as you can. Take your time with the grenade. Make sure it goes through the window. Then run back here as fast as you can. But don't pass in front of the windows. When you go to the last window and come back here, take a route behind the second row of pillars. Get going."

Lakatos, doing as Camellion had instructed, scurried back to the columns, then turned and ran to the last window. As afraid as he had ever been in his life, he placed his hand grenade on the cold marble floor, looked at the window for a moment, then raked the lower section of glass with a short burst of Zel slugs. Pieces of glass were still falling to the floor when Lakatos pulled the ring of the grenade and, first measuring the distance, threw it through the window as hard and as far as he could. Seven seconds later, the grenade exploded with a *BEROOOMMMMMM* that rattled the rest of the windows, the brief flash of flame, fifty feet ahead, winking like a giant eye in the darkness. Almost at the same time, the first of the Death Merchant's smoke canisters landed twenty feet in front of one of the personnel cars, between the car and the trees, and began to hiss tar-black smoke from the holes around the bottom of the can. Camellion flung a second and a third and a fourth canister, spacing them out as best as he could. In the meanwhile, Thomas Lakatos sprinted back to Camellion. By the time he

18

reached the Death Merchant, the smoke outside the building was almost a solid black wall, some of it drifting on a light breeze through the open door.

"We're going to get in one of those personnel cars," Camellion said, "and drive around to the truck gate in the back. But don't fire or you'll give away our positions."

Lakatos stared at Camellion, his face the color of wax. "We can't dodge machine-gun bullets!" he protested. "Why don't we go out the back way?"

"We need transportation, that's why," Camellion pointed out. "They can't see us. Once outside, we'll belly-crawl to the car. The odds are on our side."

"It seems like a good way to die, if you ask me!"

"We live in the midst of death," Camellion said with a slight laugh. "The very hour that gave us life begins our death. I'll go first."

Without waiting for Lakatos to reply, Camellion got down on his hands and knees and crawled through the door into the thick smoke, doing his best not to cough as the black fog enveloped him. He dropped to his belly and began to slither, determination giving him extra energy, just as naked fear drove Lakatos to extra effort. Then Lakatos, too, was past the steps and crawling on the ground behind the Death Merchant. They were halfway to the parked vehicles when half a dozen submachine guns opened fire. Having stepped out from behind trees, some of the AVOs fired at the window shot out by Lakatos, the others sending a storm of leaden death at the open door hidden by the rolling black smoke.

In less than two minutes, Camellion and Lakatos reached one of the personnel cars and climbed in. Up front on the driver's side, Richard put his submachine gun on the seat, sat up, made a quick search of the dash, and was relieved to see that the ignition wouldn't require a key. He settled down in the seat, pushed the starter button, and yelled at Lakatos, who was in the rear, "Rake all the trees in front when I pull out."

"I won't be able to see what I'm shooting at!" Lakatos said. Finding it difficult to believe he was still alive, he began to roll down the rear window.

"You don't have to. Sweep the trunks as best you can. The firing will keep the AVOs down."

The Death Merchant gunned the motor slightly, shifted gears, and backed the car out. Shifting again, he turned and drove along the north side of the building, the tires screaming and shrieking on the concrete.

Camellion's unexpected move didn't give the AVO guards behind the trees much time to formulate a new plan. By the time they realized how they'd been tricked, the personnel car was roaring away and Lakatos was spraying the trees through the rear window, tiny flashes of flame flashing from the muzzle of his Zel. The streams of deadly slugs banged into a lot of birch and maple and came very close to several AVOs, but didn't kill or wound anyone. Several moments later, fate stepped in and snatched away the life of an AVO—all due to the Death Merchant's turning the car sharply to the left as he turned the corner and drove up the west end of the building. The sudden shift in motion, during the height of the turn, threw Lakatos to the left side of the car and caused the barrel of his Zel to veer up. It was then that one of his slugs found an AVO officer, who was in one of the maple trees. The bullet bored into the man's left eye, made mush of his brain, and tore out the back of his skull. The Hungarian secret policeman did not even have time to cry out.

The personnel car shot up along the west end of the building. Camellion slowed at the southwest corner, again turned sharply to the left, and pressed down on the gas pedal. Jumping like a wild animal, the car streaked between the empty parking lot and the rear of the building, Camellion moving the car south toward the service gate in the southeast corner of the security fence.

Thomas Lakatos raked the windows of the first floor with his machine gun. Suddenly the weapon clicked on empty and he jerked the empty magazine from the automatic weapon.

"I'm out of ammunition!" he yelled at Camellion, who jammed on the brakes, skidding the car to a full stop fifty feet in front of the double mesh-steel gates.

"Here's my last one," he said, and turned and handed the 43-cartridge clip to Lakatos across the top of the seat.

20

"Watch the northwest corner and make every shot count. I'm going to blow the gates."

The Death Merchant got out of the car on the driver's side and pulled a hand grenade from his Swiss army hip bag. He jerked the pin, tossed the grenade toward the line where the two halves of the gates came together, and quickly dropped down by the side of the car. The inside of his head was still buzzing from the explosion when he pulled two more grenades and Lakatos, still in the rear seat, opened fire at the second personnel car roaring around the southwest corner of the Institute. Four AVO men had piled into the second vehicle and were foolishly rushing in to attack the Death Merchant and Lakatos. None of the four realized it, but all they were doing was hurrying to their own executions; and although Frigyes Huszar, the driver, began to swing the car from left to right, he couldn't escape the second blast of Lakatos' high-velocity Zel projectiles. Neigher did Lajos Nemes, the man next to him in the front seat. They didn't hear the roaring of Lakatos' submachine gun either, the rapid four-second blast lost in the two thunderous detonations of the two hand grenades, which blew open the closed gates, the two inward ends flying outward.

Within the car there was no time to think, no time to do anything but die. The front windshield of the AVO car dissolved, and the lives of Huszar and Nemes instantly terminated, lead 7.62mm projectiles puncturing their faces and necks, the forward motion of the car sending a wave of blood washing over Jeno Benkei and Mihaly Apro in the rear seat.

"The wheel! Grab the wheel!" yelled Jeno Benkei, who was on the right in the rear seat. Looking as if he had just overdosed on a thundercloud, Benkei was utterly helpless, and so was Mihaly Apro, who leaned over the front seat and tried frantically to push aside the dead Huszar, who had collapsed over the wheel, his foot jammed down on the gas. But it was die-time for Benkei and Apro. Huszar's arm, caught in the wheel, turned it sharply to the right as Apro tugged at the corpse. The car veered to the right and, with a grinding and a screaming of metal

21

and men, turned over twice, rolled into the high steel-mesh fence, and exploded into a bright ball of flame.

The screaming stopped. The flames, edged and laced with oily black smoke, grew larger. Suddenly the gas tank exploded, scattering fire and parts of metal and men as Camellion and Lakatos roared through the jagged inside ends of the truck gate. The personnel car sped along the short drive to Kozma Street, Camellion hunched behind the wheel. At the end of the drive, he turned to the left and headed into the thin traffic, his mind clicking out calculations with the speed of a computer. *Only six blocks to Rakocziut Boulevard. After that, only three blocks to the second transfer. Then two and a half blocks to the Szechenyi Bridge over the "Beautiful Blue Danube." We just might make it over to the Buda side of the city!*

"I'm beginning to feel like we're freaks in some kind of circus!" Lakatos said, wiping his face. Having crawled into the front seat, he turned and looked through the rear window to see if anyone was following.

The Death Merchant smiled. "It's a circus all right, and we're the two clowns in the center ring. Cheer up. The worst is over. If we can get to Frantisek and Mihaly in the first car, our chances for escape will have increased fifty percent."

Camellion's eyes bored into the pavement ahead. Since it was after midnight, traffic was scanty. This was the middle of the week. Tomorrow was another long workday, and most Hungarians were asleep. There were, however, some pedestrians on the streets, and already several cars, going in the opposite direction, had passed Camellion and Lakatos, their occupants staring fearfully for a moment at the bullet-riddled personnel car. The only advantage Camellion and Lakatos had was that the streetlights were burning only in the middle and at each end of every block. The windows of storefronts were dark.

Camellion kept to forty miles per hour, the legal limit, every now and then glancing into the rearview mirror. He and Lakatos had covered only a black and a half when he spotted the four-wheel, light armored AVO car turning from the Institute's back drive onto Kozma Street.

"Oh, my God!" muttered Lakatos. Twisted around in

the seat, he stared at the three-man armored car, with its twin 7.62mm Pekhotni light machine guns protruding from the boxlike turret. Its two recessed lights glowing, the armored car speeded up when the driver caught sight of the fleeing personnel car.

Lakatos turned to the Death Merchant, looking like a man about to ride piggyback on a buzzsaw. "What are we going to do now?" he asked and reached into his coat pocket. "They'll rip us to pieces once they get close enough to use those machine guns. They've seen us and they're coming in fast!"

Camellion glanced up at the rearview mirror and pushed down on the gas pedal. The car shot forward.

"Yes, but only if they get close enough," he said. "Hang on!"

The personnel car was only a short distance from Eotvos U., which intersected Kozma Street and stretched out in a north-south direction. The car tore by another car that was headed west, the Death Merchant amused at the startled face of its driver. Looking in the rearview mirror, Camellion saw the man pull over to the curb and park, as required by law at the approach of any speeding AVO vehicle.

Just as Camellion turned the car to the right and swung around the corner onto Eotvos U., the AVO gunner in the turret of the armored car opened fire. Several minutes earlier, the alarm siren at the front gate of the Scientific Race-Protecting Institute had quit howling, and the roar of the brace of Pekhotnis shattered the quietness of the night. Luck wasn't with the AVOs. Camellion had turned too quickly, and the gunner's thirty or forty projectiles cut through empty space.

Holding onto the steering wheel with his left hand and fumbling in his kit bag with his right, Camellion headed south at seventy miles per hour. He surprised Lakatos by slowing the car almost to a stop in the middle of the pavement halfway down the block. Then Camellion came to a full stop. The motor continued to run.

"We can't fight it out here, not in the middle of the street!" protested Lakatos, his voice quavering with fear. Grimacing with suspense, his mouth fell open and he

23

stared at the Death Merchant, who had taken three P-T burn bombs from his bag, opened the door on the driver's side, and was now putting the three bombs side by side on the pavement.

Camellion closed the door, put the car in gear, and fed it gas. The car leaped forward, its engine roaring. The Hungarians made more than excellent wine; they also turned out excellent automobiles.

"If you're going to try what I think you're going to try, it won't work!" yelled Lakatos. "We're out of machine-gun ammo!"

The Death Merchant's expression was enigmatic. "I'll use the twenty-two," he said, his voice carrying a well-honed measure of ridicule. "How can I miss? I have all the light I need from the two streetlights in the middle of the block."

He pulled the Dieckmann P-66 pistol from its shoulder holster and jammed on the brakes when the personnel car was almost at the end of the block, the tires protesting loudly on the pavement.

Perspiration pouring from his face, Lakatos pulled out his own Dieckmann Destroyer as Camellion jumped from the car on the driver's side, got down on one knee, and raised the weapon military style, his left hand around his right wrist. He waited, sighting in on the first P-T bomb a hundred feet to the north.

Across the street, on the east side, an old begger, suspecting a lot of trouble was about to explode, ran to the door between the front windows of a clothing store and crouched down.

The Death Merchant got what he was waiting for. The armored car slowed, tore around the corner onto Eotvos U., and then, when it was on a straight stretch, increased speed. The driver, seeing the personnel car parked in the middle of the pavement at the end of the block, pushed down even harder on the gas pedal and yelled up to the gunner in the turret, "Don't waste ammunition. Wait until we're close before you open fire."

The radioman, next to the driver, said, "Those pigs have probably deserted the car and are on foot. The report said there were two of them."

24

The driver, a hotshot with a great mop of red hair, spotted the three gray P-T packets when he was forty feet away from them, but he didn't realize what they were. Anyhow, he knew he could drive around the objects, whatever they might be. It wouldn't have mattered if he had tried to stop: the armored car was moving at about seventy-five miles per hour. The driver was confidently turning the wheel as the Death Merchant sighted in and pulled the trigger of the Dieckmann three times in quick succession. There were three *bzittss, bzittss, bzittss.* Three .22 Magnum bullets struck the first and second P-T bombs, which exploded as a single unit. The right front wheel of the armored car was only two feet away from the third P-T packet, which the first two touched off a micro second later.

A blinding flash of light enveloped the right side and the sloping hood of the armored car, and so did the liquid fire of the phosphorus and thermite.

The AVO car had less of a chance than a moth caught in the flame of a blowtorch! Instantly the gunner, standing in the open turret, became a shrieking human torch, the droplets of molten fire, burning at 1,300 degrees Fahrenheit, eating to the bone. Other droplets of P-T began exploding the cartridges in the belts of the Pekhotni light machine guns.

Rolling waves of fire washed through the air vents on the right side and into the vision slots in front of the driver and the radioman. In less time than it takes to blink, both men were suffering the agonies of hell. White-hot phosphorus and thermite turned their uniforms into flames and began to dribble the flesh from their bones. So unbearable was the agony that within a few seconds the three men were—for all practical purposes—demented. Their pain, however, was very brief. Not only did the intense heat burn all the oxygen from around and inside the car; the flames rolled down the throats of the men and into their lungs as they inhaled.

A mass of blue-white flames, the armored car charged down the street—a gigantic fireball pushed along by its own momentum. Not more than fifty feet from the personnel car, the blazing metal coffin careened wildly to the right, helped along by the Death Merchant, who had put three .22 Magnum projectiles into its right front tire. Like a runaway comet, the armored car jumped over the curb, slammed itself across the sidewalk, and crashed through one of the plate-glass windows of a furniture store.

From the corner of his eye, Camellion saw Lakatos raise his Dieckmann Destroyer and yell a warning—"Behind you! Coming in at the end of the end of the block from Dozsa Gyorgy Ut!"

Reacting by instinct, Camellion threw himself forward in time to avoid several Model 48 Kal pistol slugs, which zipped several inches over the broad part of his back. But he didn't have time to speculate on near-misses. He was too busy diving behind the personnel car, then swinging around to face the new threat—the green and white car of the *Nepkoztarsagyi,* the regular People's Police. *The damn car is coming straight at us!* Worse, one of the cops in the front seat was leaning out the window and firing his service Kal, in an effort to hit Camellion and Lakatos. It was the last act of his life.

The Death Merchant fired twice. Thomas Lakatos fired three times. Camellion's two bullets shattered the windshield. One missed the Nepko with the pistol; the second bullet chopped into the left side of his chest. The driver was just as unlucky. Two of Lakatos' slugs had smashed the other side of the windshield, but had missed the driver. Lakatos' third .22M hit the driver in one cheek, cut sideways through his mouth, and went out the back of his neck.

Out of control, the police vehicle was by now too close for either Camellion or Lakatos to try to turn it by firing into one of the front tires, or, in turning, the vehicle would have crashed into the personnel car.

The police vehicle—the driver bouncing around like a rag doll, his partner hanging out the window on the opposite side—tore past the left side of the personnel car. For a moment it seemed to Camellion, who jumped far to the right, that the police car was so close it would have to crash into the side of his own machine. Fortunately, there was no grinding of metal. The police car streaked on by and its front wheels, at an angle, finally struck the curb.

The car turned over and lay upside down, its wheels spinning.

"Let's get out of here!" Camellion yelled, jumping up.

He and Lakatos piled into the front seat of the personnel car, both aware that they were skipping close to the whirlpool of death. They had exhausted their submachine gun ammunition and were down to their last few clips of .22 Magnum cartridges. If they met another force of AVOs or Nepkos, the end would come swiftly.

Lakatos took a pint of *bikaver* wine—"bull's blood"—from his coat, pulled out the cork, and took a long slug, muttering, *"Vakulastol vakulasig!* From blind darkness to blind darkness. That's all we've accomplished this night."

The Death Merchant turned the car to the left on Dozsa Gyorgy Ut and glanced furtively at Lakatos, who was putting the bottle in his coat pocket. They could hear sirens wailing two or three blocks behind them and knew that more AVO vehicles were pulling onto the grounds of the Institute. In all probability, the first armored car had arrived so fast because it had been in the vicinity.

"All we need is a little luck," Lakatos said. Leaning back, he rubbed his knees and stared ahead through the windshield.

"It's only four blocks to Rakocziut Boulevard," Camellion said. "We'll get to the moving company lot if we don't bump into any AVOs or Nepkos."

Camellion made a right turn at Lehel Ut and forced himself to maintain the forty-mile-per-hour speed limit. Ahead, two cars were approaching. Lakatos hunched down and pulled out his Magnum automatic. The Death Merchant remained icy calm. The two cars, much closer now, revealed themselves to be ordinary citizens' automobiles.

He drove to the end of Lehel Ut and made a left turn onto Kelenhegyi Korut. Five minutes later he turned right on Mizavirgu, a short street that intersected Rakocziut Boulevard. There was a couple walking on Mizavirgu, on the right-hand side of the street. Hurrying along as if they were late, the man and the woman didn't bother to look at the passing personnel car.

Rakocziut Boulevard came closer and closer, its tall,

curved streetlights giving a silent welcome. The Death Merchant turned left, drove half a block on the wide boulevard, and made another left, swinging into a narrow, dark alley.

"We'll park in the alley and go the rest of the way on foot," he told a startled Thomas Lakatos, who had expected him to drive straight on Rakocziut Boulevard. "We'll take the alley that cuts through this one."

Thankful that the People's Republic of Hungary still had private enterprise, even if all privately-owned businesses were tightly regulated by the central government, the Death Merchant drove very slowly until he saw the mouth of the other alley. He stopped the car, turned off the motor, and switched off the lights. Without a word, he and Lakatos got out of the car, listening to the sirens in the distance. One of the sirens was getting closer. Ahead in the alley, a dog barked.

In single file they headed west in the opposite alley, Lakatos going first, since he had been born in Budapest and was familiar with the area. They kept to the side, in the deep shadows, carefully avoiding trash cans, boxes, and other refuse.

At the end of ten minutes, they were approaching the fenced-in parking lot of Arpad & Sons Moving Company. The main traffic gate was in front, on Rakocziut Boulevard. Another truck gate was on the west, facing Veritzog V. A narrow man-gate was on the south side by the alley.

For several minutes, Camellion and Lakatos studied the entire area. The small, two-story building on Rakocziut was pitch dark. The garage, on one side of the region, was only a shadowy rectangle. A dozen vans of various sizes, some attached to tractors, were on the lot, as well as a few cars and minibuses. The entire area seemed devoid of life.

Lakatos turned and noticed that the Death Merchant's eyes shone like a cat's in the night. It occurred to Thomas that the first thing he had noticed about Richard Camellion had been his unusual eyes. Blue they were, a cold kind of burning blue, at times glowing with an eerie, peculiar sheen. There were other times when the eyes seemed glazed over, almost lifeless, the luster gone.

Lakatos whispered, "What do you think we should do? Stick with the original plan and signal, or try to go over the fence?"

"I'll signal in a moment," Camellion said in a low voice. "But stay down. Let's wait and see what the cop car on the next street does. If it turns and comes our way, we'll have to kill them before they get us. That's how things are." He pulled the Magnum pistol from his shoulder holster.

Its siren howling, the screaming becoming louder and louder, the AVO patrol car sped across the mouth of the alley, racing north on Veritzog U. Then the secret police car was gone, continuing north across Rakocziut Boulevard.

The Death Merchant and Lakatos hurried in the darkness to the man-gate. Camellion pulled out his penlight, held it over his head, with the end pointed toward the truck area, and three times pressed the small button at the end of the metal tube.

Presently they could see several figures hurrying toward them in the darkness, moving between the vans and the cabs. Finally Tibor Arpad was unlocking the padlock and pulling the chain from around the gate and the fence posts. Dr. Frantisek Palfecky was with him.

"You're twenty minutes early." Palfecky's tone sounded almost like an accusation. "What went wrong?" He closed the gate after Camellion and Lakatos stepped inside and began to fasten it with the lock and chain.

Camellion explained how the mission had fallen apart as Arpad and Palfecky led him and Lakatos to the side of a van in the center of the pitch-dark area. The four men crouched down by one side of the big cab, Dr. Palfecky whispering in his thick voice, "AVOs will be racing around this section of Pest for the remainder of the night. I suggest that the two of you remain in the office all night and leave tomorrow when the roads and streets are heavy with traffic."

Tibor Arpad, a well-muscled man with a stern face and very bushy eyebrows, flatly vetoed Palfecky's suggestion. "It's too dangerous," he said, shaking his head from side to side. "It will be impossible to get them out without my

29

workers seeing them, especially the four girls in the office. One of the bookeepers is a fanatical Communist. The AVO would know before the end of the day. No, they cannot stay here."

"Thomas and I must get back to St. Matthias Church tonight," Camellion agreed with Arpad, although he wanted to leave the Pest section of the city and cross the Danube over to the Buda side about as much as General Douglas MacArthur must have wanted a date with Tokyo Rose.

"If we don't get back to the church tonight, we'll be missed in the morning," Camellion pointed out. "Right now, Father Redlich thinks that Brother Schmid and I are in our room. If I'm not at breakfast and if I don't show up for mass, he might become suspicious. Leaving in the minibus is the lesser of the two evils."

Lakatos, who was a janitor at St. Matthias Church and Father Csoki's chauffeur, agreed with the Death Merchant. "And if I am also missing in the morning, it would indeed seem odd." He looked from Arpad to Palfecky. "We could have driven to meet Mihaly in the AVO car if we hadn't been early and hadn't been anxious to get here. It would have been too risky. Szechenyi and his two helpers would have been suspicious at the sight of an AVO car. But as the situation is now, we have more than enough time to drive the three blocks to Jeno Street and meet Szechenyi. His garbage route will take him by the church about four-thirty."

"Doctor, you did make arrangements with a patient, didn't you?" The Death Merchant stared at Palfecky, who was losing more and more of his nerve by the second.

Palfecky nodded and wrinkled his thick nose. "That is not a problem. If the AVO stops us and checks out my story, they will find that I'm on the street at a late hour because I am making a house call. My patient—he had a genuine heart attack a few months ago—will confirm my words." His voice rose in fear, becoming more intense. "But if we're stopped, suppose the AVO searches the back of my bus? What do we do then?"

"A search of that nature is not likely to occur," the Death Merchant said. Sitting on the running board of the cab, he leaned over and folded his hands between his knees. "Those box seats have been put together very cleverly. It would require an expert to detect the push-out panels. Yet, if Tom and I are discovered, there'll be two or three or more dead AVOs. I guarantee it."

"I wish you could guarantee our lives," Palfecky said hollowly.

"Doctor, when one fights for freedom, the price is never cheap," Camellion said in annoyance. "That's what liberty is all about—being able to live without having to worry about a knock on your door in the middle of the night, and having a free press. If you want those things, if you want that kind of freedom, you must be prepared to fight for it, and, if necessary, die for it. . . ."

CHAPTER THREE

The charred bones, blobs of burnt flesh, fire-blackened belt buckles, and discolored metal that had been on the AVO uniforms had been picked up from the third-floor corridor of the Scientific Race-Protecting Institute. The entire building had been aired and sprayed with aromatic disinfectant, measures that had not been entirely successful: the nauseating stink of burning death was still strong. Now, at nine-thirty in the morning, workmen were replacing the blackened floor tiles and the deeply singed wall paneling.

The group of workers was more than slightly nervous. They had every reason to be discomposed: General Bela Skedfu, the commander of the entire *Allemvedelmi Osztaly,* and Lieutenant General Sigismund Barthory, the chief of Section 4-DII, the intelligence branch of the AVO, were standing in the hall watching them work.

General Skedfu and Lieutenant General Barthory finally turned and walked slowly to Dr. Imre Meleter's office door. The two AVO guards saluted smartly as Skedfu and Barthory walked into the office.

Barthory closed the office door and followed his boss

and old friend into the inner office, watching Skedfu, who strode over to the vault, touched the combination-dial below the spin-wheel, and slowly nodded his head. Tall and thin, with a neat mustache and tailored uniform heavy with decorations, Skedfu impressed most people with a sort of Old Testament melancholy and a professional intensity that bordered on the fanatic. He removed his olive-green uniform cap and placed it on Dr. Meleter's desk.

"Did those two, whoever they were, think the old safe was still here, or did they know that the new vault had been installed?" Skedfu, speaking rhetorically, stared at the shiny vault, as if it might be the answer to his question.

"Bela, I feel that they came here intending to open the old vault," Sigismund Barthory said. He reached underneath his coat, took a pack of cigarettes from his shirt pocket, and tore open one corner. "If the two had known the new vault had been installed, they wouldn't have attempted the burglary. They would have known they wouldn't have had the time to drill it open, and they knew they couldn't use explosives. Their getting the two safes mixed up does give me a clue, however."

"How can we know that they didn't have some kind of new equipment which would enable them to do the job in a hurry?" asked Skedfu, sitting down in a swivel chair and crossing his legs. He went on amiably, "The device they used on the window to neutralize the electric eye reveals a high degree of sophistication, which leads me to believe that this could be very serious, that we're not dealing with the Society of the Double Cross, but with highly trained foreign agents—specialists." He looked at Barthory with new interest. "What kind of clue?"

Having finished lighting his cigarette, Barthory returned the silver lighter to the corner of Dr. Meleter's desk and exhaled twin wisps of blue-gray smoke from his long nose.

"Not even the Russians or the American CIA has equipment that can open such a modern vault in less than—oh, I should say three to four hours." Barthory sat down on one corner of the desk. "To me that is evidence that the two men thought the old safe was still here. An expert could open a pile of junk like that in half an hour. In turn, I'm led to believe that whoever tipped them off works right in this building. But whoever the traitor is, he or she wasn't working day before yesterday when the vault was installed, unless he or she couldn't get word of the change in vaults to the men who broke in last night. I've narrowed the list of possible informants down to three dozen people. Some were sick. Others were not here day before yesterday for various reasons, the vacation season being the major reason. A third are women. Some are clerks. A dozen are officials of various grades."

General Skedfu nodded, his eyes warm. He was very pleased with Sigismund's efficiency. But Sigismund had always operated like a well-oiled, well-kept machine. There was another reason—a far more important one—why Bela Skedfu was fond of his boyhood friend: Sigismund had saved his life twenty-one years ago, during the Hungarian Revolution when ordinary citizens were killing any AVO man (or woman!) they could get their traitorous hands on.

Both men had been born in Esztergom, the birthplace of St. Stephen, and were the same age. Without formal education or influential friends, both men had decided at the age of twenty-three that if they were to have any kind of future, they had better join the AVO. Men wearing the blue uniform of the AVO were respected—and feared. It was on the AVO that Communist Hungary was going to build its greatest defense. The men of the AVO would be the new national heroes, watching day and night. The AVO would seal the borders hermetically, transform the frontiers into impassable fortresses, and weed out traitors at home. Finding traitors meant incriminating every living Hungarian and many of the dead, the psychology being that when everyone was incriminated, then any normal social relationship was impossible, and only the AVO could thrive.

Skedfu and Barthory were first sent as guards to the prison five kilometers outside the little village of Recsk, northeast of Budapest. All new AVO recruits were sent to Recsk, the most terrible prison in all Hungary, for "condi-

33

tioning," to become hardened to and experts in calculated and systematic brutality. In the cases of Bela Skedfu and Sigismund Barthory, the AVO was wasting its time. Both men, cruel by nature, could have given lessons in sadism to the worst psychopaths in Hitler's SS.

Within the cold walls of Recsk, the two boyhood friends could work out their frustrations on helpless political prisoners. Using steel-corded rubber hoses or clubs or chains, they could break bones, wreck kidneys, smash testicles, or puncture eyeballs and receive praise and be rewarded for their efforts. Naturally each man had his favorite torture. Skedfu liked to take a pair of pliers and half-pull a man's teeth, then calmly sip wine and watch as the chained prisoner went half-mad with pain. Barthory was much more imaginative. He and other guards would clamp a man to a table, and Sigismund would ram a thin hollow glass tube up the victim's penis. Then he'd beat the poor devil till the tube broke into a million pieces. Thus it became not uncommon to see men scream and faint as they urinated. Weeks or months later, Sigismund would single out such a victim, force him to drink a couple of quarts of water, and later roar with laughter when the man, suffering the agonies of the damned, urinated.

There were no doctors at Recsk. And because there weren't, it was a common sight to see prisoners stumbling along on weirdly bent legs or with arms jutting off at queer angles. Why waste time to set a prisoner's broken bones?

At Recsk, there were daily tortures, prolonged beatings, water cures, burnings, and psychological measures that reduced brave men to mental and physical wrecks.

There was also Sunday. . . .

Because Sunday was a holiday for the guards and because the AVO was determined to defile a day still held in affectionate memory by the majority of the prisoners, Sunday was a day of special sport—or of horror, if one happened to be a prisoner. The AVOs would play various games with the prisoners. Prisoners would be forced to stand up, hands at their sides, while AVOs knocked them flat to the ground with gigantic blows to the mouth.

There was the game called "the White Mare." AVOs

would insert a broomstick under a prisoner's knees, then double him up into a tight ball, lashing his wrists to his ankles. The prisoners were deathly afraid of this terrible punishment, for it placed a stress upon the stomach and heart that they knew no man could bear longer than two hours. Now and then the AVOs would forget a man made into a white mare, and the man would die without anyone caring.

It was Bela Skedfu who had invented one of the cruelest Sunday punishments. The AVOs would force prisoners to stand facing a row of bright electric lights. "Now stand on one foot, scum!" Skedfu would order them. The combination of intense light and one wavering foot would bring forth unexpected reactions. One man would begin to scream, another would faint, a third would start dancing! But if a prisoner made so much as a single move, all the others would be savagely beaten. Not the one who moved. He was safe.

Barthory made his Sunday contribution, one that was both extremely simple and extremely effective in subduing difficult prisoners. He would force a prisoner to face a wall where a bright light shone into his eyes. Against the man's forehead he would place the point of a pencil, putting the other end against the wall. "If you let the pencil fall, I'll break both your arms and legs," Barthory would warn the terrified prisoner. And there the man would stand, pressing the pencil against the wall with his forehead, trying not to faint because of the bright light in his eyes, trying not to think of Barthory waiting with his crowbar. Sometimes when a man left this punishment after a couple of hours, the pencil would go with him, imbedded in the thin flesh of his forehead.

There were other aspects of Sundays at Recsk prison there were the women guards, who would drag male prisoners to their own quarters and force them to undress. Then they would torture them in hideous ways, using knives and hairpins and cigarette lighters.

Skedfu and Barthory married two of the women AVO guards.

After twenty-seven months at Recsk, the two men were transferred to the AVO main prison in Budapest. One

35

block in from the Danube, on the Buda side, ran Fo Street, the main thoroughfare of the right bank, and on its handsome flank, where the Kossuth Bridge crossed from Pest, stood the main prison and headquarters of the AVO. It was housed in a sprawling complex of buildings whose five-story facade was nearly four hundred yards long. The first two stories were heavily barred, giving it the appearance of a prison; but it was another feature, not visible from the street, which made this building particularly attractive for the purpose to which it had been put. It had a series of deep cellars.

Bela Skedfu and Sigismund Barthory were assigned to the torture cellar. By the spring of 1956, Skedfu had been promoted to lieutenant and Barthory to first sergeant. Barthory, at his own request, had been transferred to the intelligence section of the AVO. Both men were at the AVO main prison and headquarters in November of 1956 when the revolution exploded in Hungary and an enraged citizenry stormed the prison. Scores of AVOs were shot, torn apart, or beaten to death. But it was Sigismund who had thought of the idea that had saved his and Bela's life. The two men had put on civilian clothes and had armed themselves with identification taken from prisoners in the cellars. In an effort to escape the revenge of the people, who were killing every AVO they could get their hands on, Skedfu and Barthory had hidden, concealed behind some boxes, underneath a staircase on the first floor. After the revolutionaries had broken down the doors of the building and were shooting terrified AVOs and storming the dreaded cellars and freeing prisoners, Skedfu and Barthory had mingled with the raging crowd and had managed to leave the building before any of the released inmates could see and recognize them.

While history was on the side of the Hungarian people, victory wasn't. The Russian army invaded Hungary and, with a ferocity and barbarism unmatched since the days of Adolf Hitler, moved its brutal tanks against a defenseless population seeking to escape the horrors of Communism. Hundreds of men, women, and children were blown apart and machine-gunned. Flame-throwers murdered hundreds more. Thousands of Hungarians were rounded up like animals and shipped in sealed boxcars to the USSR.

Russia introduced her terror into Hungary by other measures: she stole the produce of the land and called it "elevating the peasants." The Soviets victimized the workers and calmly told the world press it was "the rule of the proletariat." The Russians corrupted every institution of the Hungarian government, a government already made putrid by the Hungarian brand of Communism, and called it the New Society. The Russians stole from housewives, raped teenage girls, contaminated children, allowed the elderly to die in poverty, and called it "world brotherhood." And through the AVO, the Soviet Union declared war on every Hungarian worker and called it peace.

After escaping from AVO headquarters on Fo Street, Bela Skedfu and Sigismund Barthory stayed in hiding until the Russian army arrived. The two men, and other AVOs, then helped the Russians smash the uprising.

Ambulances and Red Cross workers were mercilessly machine-gunned. Even nurses attending wounded Hungarian Freedom Fighters were executed at point-blank range. Children were murdered, hospitals fired upon, and young men were executed merely upon suspicion. Crimes against inanimate objects were as bad. A Russian squad of flame-throwers attacked the National Archives and burned it out; when foolish but patriotic firemen tried to save the building, they were shot. Stores were completely looted, even though the Russians did not need the food. Russians machine-gunned 322 old people at the old folks' home at 47 Nepszinhaz Street.

The bad fortune of the Hungarian people was the good fortune of Lieutenant Skedfu and Sergeant Barthory, both men continuing to prosper within the AVO, which KGB specialists reorganized. As a reward for helping the Russians confiscate all the blood and blood plasma at the Hungarian central depot on Daroczi Street and take it to the Szabolcz Street hospital, which the Russians had reserved for themselves, Skedfu was promoted to captain and Barthory to Second Lieutenant.

As the years passed, Skedfu and Barthory continued to prosper within the AVO. Life was good. They and their

37

families had special privileges—the best food, the best housing, the best clothes, the best medical attention. They could shop at special "M-Stores" and buy scarce goods at discount. There were yearly vacations at Lake Balaton, the exclusive resort area.

By 1974, life was even better for Skedfu and Barthory. The Central Committee of the Hungarian Communist Party's Politburo promoted Major General Bela Skedfu to full general, the promotion giving him command of the entire AVO. Skedfu then proceeded to use his influence and have Colonel Barthory promoted to lieutenant general. As a lieutenant general, Barthory was made chief of the non-uniformed AVO.

The two men had reached the pinnacle of power. Together they controlled 26,000 uniformed AVO, 9,000 plainclothes men—3,000 of whom worked in Intelligence—and 2,000 spies, men and women who reported any loose talk and any person they considered suspicious and dangerous to the regime.

General Skedfu fixed his eyes on Barthory with a basilisk stare.

"The possible informants you mentioned. What action are you taking to find the guilty one? The suspects are all minor officials. I assume that since they all work at the Race-Protecting Institute, hidden transmitters have been monitoring their homes. Ah, but if the suspects had said anything incriminating or slanderous in private against the government, they wouldn't be working at the Institute or be suspects!"

"Bugging is usually a waste of time." Barthory was dismal as he contemplated the burning end of his cigarette. "People always suspect their homes are bugged and never have anything but praise for the government. Forget wireless transmitters, Bela. They're not the answer to our problem. You of all people should know that."

The tone in Barthory's voice indicated he regarded Skedfu as an equal, a tone that no other man in the AVO would even dream of using, nor would Sigismund have been that familiar if a third person had been present (the exception being the wives and children of the two men).

Skedfu didn't even seem to notice Barthory's lack of respect. Long ago, with a peasant's natural cunning, he had become aware that he and Barthory were dependent on each other, that their careers in the AVO was intricately interwoven, as were their lives. Barthory also knew that he and Bela were like a hand and a glove. Skedfu was the hand, a man who could command and was willing to take responsibility. Barthory was the glove. More devious and paranoid than Skedfu, Barthory preferred to remain in the shadows, to watch and wait, to play at power the way one would patiently work at a jigsaw puzzle. He was the perfect type for intelligence work.

"This matter must be handled promptly," Skedfu said in a low voice with quiet firmness. He put his elbows on the arms of the swivel chair, raised his arms, and began tapping the ends of his fingers together. "Kadar himself phoned at three o'clock this morning and demanded to know what had happened, who was responsible, and what we were going to do about it. I told him that you and I were convinced it was the work of the Double Cross scum. The press will blame the Society without mentioning the Solenoid-Inductor Intensifier."

Barthory frowned severely. Many people feared Barthory and Skedfu, and they feared Janos Kadar, the Premier of the Hungarian Communist Party. The other high government officials didn't count; they were only rubber stamps. It was different with Kadar: he represented the Soviet Union. He was the Kremlin's man.

Kadar had been around a long time. In 1948 he had been head of the AVO but had fallen from grace and had been imprisoned. After his release, he had gradually regained power and had supported Imre Nagy, the Premier, during the 1956 revolution. Then, seeing his chance to grab full power, Kadar had formed a counter-government, which had presided over the Soviet suppression of the revolt. Ever since then, Kadar had been controlled by the Soviets. When the Kremlin said, "Jump!" Kadar was the man who asked, "How high?"

"Did you tell Kadar that only two men were involved in the attemped burglary?" Barthory asked. Of medium height, weighing one hundred sixty-seven pounds, he had jet-black hair, sneering black eyes, a stubborn chin, and a great capacity for work. "But I know you didn't."

Skedfu favored Barthory with one of his rare smiles.

"I told the Russian kiss-ass that there were nine or ten of the traitors, and the guards will swear to that number. That was the first thing I made sure of. The point I wish to stress is that unless we do something and fast—I mean today—we could be in for trouble. We've got to make some arrests today. We must give Kadar what he wants, and fooling that foxy bastard won't be easy. The uniformed AVOs can pick up a couple of dozen people, but your intelligence people will also have to show some measure of success. Do you have any actual leads, any idea at all that will help?"

Barthory yawned. He had been awake since three o'clock in the morning, was worried, and had had an argument with Eva, his wife.

"Bela, before you start jerking people in off the streets, clear their names with my department. We don't want to arrest any person we might be watching in the hope he'll lead us to bigger fish. My department hasn't made any progress. Here in Budapest we're watching a hundred or so people, both men and women. We suspect that a third of them are Double Cross members or at least sympathetic toward the organization. When we leave, I'll go over the list and have twenty or thirty of them—the most innocuous—brought to Fo Street for questioning."

Barthory eased himself off the desk and sat down on a plain wooden office chair, adding, "But I can tell you right now, we're not going to learn anything about last night's breakin."

General Skedfu shot him a quick, calculating glance. "I think I know why we won't, but tell me anyhow."

"The Double Cross operation last night must have had top-level approval," Barthory said simply. "Only the most trusted members were involved. The SDC has cells of three and seven and nine members. It's that type of extreme secrecy that has made it impossible for us to smash those freedom-loving bastards! It's like a cancer that's spread throughout the body. You cut it out in one place and it breaks out in another. We've smashed SDC cells all

40

over the country during the past six years, but look what happened last night. Now they're aware of the gas development!"

"We can't be absolutely certain that the SDC knows about the gas." Skedfu's voice was hopeful.

"Quit kidding yourself, Bela. Why else would they try to get into Dr. Meleter's vault? Fortunately, Meleter was at the castle. If he had been in his office, the sons of bitches would have killed him." Barthory, making an angry face, his black eyes glinting, reached underneath his suit coat, pulled out another king-size cigarette, and began toying with it. "Personally, I wish the damned Russians had moved the entire gas project to Russia. It's an insult to our intelligence, the KGB's telling us that the project should be carried out in Hungary because Dr. Meleter originated the formula."

"Sigismund, stop complaining and be that realist you're always talking about," Skedfu sighed, putting his hands on the lapels of his uniform coat. "There is no more independence in politics than there is in jail. We both know why the KGB insisted that the project be developed in our country—in case something goes wrong and there's an accident! If that happened, it would be our people who became demented! Why, if the gas escaped it could drift even to the Balaton area! But we also know we can't argue with the Russians. Remember, years ago, how General Borshenovitch insisted that the uniforms of the AVO be changed from blue to green? As if a change in color could make the people forget!"

Barthory finished lighting his cagarette and looked thoughtfully at Skedfu. "Has the Russian embassy phoned you about last night? But I suppose Lysemki won't call until after he's had a conference with Kadar."

"I anticipate a visit from Comrade Lysemki—that KGB pig—this afternoon. I'll tell him I've ordered extra guards posted around the castle and that I've given orders that Dr. Meleter is to be guarded day and night. I don't think it's at all necessary, however. With all the alarms at the castle, no one could reach Meleter. Why, if anyone tried to get past the microwave field surrounding the lab, he'd be fried to a crisp within a few minutes. I expect Ly-

41

semki will bring up the procession, but I don't think he'll demand that we call it off." Grinning, General Skedfu rubbed his hands together gleefully. "The damned Russians learned their lesson in Poland. They know you can do almost anything to a people ... torture them, execute them, or whatever. But take away their religion, their security in the hereafter—never! The Russians don't want another revolt here in Hungary!"

"Bela, you're wrong!"

Surprised, Skedfu sat up straight and blinked at Sigismund Barthory. "Wrong? What the hell do you mean? Not even the Russians would dare go so far as to cancel the pilgrimage to that ridiculous shrine!"

"Forget that damned shrine!" Barthory was annoyed and waved one hand impatiently. "I know the Russians won't cancel the pilgrimage. I didn't mean that at all. I am saying that we can expect some kind of an attack on the castle!"

General Skedfu looked as if he had just swallowed a goldfish. "An attack on the castle—impossible!" He laughed, a guffaw that was forced and ragged with doubt. "Why, there is even part of an army unit at the castle. Ah, Sigismund ... you're overestimating the Society of the Double Cross! Come now, tell me your reasoning behind this madness—and don't say the underground might attack because the castle is only six miles from the shrine!"

"Friday afternoon people from all over Hungary will begin the journey to Fonyod," Barthory said, not at all insulted. "Saturday afternoon the pilgrimage will assemble at Fonyod and begin the march to the shrine for religious ceremonies that will culminate at the shrine itself Sunday night." He turned and looked slyly at a frozen-faced Skedfu. "Think of how easy it will be for revolutionaries to conceal themselves among all the thousands of people who will make the pilgrimage!"

Bela Skedfu's expression became very serious. "Suppose you are right. How would the revolutionaries cover the six miles from the shrine to the castle—and do it without our spotting them?"

"Bela, you know that intelligence is not only my job—

42

it's also a hobby with me," Barthory said smugly. "You're aware that I keep very extensive files and—"

"Get on with it! Make your point!"

"Bela, have you ever heard of an international agent called the Death Merchant?"

CHAPTER FOUR

Decorating the float was a slow and tedious job for the four men. Each individual artificial blue hydrangea and white azalea had to be carefully attached by hand. Friday morning, an hour before the procession would form, freshly cut red roses would be fastened to the wide streamers leading from the five-foot statue of the Immaculate Conception to the four corners of the float. The float itself was a flat, wooden bed with four rubber-tired wheels. A false siding would hide the wheels as the float—it would be only one of hundreds—moved in the mile-long procession down Nepkoztarsasag Utia, crossed the Margaret Bridge, then moved slowly along Attila Ut.

One of the men working on the float was Father Peter Csoki, the high priest at St. Matthias Church. He didn't look like a priest—at least how one thinks a priest is supposed to look. Dressed in shorts and a T-shirt, he was fifty but looked forty. He was about five feet eleven, a rugged, brown-eyed, bushy-haired man with deep lines in his face indicating a resolute character, and a dimple in his chin showing a love for the good life. Two decades and three years earlier, his father and mother had been murdered by the AVO. The Russians had murdered his brother in the 1956 Hungarian revolt.

Father Csoki often described himself as "only a priest doing his best to obey the will of God." He hadn't even tried to guess the true identities of Richard Camellion and Raymond Merrit. He considered it the "will of God" that he didn't poke and pry and try to find out. He did know that the two men from West Germany were not members of any monastic order; instinct alone told him that. As far

43

as he was concerned, the lean, hard man with the closely cropped brown hair and strange blue eyes was Brother Helmut Krim, and the big-boned, blond, wavy-haired man with him, Brother Hugo Schmid. Monsignor Csoki was not concerned with the two brothers—nor with the procession, for that matter. He was burdened with the same problem eating at Brothers Krim and Schmid, and Paul Tisza: how to move the two stolen launchers from George Rakoczi's house to the float, which was being decorated in the shaded courtyard between the rear of the church and the priests' home.

The two Russian RPG2s, and ten rocket missiles, were to be attached to the underside of the bed of the float. In this manner, hidden by the four pieces of siding, which would fit together like an open box, the rocket launchers and missiles could safely be smuggled to the Bakony Mountains, to the shrine of Our Lady of Bakony.

But moving the antitank launchers and shells was only half the problem. Even if the weapons could be brought to the courtyard, how would it be possible to move the ordnance from the car to the float without Father Dominic Redlich or the other two guests seeing the transfer? The other guests were a man and wife, and the couple had arrived from Poland the day before. Were they agents of Polish Intelligence—or plants of the AVO?

Monsignor Csoki picked up another hydrangea from the large carton and, using a stapling gun, fastened the plastic stem to the tiny railing on the right side of the float.

Standing on top of the float, Paul Tisza was busy attaching the ends of white satin streamers to the crown of the statue of the Immaculate Conception. A former Professor of Philosophy at the University of Budapest, but now an electrician, Tisza was a spare man in his middle fifties. Almost gaunt-looking, he was bald, had a small mouth, and a long, crooked nose. In 1955, the AVO had smashed his nose and it had not healed properly. For the same brutal reason, Tisza walked with a slight limp. The bones of his right leg, broken by the AVO, had not been set by a doctor.

Brother Krim and Brother Schmid worked on either side of Monsignor Csoki.

"I'm thinking that this float is going to have the national colors of the United States—red, white, and blue," Raymond Merrit/Brother Schmid commented, giving Father Csoki a brief glance.

"I think you have forgotten the sides and the ends of the float, Brother Schmid. They will be covered with thick evergreen ivy," Father Csoki said. "The evergreen will give the float the green of the Hungarian flag."

Richard Camellion, several blue hydrangeas in his hand, moved closer to Monsignor Csoki. "We'll have to drill holes in the wagon bed to support the clamps underneath," he said. "The bottom of the statue, which is also in the center, is slightly indented and will hide the bolt heads. We can put the other bolts at each end and cover the heads with evergreen."

"Are you not putting the cart before the horse, Brother Krim?" Father Csoki chided Camellion. "We don't have the two launchers and the missiles, and it doesn't look like we're going to be able to get them. Rakoczi's house is across the city, and even though it has been three days since the trouble at the race institute, the AVOs are still stopping anyone they consider suspicious. It is much too dangerous to go to Rakoczi's house."

"Today is Thursday," Camellion said matter-of-factly and stapled a hydrangea to the railing on the float. "High mass is tomorrow at ten in the morning. Then comes the procession to St. Stephen's Basilica and the beginning of the journey to Fonyod. By six tomorrow morning we must have the launchers and missiles in place. Either Brother Schmid and I risk going after them and bringing them back here, or else the launchers and shells remain behind."

"In which case we won't be able to destroy the Russian tanks at Karolyi Castle," added Brother Schmid, "and our chances of getting inside will have taken a seventy-five-percent nosedive!"

Monsignor Csoki pulled a handkerchief from his back pocket, wiped his tanned face, sighed, and recited a proverb in Hungarian, *"Huncut a paraszt, mihelyt egy araszt"*:

"Crafty is the peasant as soon as he is an inch long." He folded the handkerchief and returned it to his pocket. "But it would seem we're not being too crafty. Why, it was all I could do to talk Father Redlich into helping Fathers Donyar and Sarsesapak decorate the altars in the church for tomorrow's festivities. He wanted to help out with the float. And that Polish couple, Mr. and Mrs. Kobalinsky! Now we have to outwit them as well as Father Redlich. Oh, the powers of evil must be smiling!"

"I always thought that the nuns decorated the altars in a Catholic church," Ray Merrit said, then looked as if he were remembering. "But, St. Matthias no longer has sisters."

"That is right, Brother Schmid. The Communists suppressed all orders of nuns," Father Csoki said bitterly. "There are no parochial schools in Hungary, only state schools. Catholic children must learn their catechism at home. The only people we don't have to worry about are Father Szell and Father Kodaly. They aren't members of the underground, but they have made their senses blind to our efforts. Thank the good Lord for that."

Brother Schmid stapled a white azalea to the float, flipping his drooping cigarette up to a better angle by twisting his lips.

"It seems to me that Szell and Kodaly will have their heads on the AVO block once we escape across the border into Austria."

Merrit turned and grabbed Father Csoki with a hard stare. "They don't know, do they?"

"I don't think they even suspect," Father Csoki replied. "They will be questioned by the AVO, detained for a few days, and then released. It will be obvious to the authorities that they were not a part of the scheme, or they wouldn't have remained behind. Yes, Father Szell and Father Kodaly will be safe enough."

"Suppose the big helicopter isn't at the castle?" Paul Tisza, on the bed of the wagon and untangling a satin streamer, sat down on his heels and cast his mournful eyes at the Death Merchant, to whom he was speaking, sensing that the man with the icy blue eyes was the real decision-maker. "It's thirty-five miles from the castle to

46

the Austro-Hungarian border. We could never cover that distance on foot."

It was Father Csoki who answered, "The troop-carrying helicopter is always there at Karolyi Castle. Our agents watching the castle from the surrounding mountains report that three helicopters are usually on the pad. The big one and two smaller craft. Try to have faith in God, Paul."

Tisza's thin lips twisted into a smile. He did not reply as he resumed untwisting the long streamer. Father Csoki suddenly felt foolish, like a modern-day Don Quixote tilting at giant concrete windmills. How could a convinced atheist, such as Paul, have faith in God? The priest, who had known Paul for almost eighteen years, felt very sorry for the ex-teacher of philosophy. Tisza had lost so very much to the AVO, including his wife and eldest son. The government had forbidden him to teach. Get yourself an honest job! the Ministry of Education had told him. The only philosophy that Hungarians need comes from Marx and Lenin. Such a waste, such a terrible waste. Paul was a brilliant man, even if some of his ideas were ridiculous. For example, Paul even had the theory that racial memory could be carried in one's genes. He used this theory as a basis for his belief that schizophrenics suffered from a mind split because they were torn between their Hominid and their Starman heritages.

But worst of all, Paul had lost his belief in God, his faith in Holy Mother Church. Yes, Satan was after Paul's soul. Father Csoki recalled part of a conversation he had once had with Paul. Paul had mused, "We're supposed to be in a time of creation. If that's the case, God had to create Himself from a previous absence of any quality or quantity. How could this be? How could God start to create Himself? He had nothing to begin with because He didn't have any existence if He had to create Himself. How can the idea of time make sense when there was absolutely nothing in the universe—which hadn't yet been created—to measure it with? It has to follow that before God created Himself there were no events, and if there were no events, there was no time. How did God know when to begin His remarkable act of creation? How could

47

He even know when to begin, if He didn't exist, but had to create Himself from nothing? And if He was nothing, where did the something He used for creation come from?"

Father Csoki made up his mind to say a special novena to Our Lady of Bakony for the salvation of Paul's soul. The priest was pulled from his reverie by the quiet voice of Brother Helmut Krim.

"Father Csoki, we must have the Russian launchers and missles," the Death Merchant said. He didn't look at the priest as he attached another artificial flower to the float. "It's now eleven o'clock. Brother Schmid and I will leave after lunch. Mr. Tisza said we could use his small truck. There is no other way."

Father Csoki could hardly believe what he had just heard. "What you are proposing is suicide," he said half-angrily, loading staples into the handle of the stapling gun. "What will you and Brother Schmid do if you're stopped by the AVOs or the Nepkos? Don't you suppose the police will wonder why two Benedictine brothers from West Germany are driving around Budapest in a delivery van? If you manage to get the weapons from Rakoczi— and he lives miles from here, in the Budakalasz section of the city—and the AVOs stop you and search the back of the truck, then what? Or if you have to make a run for it and some policeman takes the license number? No! Never! I cannot consent to such a wild, fantastic scheme."

"Brother Schmid and I would venture from here disguised as workmen," Camellion said softly and very insistently. "With the materials in my makeup kit, I'll change our appearance; and we have numerous sets of false identity papers from which to choose, including membership books that identify us as members of the Communist Party's Kontakta toy factory group. We have false license plates for the van; we obtained those earlier in the week from Tibor Arpad."

"Yes, and that night you and Thomas came very close to being discovered." Csoki's voice was low but sharp with irritation. "Both of you got back only minutes before Father Redlich was up and about!"

The Monsignor turned and stared at Camellion. "May I

48

ask how you and Brother Schmid propose to leave here—and in disguise yet—without Father Redlich or the Kobalinsky seeing you? Christ walked on water, but I daresay the two of you don't know the secret of invisibility! And suppose you do succeed in getting back here with the launchers and shells. How do you propose we move them from the truck to the float? The privacy hedge would hide us from the street. But what would hide us from Father Redlich and Mr. and Mrs. Kobalinsky?"

The Death Merchant smacked his lips. "Well, Father, I haven't figured all that out yet, but I'm working on it!"

Ignoring an amazed Father Csoki, Brother Krim picked up another hydrangea and stapled it to the float.

Brother Schmid's wide face broke out into a big grin. "The Predtridecarone would knock them out for hours," he whispered in a husky voice. "The catch is, they'd smell somebody's dirty hands after they woke up. So we can forget Predtridecarone."

Father Csoki looked as startled as a snake with a sudden backache. "We can forget any plan to get the rocket antitank launchers and shells," he said adamantly. "To go across the city and risk being stopped by the AVOs, that would be courting death. Here the two of you are safe."

The pleasant fragrance of Madonna lilies—there were several beds of them to the rear of the church—drifted to Camellion, who felt sorry for the bushy-haired priest. The man was so damned afraid of death!

"Father, the entire purpose of life is to reach death," Camellion said in an easy voice. "As a man of God, you should know that birth and death are joined together by life, by a short period of time. So the only reason for our existence must be to prove that time exists. One might say that the only positive thing we discover in life is that time is eternal. The irony is, though, that in eternity time doesn't exist. It's all the forever now."

Father Csoki turned and stared disapprovingly at the Death Merchant.

"Well, I must say, Brother Krim, your Kantian view of existence is as silly as some of the things I've heard Paul say. I know he has a death wish. I didn't know that intelligence agents from the German Federal Republic—or are you members of the American CIA?—were similarly afflicted with the desire to terminate their life by acts of violence. The purpose of our existence on earth is to love and serve God!"

Raymond Merrit said mildly, "We're only simple brothers from West Germany—and God is not going to get the launchers for us."

Paul Tisza added, "God helps those who help themselves!"

"Like Brother Schmid said, he and I are only brothers," Camellion said, half in jest. He paused in his work and stepped back from the float to get a better perspective.

"And I'm St. Peter!" snapped Father Csoki, also taking a few steps backward and stabbing Camellion with sharp stares. "If you were a sensible man, you would realize that there isn't any way we can get the launchers, just as you would know that by assuming a future, man makes his present endurable and his past meaningful."

"Father, if Brother Krim and I were sensible men, we wouldn't be in this business!" Ray Merrit said with a low, chilling laugh.

Monsignor Csoki ignored the big man. The priest had never liked him. He smiled too much and too often. Csoki disliked Camellion even more. Brother Krim was too cold-blooded, too computerized. Worse, he could discuss theology like a theologian! Could he be an ex-priest?

Feeling that he had Brother Krim backed into a corner, Father Csoki took another artificial flower from the carton by the float and said slyly, "Besides, you have admitted that Father Redlich and the Kobalinskys pose an insurmountable obstacle. You can't just snap your fingers and make them go away."

The Death Merchant ignored the irony and said coldly, "Wrong! I didn't say 'insurmountable.' And you're right. Brother Schmid and I can't make them go away. But we can use direct action."

"What does that mean?" the priest asked, childlike.

"We can kill the three of them!"

Too stunned by the unexpected, Monsignor Csoki did not reply.

There was silence, except for Camellion's humming Liszt's *Les Preludes*. Working with religious people always presented the same problem: it was always difficult to gauge how much one could depend on them.

Until about ten o'clock at night, the Elizabeth Bridge, the largest bridge spanning the Danube, which divides the Buda and the Pest sides of the ancient Hungarian capital, was usually a permanent traffic jam of buses, taxies, trucks, and private cars, as were the other six bridges, the boulevards lined with beautiful old buildings, and every major street and thoroughfare in Budapest.

Downtown in Pest, the famous pastry shop on Voros-Marty Square, a Budapest landmark since the days of the Austro-Hungarian empire, was often a mob scene combining the past and modernity. Inside, young people in bluejeans (Hungarian made because only the new, gilded youth could afford the real thing from the United States) crowded the counters to buy the fantastic "Dobos" chocolate cake. Outside, there was a battle for the sidewalk tables, where the old and the young sipped espresso coffee or beer, ate more pastry, and watched the afternoon shoppers and strollers.

Along the Danube, as far as the Visegrad mountain-and-river resort forty miles west of Budapest, modernistic weekend homes and cottages, belonging to Hungary's new wealthy class, sat next to each other in contented affluence. The truly powerful had weekend and vacation homes in Tihany, on the shores of fifty-mile long Lake Balaton.

Underneath this phony national smile was deep discontent, existing not only in the intelligentsia, but in the middle class, concerned with traditional Western freedoms. Resentment of the government and discontent ran deep in the universities and in such huge industrial complexes as Budapest's Csepel Island on the Danube (still called the "Red Csepel"), where students and workers had developed hatreds on practical as well as ideological grounds against the wealth of the new bourgeoisie.

There was inflation (although the word "inflation" was taboo) that burdened most industrial workers—sixty percent of the Hungarian work force was in industry—

51

and white-collar employees in government offices. As in most Communist nations, it was impossible to explain statistically how, for example, there could be so many private cars in Hungary, since an imported Soviet Fiat costs 80,000 forints, and an East German Trabant 40,000 forints, and a worker or a teacher earns about 3,000 forints per month.

"We have our ways," Paul Tisza had told Camellion, with a twinkle in his deep-set eyes. "Our ways" meant dealing in everything from specialized "private sector" services to sophisticated forms of black-marketeering, both of which had become part and parcel of the complex social system.

Richard Camellion reflected that Communism was similar to the prohibitions against liquor, gambling, and prostitution. *A good idea, but it won't work and can never succeed! Neither will this mission if I don't put my foot down and tell Father Csoki who's boss.*

He began to go through the files of his mind, glancing toward the rounded back of St. Matthias Church, which was also called the coronation church. it had been built by King Bela IV in the thirteenth century and had been rebuilt by King Yok in the fifteenth. Its Loretto Chapel contained a fine seventeenth-century marble figure of the infant Jesus and a madonna from the workshop of Lucas Cranach. The Trinity Chapel held the remains of King Bela III and his queen. There were also some paintings in the church by the Hungarian artist Michael Zichy, who had been court painter of the Czars in the nineteenth century, and by Bertalan Szekely. The edict of Pope Calixtus III had been proclaimed in St. Matthias Church, ordering the bells of the whole Christian world to be run at noon in memory of the victory of the Hungarian warrior Hunyadi Janos over the Turks.

Thinking about the inside of the church won't help me figure out what to do about Father Redlich and the couple from Poland.

How the Company had smuggled the makeup kit, the drugs, and the explosives to Father Csoki was a mystery that the Death Merchant had not tried to solve. He didn't know, knew he would never know, and didn't care. He also knew that Monsignor Csoki didn't know the over-the-border from Austria route.

The 3' x 1' x 1' wooden case had been brought to the priests' home by members of the Society of the Double Cross when Father Redlich and Father Szell and Father Kodaly were not around. The box had then been hidden beneath the floor of the garage, in a secret compartment that had previously been prepared by Thomas Lakatos and the four other janitors of the huge church.

Emytusidrex is among the drugs! I think that might be the answer.

Camellion picked an artificial white azalea, looked at the tiny clip of paper attached to the stem—*Made in Japan*—and said, "Father Csoki, very possibly I have the answer to the problem of Redlich and the couple from Poland. Could you tell me what is being served for lunch?"

Raymond Merrit grinned, showing big, white teeth. Paul Tisza paused in his work at the top right-hand corner of the float and looked at Camellion with interest.

Monsignor Csoki appeared to be twice as surprised as a subversive termite trapped in the beam of a searchlight. "Lunch? What does lunch have to do with it?"

"What will be served?"

The priest thought for a moment, moving a skinny hand through his heavy hair. "I think . . . yes, I'm sure. We'll be having *Szegedi halaszle*, wine and—now see here, Brother Krim! I demand to know what this is all about!"

"This *Szegedi halaszle*. It's a kind of fish stew, is it not?"

"Yes, but I fail to see the connection."

"Brother Schmid and I have an all-purpose drug called Emytusidrex," Camellion explained. "A drop of Emytusidrex, when put into someone's food, will give all the symptoms of staphylococcal food poisoning, complete with nausea, the G.I. trots, and severe abdominal pain. All we have to do is put one drop into the plates of Redlich and the Polish couple, and by three this afternoon, they should be in the hospital and out of action at least overnight."

53

"My God in heaven!" Father Csoki's eyes widened with amazement and the blue hydrangea slipped from his fingers and fell to the flagstones.

"The—'G.I. trots'?" echoed Paul Tisza, who had moved close to the Death Merchant.

"Diarrhea," Brother Schmid said. "And there is no way the drug can be traced."

"The two cooks and their two helpers are with us," Tisza said. "They will be glad to assist."

"Each individual plate is filled in the kitchen and brought into the dining area," Camellion said with cool deliberation, throwing the words at a confused Monsignor Csoki. "The drug won't kill them or do any kind of permanent damage."

Father Csoki gestured eloquently in indecision. "You're not lying to me?"

Brother Schmid answered him, quietly and frankly: "He doesn't have to lie, Father. Either we use the drug or take direct action. One thing is certain—we're going after the rocket launchers!"

"Father, the decision is yours," the Death Merchant said.

CHAPTER FIVE

At the last moment Camellion had decided that it would be too dangerous to use Paul Tisza's truck. Should they be forced to abandon the vehicle for some reason, the false license plates would not conceal the true ownership. The police would trace the truck to Tisza through the motor and body numbers on file at a central registry. The Death Merchant and Merrit had done the next best thing: they had gone out and commandeered a car.

The Emytusidrex was a marvelously sneaky drug. Two ambulances had taken Father Redlich and Emil and Mary Kobalinsky to the Ptzizutit U. hospital at 3:30 in the afternoon. Some kind of food poisoning, the doctor said. Probably of the staphylococcal type. The others who had eaten the *Szegedi halaszle* should come to the hospital if they had any symptoms. It was nothing to worry about. The doctor said that Father Redlich and the Kobalinskys would be all right in a few days.

Freed then from curious eyes, the Death Merchant had gone to work with his box of makeup and cosmetic goodies—the cytex skin-tight, tissue-paper-thin face masks were a great help—and when he had completed the job on himself and on Merrit, the true features of both men no longer existed.

Camellion had been turned into a man in his late forties (ten years older than he actually was). His face was blotched, his cheeks webbed with telangiectasistic veins. His nose had been lengthened and the nostrils widened. He was bald as a rock. And since his *Terkep,* or Hungarian internal passport, Communist Party membership book, union book, and other papers identified him as a lathe operator at the vast Ponchek Electrical Works, "Donath Pal" was dressed in accordance with his occupation, wearing a brown cotton work shirt and pants to match.

Merrit, who was also a machinist at the Ponchek Electrical Works, was dressed in a similar manner, his face identical to the photograph in his Terkep book. A wig of thick brown hair covered his own wavy blond locks. His face was a field of wrinkles dotted with freckles. Three of his upper teeth appeared to be stainless steel, and he sported a small beard.

The rest had been easy. Each armed with a Sterling .25 caliber automatic and carrying a cheap imitation leather attaché case, the Death Merchant and "Sandor Hadjok" had walked four blocks to Andre Szn U., where they had hailed a taxi and instructed the driver to take them to Hero Square, at the end of the Avenue of the People's Republic.

There wasn't anything suspicious about the two attaché cases. Like the Russians, most Hungarians of the working class always carried attaché cases. Who could tell when one might see a scarce item in a store and have to buy it? An attaché case was ideal for carrying such hard-to-find items.

Camellion and Merrit had fully realized the terrible risk

55

they had taken. If they had been stopped by the AVO, a gun battle would have been the result, for each man's attaché case contained an Ingram pistol, which could be fired either on semi- or full automatic, the latter making the weapon a submachine gun. There were four extra magazines for each Ingram, every magazine containing thirty 9mm Kurz cartridges.

They had found the transportation they wanted parked in front of the *Snabad Nap* (Free People) bookstore at 276 Lovolde Tor: a compact walk-in van with Czech license plates.

"Perfect!" Camellion had said to Merrit, who had grinned and said, "They have to be in this damned country on a summer vacation. That van is ideal. I hope there's not four or five Czechs traveling in it. We can't handle that many without attracting attention, and we'd have to stash them like cord wood."

Patiently, Camellion and Merrit had waited, the Death Merchant glancing at his wristwatch every now and then, to give the impression—in case anyone was watching—that he and Merrit were waiting for someone. Which they were.

After ten minutes, a young couple, in their middle twenties and dressed in gaudily colored shorts and shirts, came out of the bookstore and walked to the van, which was painted a bright pink. Against the pink background had been painted bouquets of flowers of every shade and color.

Camellion and Merrit had moved in right behind the young man and the young woman and had climbed into the van before the woman could slide the door shut.

Ten minutes later the van (a Czech-made Vedasko) was moving down broad Ferenc Boulevard, Merrit, as cool as an icicle, doing the driving. The van was not air-conditioned, and his face was dotted with tiny beads of perspiration.

"You're sure the Thorasulfil will keep them unconscious?" Merrit asked, watching the heavy traffic ahead of him through dark brown sun glasses. "I've never used the stuff, but I'm told it will knock out an elephant."

"I've used it," Camellion said. "They'll remain in dreamland for three hours, perhaps a little more or a little less. We'll have more than enough time to pick up the shells and launchers and get back to the church. After we unload in the garage, we'll drive the van a quarter of a mile from the church and Lakatos can pick us up in one of the church cars."

"I have an itch on the back of my neck that tells me Father Csoki won't go for that idea," Merrit said. "I also have the feeling we're going to have trouble with him when we reach the shrine next Sunday."

"We can always put his morality to sleep with a good stiff dose of Thorasulfil," Camellion said. Thinking of how he had drained the hypodermic on the two young people, he turned halfway around and looked at the unconscious couple in the rear of the van. Lying between rolled-up sleeping bags and other camping gear, the man and woman appeared to be enjoying a deep, peaceful sleep.

"Speaking of drugs, I still think we should have used the Emytusidrex on Father Szell and Father Kodaly," Merrit said. "There were eleven of us at the table, and for only three people to come down with food poisoning seems kind of suspicious to me. Of course, like the doctor said, that's how food poisoning often works. It can strike two or three and skip over everyone else, or else hit the whole group."

"Not only that, but we might have gotten Szell and Kodaly into serious trouble if we had dosed them with Emytusidrex," Camellion said. "Once we escape to Austria, the AVO could accuse Szell and Kodaly of not escaping with us and the other priests because they had been stricken with food poisoning. But what about directions? Are you positive you can get to Rakoczi's house on Tized Street?"

The big man chuckled. "No problem there. This is my fourth time in Budapest. I can get to Tized Street OK. It's the damned language that throws me. All I know are the usual phrases—*igen:* 'yes'; *nem:* 'no'; *elnezest kerek:* 'excuse me'; *jo napot kivanok:* 'good day'—key phrases like that. And that bird George Rakoczi worries me. We know what he looks like from his photograph. But he doesn't

57

know us from Molly's cow. If he doesn't accept our code words, we could have trouble with him."

"He knows we're coming. At least he's expecting someone to come to his house and pick up the ordnance hidden in his attic. I don't anticipate trouble, not unless we're stopped by the Nepkos or the AVOs. If worst comes to worst . . . there's always our L-pills."

"Yeah, of all the Commie cops in Communist Europe, the AVOs are the worst sadists," Merrit said in disgust. "And those two ding-dongs in power now—Skedfu and Barthory—belong in a funny farm. I don't know about this new bunch of modern terrorists, but in the old AVO, before the revolution, many of them were homosexual. Some had been sex perverts and others had been petty criminals. But I can tell you one thing about the old AVO that damns Communism to hell and makes it doubly hypocritical: the typical AVO officer had been a bully boy for the Horthy regime, a servile tool of Hitler's Nazi occupiers, and a brutal operator for the Szalasi dictatorship. These were all fascist governments, and fascism was supposed to be the deadly enemy of Communism. But when the Soviets assumed control, they adopted into their system the worst elements of the fascist police force and called them good Communists. Crap! Many of those goddamn AVOs didn't even know what Communism was."

A ghost of a grin twitched the Death Merchant's lips, and he said, without emphasis: "I'm not sure who is right, I in my belief that an AVO matures by a process of inevitable deterioration in a Communist society, or Father Csoki, who believes that the AVO is the end result of Lenin's preaching terror and the liquidation of opposition as a calculated strategy of power."

The van passed the Hungarian Parliament building, a neo-Gothic masterpiece, with a long facade, slender pinnacles, and an imposing central dome. Ahead was Szent Istvan Korut.

"I am sure that if Japan, or West Germany for that matter, were to go Communist tomorrow," Camellion said soberly, "within six months there could be Communist secret police. Communism must have its secret police in order to exist, in order to silence the people it has de-

58

frauded. And make no mistake about it, Merrit: it could happen in the United States. That's why you and I are risking our lives right now in Hungary—to make damn sure that it doesn't happen in America."

"I can't argue with your reasoning," Merrit said with a long sigh. "I hate to admit it, but there are millions of people in the U.S. who hate blacks, or despise Jews, or Catholics, or whatever. Crap! What the whole damn world needs is dirtier fingernails and cleaner minds!"

Merrit stopped for a red light at an intersection. Several minutes later, he turned left and drove on Szent Istvan Korut, the street that led to Margit Hid, or, in English, Margaret Bridge, and to Buda, on the right bank of the Danube. Very soon the van was on the bridge, and Camellion and Merrit could see, to their right, the lovely, boat-shaped Margitsziget—Margaret Island. Poets had been singing about this fairy-tale islet in the Danube ever since a Roman garrison commander made it his summer residence two thousand years ago. Seven centuries have passed since a young princess named Margaret—her father King Bela IV having been defeated by the Mongols—retired to a nunnery on the island, where she died at the age of 29. A few years ago, Margaret was canonized by the church and is revered as Budapest's patron saint.

Noticing that the Death Merchant was studying Margaret Island, Merrit said in a cheerful voice, "I was down there a few years ago. It's a fun resort. Its banks are lined with boathouses and beaches, and there's a hotel at the far end of the island. Believe it or not, it's called the Grand Hotel. Just like out of a movie, right?"

Then, seeing that Camellion had opened the two attaché cases and was shoving magazines into the Ingrams, Merrit twisted his mouth into a crooked grin. "You think we're going to need them?"

"I hope not, but we had better be prepared in case we do," Camellion said. He ran his tongue over the tiny metal capsule attached to the last molar on the right side of his mouth. In case of capture, the L-pill would be the last resort.

A green AVO car passed by as Merrit turned the wheel

to allow the van to continue on Martirok Utja, the wide street that led from Margaret Bridge.

"We'll stay on this street," Merrit said. "It will take us to Szena Square, which is only a few blocks from Rakoczi's house on Tized Street. What's your plan? I don't propose that we drive up to his front door and wave an American flag!"

The Death Merchant returned the second Ingram pistol to its attaché case. "We'll drive by his house and case the place," he said. "According to Father Csoki, Rakoczi has the stuff in his garage. We'll have to pull inside his garage to load up. Depending on his neighbors and how nosy they are, it's a risk, but there isn't any other way."

In a very short while the van was moving through Szena Square, which was filled with bicycles and cars. Merrit made a right turn onto Retuk U., slowed slightly, and said, "Another block and we'll reach Tized. Tized is only a block long and runs north and south. George Rakoczi's number is a hundred and twenty-four. His house should be in the middle of the block."

They were almost to Tized Street when they saw the green AVO patrol car parked on the corner of Retuk and Tized, the front of the car facing the west. A ding-dong warning drummed in both Merrit's and Camellion's head.

"I have the feeling that we should continue straight on Retuk," Merrit suggested, ignoring the AVO vehicle, in which four uniformed agents were sitting. "Those four jokers don't represent the Good Fairy. . . ."

"Neither do we," Camellion said grimly. "Let's turn on Tized and see what the score is. We've come this far and there's no use turning back."

Merrit shrugged and thrust out his square jaw. "Why not?" he muttered. "I'd just as soon get killed in the sunshine as in a snowstorm!"

Easily he slowed the van and turned onto Tized Street. And immediately he and Camellion saw what they didn't want to see. Four AVO cars were parked by the curb, halfway down the block, three in front of George Rakoczi's house, the fourth one across the street.

"It would seem we have walked into a mess!" Merrit

said with a deep sigh. "We can't turn around. There isn't room, unless we turn into someone's drive."

"Or go over the curb and turn around on somebody's lawn," Camellion said. "Either way we'll look as suspicious as two black men at a KKK meeting. All we can do is drive straight ahead and ice them before they get us. Take a look at that; Rakoczi's had it."

Two AVOs were dragging George Rakoczi down the steps of his porch. His hands were handcuffed behind his back, and an AVO man was holding on to each of his arms. AVO men were shoving a weeping woman and a teenage boy ahead of them out the front door. Coming around from the north side of the house, half a dozen AVOs were carrying two Russian RPG2 rocket launchers and two cases of missiles.

"Those are two launchers we can forget about," Merrit muttered.

Guiding the van with one hand, he reached out and began stuffing the spare Ingram magazines into his belt. Then, with his right hand, he picked up the Ingram pistol, his trigger finger resting lightly against the trigger guard.

At the end of the street, two more AVO squad cars were parked on the corners of Tized and Lovohaz streets, the cars parked horizontally, their fronts facing each other.

The van was passing slowly between the four cars in the middle of the block when the two AVO patrol vehicles at the end of the block pulled together, blocking the street.

Ray Merrit slowed the van even more. "You figure they're wise?"

"They're only checking everyone who turns in just to be on the safe side," the Death Merchant said. "We'll use *aktivniye meropriyatiye*—'active measures,' as the Russians say. We'll kill them when they come over, then escape in one of their cars. This van is too slow, and I don't want the young couple in back hurt."

"I'm more worried about us," Merrit said, then brought the van to a halt ten feet from the two AVO cars blocking the end of Tized Street. Holding the Ingram pistols in their laps, Camellion and Merrit thumbed off the safety catches and switched the weapons to full automatic, watching as two AVOs sauntered to the van from the left, another approaching from the right. A fourth unsmiling agent remained leaning against the front fender of the police car parked to the right of the van. All four looked meaner than a cobra at mating time.

The two AVOs to the left were only five feet away, and the one to the right was about the same distance, when the Death Merchant and Merrit stuck the Ingrams out of the open windows and opened fire, the sharp, rapid cracks of the two deadly weapons shattering the regular everyday noises of the usually quiet street.

The two AVOs to the left crashed backward, wide-eyed and bloody, the half-dozen power-point projectiles popping off bits of green uniform cloth as they cut into the chests of the men and smashed away their lives. The AVO to the right, catching two of the Death Merchant's 9mms in the chest, shook for a few seconds, a look of pure horror and disbelief on his face. Then he wilted to the ground, jerked, and lay still.

The AVO leaning against the fender of the patrol car had time only to look startled before the Death Merchant popped two nine-millimeter projectiles into his chest.

"The ones behind us—put them to sleep forever!" Camellion said.

Automatically, he and Ray Merrit pushed back the sliding doors of the van, jumped out, spun around, and opened fire on the amazed AVO in the middle of the block. Four of the green-uniformed goofs were shoving Mr. and Mrs. Rakoczi and their son into a car, while the others were placing the antitank weapons and the missiles into the trunks of two other cars. The Rakoczis, already in one car, dove to the floor, Mrs. Rakoczi screaming and falling on top of her husband. The AVO agent, who had been shoving her into the car, cried out and fell sideways, his left side ripped and slashed by slugs. The man next to him, Captain Stephen Badulas, the AVO commander in charge of the party, stopped a slug in the left shoulder bone, cried out, spun around, and tried to draw his Kal pistol from the holster on his belt. His hand got as far as the flap of the holster but no farther. He died in a splatter of bone chips when a 9mm Ingram slug scattered the front of his skull.

Caught by the totally unexpected, four more AVOs went down, riddled by the Death Merchant's and Merrit's deadly spray of copper-coated lead. One AVO, playing it as smart as Einstein, flopped to the parkway and pretended to be dead.

The three AVOs who had loading shells into the trunk of the car parked on the opposite side of the street attempted to throw themselves underneath the vehicle. Two succeeded; one didn't. He caught two 9mm slugs in the back of his right thigh. In agony and slowly bleeding to death from a severed femoral artery, the man fell into the open trunk of the car. As he fell, his hand grabbed one of the missiles, and the cone-shaped rocket fell to the pavement.

In the meanwhile, the two other men belly-crawled to the front of the car. They were crawling out underneath the front bumper as the AVO patrol car that had been parked on the corner of Retuk and Tized streets came roaring down the street, the man next to the driver firing at the van.

"Come on! Let's get the hell out of here!" yelled Merrit, who was down in front of the van, listening to Kiraly submachine gun slugs thudding into the van and stabbing hotly through the air.

"Patience is the reward of all virtue," the Death Merchant said.

Lying flat on the pavement, he was aiming the Ingram underneath the van.

"Uh huh. And proverbs are the final sayings of dead men!" growled Merrit. He turned and judged the distance to the nearest AVO car parked in front of the van.

"But not in this case," the Death Merchant said, half in amusement. Watching the speeding AVO car tearing down Tized Street, he waited until it was practically side by side with the vehicle from whose open trunk the missile had fallen. Taking careful aim at the rocket shell, the Death Merchant fired.

The explosion must have been heard all over Budapest. There was an earth-shaking roar and a brief flash of smoke and flame. The car in whose trunk the other shells were stored rose eight feet in the air and came down with a crash that crushed one of the AVO men, who hadn't crawled out from underneath the front in time. Half a dozen missiles rolled out of the trunk against the AVO car that had been tearing down the street and had been turned over by the explosion, killing the driver. The three other cars had not been damaged, although the explosion had turned two of them sideways, so that their rears faced the houses on Tized Street.

"The best magic show in town," Camellion said. "Now you see them, now you don't!" Jumping up, he rushed over to the AVO car, whose engine Merrit had already started. The CIA agent was waiting impatiently and watching the car in whose trunk the rocket missiles had been stored. The car, a Russian Volga, had caught fire and flames and smoke had engulfed the machine. An AVO man and the three Rakoczis had jumped from one of the cars that had been knocked sideways and were running across the yard to the porch of the Rakoczis' house. They reached the porch just as the gas tank of the burning car exploded into a ball of orange and yellow fire. Flaming pieces of automobile went flying through the air, some of the burning wreckage falling on the scattered missile shells.

"Like General Custer once said, 'Let's get the hell out of here!' " the Death Merchant joked.

Merrit guided the AVO car onto Lovohaz Street, he and the Death Merchant ignoring the other streams of traffic moving in both directions on the wide street.

"Don't exceed the speed limit," cautioned Camellion, hunching down in the seat. "As far as anyone knows, we're plainclothes AVO. No one had time to recognize us. We should be all right after we ditch this car."

"Right on, pal," Merrit agreed. "The AVOs we blew up didn't have time to get a message to Central on their radios. We should have at least fifteen minutes to get rid of this green job and lose ourselves. We can take a trolleybus back to the other side of the city. I'll drive another—" He glanced and grinned at the Death Merchant when another roar sounded behind them. Another rocket missile had exploded. "I'll drive a few more blocks and turn left on Fizeto. Getting out of this will be easier than shooting whales in a barrel."

The Death Merchant turned and stared through the rear window. Everything appeared to be normal. No one was trailing them.

Ray Merrit turned on Fizeto, drove several more blocks, then made a right onto Ztarsog Utja. Several blocks ahead, to the left, was the old neo-Gothic Parliament house, with its 18 courtyards, 27 staircases, and 312-foot dome. A national monument, the ancient Parliament house was open to the general public; and even at this distance, Camellion and Merrit could see numerous visitors going up the wide marble steps of the large building.

"We'll go in the front of Parliament house and vanish out the back," Merrit said jovially. "We'll cut across to Martirok Utja and stop at the Regi Orszaghaz cafe. They have a gypsy band there and serve a *porkolt*—that's a kind of veal stew with concentrated paprika sauce—that's out of this world. Their *szilvapalinka* is also very good—if you like plum brandy."

Merrit glanced at the Death Merchant, who was putting the Ingram machine pistols into the attaché cases, and who looked as unhappy as a polar bear at the equator. "What's the trouble?" asked Merrit. "In another ten minutes God won't be able to find us. We'll have lost ourselves and be as safe as two saints in heaven."

Camellion, snapping shut the second attaché case, replied, "I was thinking of those two antitank weapons. Without them we're going to have a difficult time getting close to Karolyi Castle. Of course, we still have plenty of C-4 packets."

Merrit, pulling the car to the curb several hundred feet from the sprawling Parliament house, shook his head slowly from side to side.

"We have to be realistic, Camellion. The DD/P doesn't expect us to do the impossible. This mission's a bust and we both know it."

"No, not necessarily," Camellion said. "When we get

back to the church, I'm going to send Thomas Lakatos to a sporting goods store. I have a plan that might smack out those Russian tanks around the castle."

CHAPTER SIX

Far to the west there were dark traces of dangerous rain clouds, fluffs of towering thunderheads, and blue-black cumuli that appeared silently threatening; but the sky over Fonyod was clear, the midafternoon sun a furnace torturing the thousands of pilgrims preparing for the final leg of the journey to the Shrine of Our lady of Bakony.

From all over Hungary, and from other nations, they had come—by private car, by minibuses, by camping vans, and, from within Hungary, even by horse and wagon. Friday they had marched in the procession in Budapest; there had been numerous floats, each a tribute to the Immaculate Conception, the Mother of God. From Budapest, and from other cities and towns in Hungary, they had started the journey to Fonyod—hundreds of vehicles, even touring buses furnished by IBUSZ, the Hungarian Tourist Office. The pilgrims slept by the side of the road at night and resumed the journey the next morning, the first stream of cars reaching Fonyod by noon on Saturday, the hundreds of automobiles parking close to the shores of Lake Balaton, the landlocked Riviera of Hungary. Here, at Lake Balaton, the sun shines an average of two thousand hours per year, the water tempers the summer heat, the bass bite on any bait, and children can wade out for hundreds of feet in the shallow water, which sparkles with bracing carbonic gas as well as sunlight. Both shores of the forty-eight-mile-long "Hungarian Sea" form one continuous summer resort.

There is Tihany Peninsula, a thumb of land that all but cuts Lake Balaton in two. Its three-mile area is a national park; yet few Hungarians ever dare to visit the peninsula, which contains the summer homes of the Communists in power. Bela Skedfu and Sigismund Barthory both had villas at the end of the peninsula.

A resort town, Fonyod was built around the western end of the lake, in an area riddled with extinct geyser craters. Aromatic lavender carpets of color covered its fields and nature lovers could count two hundred species of butterflies. There were those who said that the area around Fonyod was one of the loveliest in all of Europe.

Dressed in a light brown sports shirt and pants to match, the Death Merchant sat on a canvas folding stool to one side of the East German Trabant van that had brought him, Father Csoki, and brother Schmid to Fonyod.

Karolyi Castle might as well be in another galaxy! Camellion adjusted his wraparound sunglasses and shifted the brown poplin field cap farther back on his head, pushing up on the visor to give him a better view of the hazy Bakony Mountains in the distance to the northwest.

Five miles northwest of Lake Balaton was the Bakony Forest, a heavily wooded area of beech and oak that had once been the hideout of many Hungarian *betyars*—highwaymen. Beyond the forest were the Bakony Mountains, stretching northeast and southwest, 4,000 square kilometers of rugged peaks, hilly plateaus, deep gorges, ravines, and small valleys dotted with boulders of granite, basalt, and other kinds of extrusive volcanic rock. However, as mountain ranges go, the Bakony Mountains were nothing to brag about, Mount Kekes, the tallest peak, being only 3,410 feet tall.

To the west of the mountains was the Little Alfold (or plain), a region noted for its wheat. Past the plain, to the west, was Austria.

Sitting there, the Death Merchant calculated how long it would take the thousands of modern-day Crusaders to reach the shrine. *Hmmm, Sunday morning high mass at nine o'clock. Five miles to the forest. Another six or seven miles through the forest. Finally the road leading through the foothills to the area of the shrine. Another four or five miles. Considering delays, for one reason or another, we should reach the shrine between noon and one o'clock.*

Father Peter Csoki hurried out from the side of the van carrying a sleeping bag, his sparrowlike legs stabbing the ground like two icepicks wearing shoes. Behind him came Brother Schmid—Ray Merrit—lugging a Bleuet Gazi Stove and a rolled-up Back Packer nylon tent. Merrit turned and winked at Camellion, clearly conveying what he, an atheist, thought of the entire pilgrimage.

For almost as far as one could see, hundreds of other people, preparing to spend the remainder of the day and the night at Fonyod, were unloading camping equipment from various kinds of vehicles. Here and there, the Death Merchant could see a uniformed AVO cop helping people to unload and doing his best to prove to foreign visitors that life in Communist Hungary wasn't at all bad—and see how helpful the AVOs were! See how they loved and helped the workers!

Half a dozen AVOs were actually helping to move off the road a giant float, an artistic masterpiece of red and white roses, with a twelve-foot statue of the Virgin Mary in the center. This float was very special because it represented St. Stephen's basilica at Esztergom. For seven centuries, Esztergom had been the seat of Hungary's Roman Catholic archprimate, with its basilica containing the world's largest altarpiece painted on canvas.

While Father Csoki unpacked the tent, Merrit moved his big bulk back into the van and came out with a folding camp stool and a nylon duck rucksack. He placed the stool next to the Death Merchant, sat down, reached into the rucksack, and pulled out a tobacco pouch and a green pipe with a billiard-shaped bowl. He unzipped the pouch, thrust in the pipe, and began stuffing the bowl with tobacco. Removing the bowl from the pouch, he noticed that Camellion was studying the pipe with calculating appraisal. "I gave up cigarettes a year ago," Merrit said, carefully tapping the tobacco around the rim of the bowl. "That's when I took up pipe smoking."

Merrit took a book of matches from his pocket and inclined his head to the left. "I see that Father Nosbyti and Father Deak are parked close by. Personally I don't think we can depend on them. When trouble starts, they're more likely to pray then to shoot. And we have no way of knowing what the AVOs might have dragged out of George Rakoczi."

Camellion remained silent. Merrit put the pipe into his mouth, struck a match, and lit up, puffing contentedly.

The Death Merchant slowly turned his head and studied Father Josef Nosbyti, a friendly, medium-built priest in his early thirties, and Father Stephen Deak, an older man with long sideburns and a full beard. Both men had driven to Fonyod in a Volkswagen minibus owned by St. Matthias. They had parked a hundred feet from the Trabant van and were setting up pup tents.

The Death Merchant wondered how many AVO intelligence agents were mingling with the hundreds of people. Probably dozens; yet there was no way he could be sure. Even if AVO Section 4-D I-Agents were watching—so what? Since Fathers Deak and Nosbyti were among the priests at St. Matthias, it was only natural that the two priests should park close to their superior, Father Csoki, and the two Benedictine brothers from West Germany.

It was also perfectly natural that Father Lido Nanasi, the fourth priest, should have journeyed to Lake Balaton with Janos Rosmartyi, Paul Tisza, and Tibor Arpad, the four men driving a Russian Pobeda. The three laymen were members of the St. Matthias parish. Furthermore, Paul Tisza was president of the Men's League of the Sacred Heart. Tibor Arpad, who had a reputation as a fanatical Communist (which was what made him so valuable to the Society of the Double Cross), was secretary of the League. As a coverup, Arpad always reported the League's minutes of meeting to the AVO.

A hundred feet behind the Death Merchant, Merrit, and Monsignor Csoki was the fourth group of men who would risk their lives in attacking Karolyi Castle—Thomas Lakatos, Frantisek Palfecky, and Mihaly Szechenyi. They had driven from Budapest in a Volga. Realists, the three men knew the terrible dangers facing them. Even now they were skipping on a loose tightrope wobbling over a canyon of death. Should the AVO, for some odd reason, search the four vehicles that Camellion, Merrit, and the other ten men were driving, the secret police would discover items that had nothing to do with paying reverence to the Mother of God.

Regular demolition hand grenades, Kiraly nine-millimeter submachine guns, and spare magazines were hidden in the Volkswagen minibus. There were automatic weapons and grenades in the Volga and the Pobeda. As for the Trabant walk-in van, it was a four-wheeled rolling factory of explosives. In a carefully concealed compartment underneath the floor, there were two Ingram machine pistols, a crossbow with a varnished rifle stock, twenty round-nosed arrows, a box of impact-contact L-14t detonators, twenty phosphorous-thermite grenades, and thirty one-pound packages of C-4 plastic explosive. Each packet was the equivalent, in explosive power, of a hundred sticks of dynamite.

Father Csoki, having finished setting up the nylon tent, stepped back and admired his work. Fine. Every stake was in place; each rope was tight. The priest turned and smiled at Camellion and Merrit.

"Brother Krim, Brother Schmid. Aren't you going to take your sleeping bags out of the van?" There was an anxious quality to his voice.

"Oh, there's plenty of time, Father," the Death Merchant said, and stood up. He glanced up at the clear, hot sky. "Right now I'm more interested in some iced tea." He turned and started for the van.

"There's several bottles of Tokay Aszu in the ice chest," Merrit called after Camellion. "Bring one back with you, Brother."

The Death Merchant stepped into the van. Father Csoki stood like a man of stone, staring out disapprovingly across the people-packed area, his gaze feeding on the shore of Lake Balaton, where children and men and women of all ages and sizes were splashing merrily in the water. It wasn't that the man of God was against people enjoying themselves. But the way some of the women were dressed, especially the young women! In skimpy bikinis that barely covered their private parts! It was a disgrace! An insult to the Almighty! Such nudity could only cause licentious desire in young men. And older men, too! Feeling his own hormones sending blood to that stiffening

70

horn with which all men buck, Csoki looked from the beach to Brother Krim, who had come out of the van, loaded down with a folding stool, an aluminum thermos, two glasses, and a square bottle of Tokay Aszu—"liquid gold," a sweet, syrupy wine.

Merrit got to his feet and helped relieve Camellion of his load, taking the thermos, the bottle of wine, and the two glasses from the Death Merchant, who unfolded the canvas stool and set it down close to his own canvas seat. "Sit down, Father, and have a drink," he said with a smile, taking the thermos and a glass from Merrit. "Today might be our last peaceful day on earth."

Merrit, uncorking the bottle of Tokay Aszu, glanced slyly around to make sure that no one was within hearing range. "I'd feel better if we knew what the AVOs tortured out of George Rakoczi and his wife and kid," he said, pouring a generous amount of "liquid gold" into a glass. "By now, Barthory's thugs have probably broken every bone in his body. And if Rakoczi had any information about us, you can bet the AVOs got it out of him."

"No!" The word jumped from Father Csoki like a cry. "Rakoczi couldn't have told the secret police about us and our plan." The priest lowered his voice. "He belonged to a different cell. His cell had only five members, and not a single one of the members had any inkling of our scheme. And none of them, other than Rakoczi, have been arrested, as far as we have been able to learn."

Father Csoki, his hand trembling from emotion, accepted a glass of iced tea from the Death Merchant, who said gently, "Father, I'm afraid that you have no understanding of how these matters operate. The AVOs wouldn't rush out and arrest the other members of Rakoczi's cell. The secret police would watch them for weeks and try to learn their contacts. You don't worry about a pebble in China when you have a boulder in Budapest. We can be positive that is how the AVOs handled Rakoczi: they watched him for weeks, then closed in when they fingured they couldn't learn any more by watching him. Therein lies the danger. In spite of our extreme caution, it is possible that the AVO is aware of the contact between your cell unit and Rakoczi's."

71

"Yes, I must confess you're right," sighed Father Csoki, "but we must have faith in the Lord." He put down his glass, pulled a large handkerchief from his pocket, and began to tie it around his head of bushy hair. His desperation was pathetic, but the Death Merchant pressed him brutally.

"We would be making a big mistake to underestimate Section 4-D of the AVO. Hungarian Intelligence knows that the antitank weapons they found in Rakoczi's garage weren't intended to be used to shoot out the stars. And let's face it: General Skedfu and Sigismund Barthory are far from stupid."

Merrit blew out a cloud of smoke, took the pipe from his mouth, and looked thoughtfully at the glass of wine in his hand. "Well," he said, "as Sherlock Holmes would say to Watson, 'We'll eliminate the alternatives that are physically and or logically impossible. Whatever alternative remains, no matter how improbable, will prove to be the solution.' That's how old pros like Skedfu and Barthory will think. Unless they're idiots, they'll have to get the idea that someone, among all these thousands of people, is using this pilgrimage to get close to Karolyi Castle!"

Father Csoki picked up his glass of tea, a mournful look on his drawn face. Merrit took out a book of matches and relit his pipe while Camellion, sipping tea, thought of the paradox in which Father Csoki was trapped. For a priest there is always the singular comfort in the invincibility of the Faith, whose axioms and syllogisms are like a fortress built solidly on bedrock; and although the disciplines are rigid, one has a certain freedom of movement within them, a movement in which one walks naturally in the way of salvation, in accordance with a formula that makes the relationship between creature and Creator a code of pure belief based on religious logic. For priests and monks and nuns, this logic is more than real: it is eternal security, the comforting knowledge that by surrendering oneself completely to the will of the Creator, one can life in peace and die in even greater peace—and live forever in Eternity, in perfect union with God.

It is doubt that can seriously undermine this faith, an

72

uncertainty that can erode this religious logic and crumble it the way the wind can scatter dust.

With his usual perceptiveness, the Death Merchant knew that it was skepticism that was tormenting Father Csoki. The priest was convinced that in attacking the castle, he and the others would be striking a deadly blow against Communism, a godlessness which, as any fool realized, was the work of Satan. Therefore, God would let the plan succeed. Goodness would triumph over evil.

But the time of man was not the time of God!

Suppose it was the will of God that the attack on the castle fail?

What then? It was a possibility that the good priest dared not think about, as he found his eyes wandering once more toward the shore of the lake and the almost-nude female bodies splashing in the water.

Father Csoki looked quickly away and, without thinking, said in a very low voice, "I am convinced that demons walk this earth, that Communism is but the prelude to the coming of the Antichrist, to the end of the world!"

Father Csoki suddenly felt slightly foolish, having previously detected that neither Brother Krim nor Brother Schmid were religious men. The priest set his jaw in determination, ready to defend his belief. Yet Camellion's answer surprised him and even made Merrit's eyes widen slightly in surprise.

"The Jews refer to this figure as Armilus, that is, he's an eschatological figure found in the literature of the Gaonic Period. Other sources—*Midrash Va-Yosha, Nistarot de-Rabbi Shimon ben Yohai*—call Armilus the successor of Gog and depict him as a monstrosity, who claims to be the Messiah or even God, and is accepted as such by the sons of Esau, but is rejected by the Jews. In the ensuing struggle the Ephraimite Messiah and a million Jews are killed, but Armilus is destroyed by God or the Davidic Messiah. The composite Armilus legend appears to have been influenced by older concepts such as Ezekiel's Gog and Magog, the Persian Ahura-Mazda, and Ahriman. It all forms part of the eschatological *aggadah* that visualizes the messianic era as the ultimate victory of

73

the forces of good, represented by the Messiah, over the power of evil."

Father Csoki, pushing his dark glasses higher up on his nose, smiled and tried not to look toward the beach. "Very well said, Brother Krim. You have an amazing understanding of evil!"

Ray Merrit took the pipe from his mouth and uttered a low laugh.

"He should have. Brother Krim's been fighting evil all his life."

Filling his glass with tea, Camellion sealed the thermos and mused, "Then again, the Antichrist just might be the weather."

"The *weather!*" Father Csoki's lower jaw almost dropped to his knees. "Are you serious?"

"Weather scientists—climatologists, that is—tell us that the temperature of the earth has lowered 2.7 degrees F since 1945; and we're told that weather over the last fifty years has been the warmest in a thousand years, but that a cycle of colder temperatures can be expected.

"To understand weather means that we can demonstrate that man has behaved differently—but predictably—during periods of warm-wet, warm-dry, cold-wet, and cold-dry weather. Wars, revolutions, economic depressions, even tastes in art and musical expression—all of it can be predicted by weather cycles, five-hundred year climatic cycles throughout history. The first five-hundred-year cycle of our historical epoch, 500 B.C. to 1 A.D., saw the growth of Greek democracy and the beginning of the democratic pattern as we know it."

"You sound positive," Father Csoki said in an odd voice.

Merrit took another drink—the hell with the weather! It was the here and now that counted.

"Every other five-hundred-year period in history belongs to Western civilization," the Death Merchant went on, carefully crossing his legs so that the 9mm Hi-Power Browning automatic in the left ankle holster wouldn't show. "Europe and North America have dominated the five-hundred-year period that is just now ending. *The next five hundred years of history will belong to Asia.*"

74

"I can't believe what you say," Father Csoki said flat out, blinking very rapidly.

"Whether you believe it or not, the main divisions of history, ancient, medieval, and modern, are marks in the history of world climate. Old civilizations crumble and new societies are born on the tides of climatic change, the turning points occurring when cold-dry periods reach their maximum severity. At this very moment, right now before our eyes, an old world is dying and a new one is being born. Right now we are living at a time comparable to 1480, just before the advent of the great Renaissance of 1500. Out of this reshuffling, out of this present world chaos and societal confusion, there will come another Renaissance, the turning point coming sometime in the 1980s. By the year 2,000 the new age will have begun. But about the year 2040 a heat climax will occur that will bring about another time of revolution. After this heat climax, glaciers will begin to advance again, and the world's temperatures will continue to fall until a cold climax is reached around 2500 A.D. At that time, the world will experience an upheaval as complete as that which terminated the Middle Ages and inaugurated our so-called modern world."

The Death Merchant drained his glass, then smiled strangely at a confused Monsignor Peter Csoki, who simply didn't know what to say to him. To quote Scripture to a man like Brother Krim—whoever he might really be—seemed inappropriate, if not ridiculous.

Father Csoki finally said in a weak voice, "Why haven't you mentioned death?"

"Death is only a word, Father. We only transcend different realities."

Father Csoki, listening to gay gypsy music being played by various groups, looked dumbly at the Death Merchant. "Have you made final plans for tomorrow?"

Camellion nodded and continued to watch men and women dancers performing a wild and furious *czardas*, one of the Hungarian national dances. "Later tonight I'll brief everyone."

Ray Merrit, bottle and glass in hand, stood up and looked at the Death Merchant. "I'm going into the van and take a nap." He sniffed the air, inhaling the smell of mushrooms and bacon being roasted on a spit. "Wake me for supper, Brother."

The Death Merchant smiled. "Pleasant dreams, Brother Schmid."

Father Csoki stood up and cleared his throat.

"I'm going down to the beach," he said.

CHAPTER SEVEN

Truth never can depend upon any kind of democratic process; the number of believers in any idea is only an indicator of its popularity and nothing more. For a man of science to have used a bullhorn to announce to the people at the shrine that miracles are only the results of natural laws still undiscovered would have been a sheer waste of time and tantamount to proclaiming that the world was flat. The thousands of people were convinced that supernatural events occurred at the shrine of Our Lady of Bakony. They believed that the Mother of God could—and would—intercede with the Creator for them, and that was all that mattered. Faith does not require reason.

All that mattered to the Death Merchant was getting to Karolyi Castle, then getting inside the ancient pile of stones and finding Dr. Imre Meleter, the creator of the deadly NK-hk-4 hallucinogen gas. Get the formula! Destroy the lab! Escape then to Austria!

Raymond Merrit, playing the Devil's Advocate during the Saturday night briefing, had pointed out that they couldn't even be sure that Dr. Meleter was at the castle. Camellion had agreed. "We must be like the thousands of religious people around us," he had said. "We must have faith . . . and hope that Meleter will be the prize at the end of our rainbow. The risks involved? Those we must ignore."

Risks? The briefing itself, late Saturday night, had been heavily sprinkled with danger. The gathering of the twelve conspirators into one group had to appear normal. Singly

76

and in groups of two, the men had just happened to wander close to the Trabant van—and didn't Father Csoki and the two brothers have to follow custom and offer them a drink and some cold chicken or a dish of *baratfule* kept warm over the low flame of the Bleuet Gazz Stove?

Gradually, as the men had eaten and drunk, all the while pretending a half-intoxicated sociability, the Death Merchant had revealed his master plan. The men had listened attentively and then, one by one, or in pairs, had moved on to eat and drink with other campers.

Father Stephen Deak had been the last to leave, staying longer than the others because he and brother Krim had enjoyed discussing the various factors involved in the occurrence of miracles, a subject Brother Schmid had found distasteful. Merrit's opinion was that miracles ". . . are a lot of nonsense." Father Deak had agreed with Brother Schmid.

Father Csoki had said in a patient voice, "Let us not forget that the Vatican considers most reports of miracles unfounded, and indeed it's rare to find priests involved in them. On the whole, I can tell all of you that most clerics are hardened skeptics when it comes to miracles."

"More often than not, there's a perfectly normal explanation," Camellion had said.

Stroking his thick, black, lustrous beard, Father Deak had laughed good-naturedly. "To be sure. I myself once saw walls 'crying' in the rectory of St. Mark's Church in Pecs. All that was necessary to dry the 'tears' was central heating!"

The Death Merchant had sensed that Father Deak was not an enthusiast of miracles and had been surprised that the man was so outspoken in front of Father Csoki, his superior.

"Yet there is a paradox of the miracle milieu," the Death Merchant had said. "Every now and then a real cure defies medical science."

"If you ask me," Merrit had muttered, waving a hand expansively at the thousands of tiny fires dotting the landscape like flickering stars, "it's easy to see that a 'miracle' has been wrought here. The Hungarian Communist gov-

77

ernment will make—will net—at least a hundred thousand dollars from this shrine in Bakony business."

Father Csoki had replied half in anger. "Brother Schmid, it is grossly unfair to call the worship of God, of the Creator Himself, a business. Do not forget that much of the money will be used toward the upkeep of churches, toward their maintenance."

Merrit had remained unconvinced, saying in his low, deep voice, "It would seem to me that you could worship God anywhere. For that matter, at the bottom of a coal mine or even in a stable!"

"Three wise men once did," Father Csoki had replied matter-of-factly. "In a stable, almost two thousand years ago!"

Merrit had made a funny, trapped kind of face, but had not replied to Father Csoki's remark. Father Deak had said good night and walked off. At the time, the Death Merchant had considered it somewhat of a miracle that, during the briefing, not one of the men had asked how escape to Austria would be possible if the helicopters had been moved from the landing pad at the castle.

Many hours later, while the Sunday dawn was baby-new and the grass still wet with dew, Merrit remarked on the men's not mentioning the helicopters, adding as he crawled out of his sleeping bag, "I suspect the reason they didn't is that none of them expect to get out of this alive. Man, if those contact detonators don't work, those tanks will blow us to China—provided, of course, we don't get killed before we get there! Or snuffed out once we're inside the castle. Yeah, none of them expect to get out alive."

"And you, brother?" Camellion asked, pouring instant coffee into an aluminum pot. "What do you expect?"

Merrit picked up his pipe and tobacco pouch, paused, and glanced for a moment at Father Csoki, who was sitting up and rubbing sleep from his eyes. Then he looked straight at the Death Merchant. "Men like us have one great talent in common; we're masters of survival. I intend to drink Brauerei in Austria before dark. That's what I expect."

Father Csoki smiled slightly and rubbed the stubble of
78

beard on his chin. "Ah, Brother Schmid! You have just proved that all men have faith in something. A man's home may be his castle, but his field of endeavor is his own personal kingdom of faith. That is how you are able to survive, and that is how the Church continues to exist and remain strong."

The priest moved a hand through his bushy hair and looked up at the sky. There were some clouds, but they were high, wispy, and scattered, the kind that indicated that rain was far, far away.

"Today's going to be a sizzler," Ray Merrit said, then proceeded to light his pipe.

"But not quite as hot as hell!" mused Father Csoki.

At 8:30, Camellion, Merrit, and Father Csoki were waiting with hundreds of others for the high mass to begin, the Death Merchant's eyes moving over the tremendous area packed with humanity—a living testimonial to man's belief in and dependence on his God. Camellion had witnessed it all before, in other times and in other places. Father Csoki was so right about faith, even if his logic was based on Thomism, the philosophico-theological system taught by St. Thomas Aquinas and his followers—a comprehensive synthesis based on the best in ancient and medieval philosophy for all thinkers since the thirteenth century. Philosophy and theology both seek truth, the former through the agency of reason, the latter through the agency of divine revelation; they do not conflict in their conclusions but support each other. *And it's all based on faith. I've seen it in the West. I've seen it among the Moslems, the Hindus, and the Buddhists. And without that faith, not a single one of them would be able to exist ... any more than I could exist without faith in the Cosmic Lord of Death. ...*

Aside from the hundreds of cars and buses, there were thousands of people scattered over the immense area, many men and women in wheelchairs, others on crutches. Thousands were standing; more thousands were kneeling. All were silent ... waiting ... hoping ... placing faith before reason. There were hundreds of cameras. Many people carried binoculars.

There are probably more undercover AVOs here than FBI agents at a Mafia funeral! Bored, Camellion was relieved when the mass finally began, at an altar that had been built on a six-foot-high platform by the north shore of Lake Balaton. The mass was performed by no less a personage than the archprimate of Hungary, Cardinal Ferencz Keslarka, who wore a snow-white chasuble over a blood-red alb—white, the symbol of innocence and triumph, used on feasts of the Blessed Mother; red, the color of blood, to signify the Lord's Passion and the suffering of the many martyrs. Half a dozen priests, dressed in white surplices, assisted Cardinal Keslarka, who, because of the heat, hurried the mass along.

During the consecration of wine, Merrit leaned close to the Death Merchant and whispered, "If you ask me, this whole gig's a real gas!"

Without changing his expression, Camellion whispered back, "I am of the opinion that periwinkles are shameless little libertines."

The mass continued. Merrit and Camellion suffered in silence, standing when they were supposed to stand and kneeling when they were supposed to kneel and, since they were supposed to be Catholic brothers, doing all the other things they were supposed to do, such as making the sign of the cross at the proper times. *But none of this will help us get the formula of the NK-hk-4 gas!*

The Death Merchant knew only too well what the gas would be capable of doing. Familiar with the hallucinogens, he knew that the term "hallucinogen" referred to any drug capable of producing perceptual alterations, intense emotional changes, a nonrational, reverie type of thinking, and ego distortions such as loss of self and feelings of complete strangeness. Marijuana, LSD, and mescaline all belonged to this category.

There were psychoactive substances—more than forty species in the Americas alone—including morning glory seeds, psilocybin from a Mexican mushroom, and mescaline from the peyote cactus.

Most powerful and dangerous of all was *d-Lysergic acid diethylamide,* known as LSD-25 or "acid." *Colorless, odorless, and tasteless, LSD looks as harmless as water;*

80

yet it's one of the most potent mind-altering chemicals known to the human race!

The same could be said of LSD's two most popular relatives: DMT—*Demethytryptamine*—and STP—*2,5-dimethoxy-4-methyl-amphetamine*.

In all the world, there was only one mind-changing drug more dangerous than LSD, DMT, and STP—*Nusocynikamine Hithoalide-4*.

Or KN-hk-4, reputed to be the compound of four derivatives of the *Amanita phalloides* mushroom. Even more ominous was the report that KN-hk-4 was being refined so that it could be used as a gas.

The prospect of such a weapon being used to full capacity in World War III was even more terrifying than a thermonuclear holocaust. There could be no value, no logic, in demolishing an enemy nation with H-bombs, the radioactivity would render the territory uninhabitable. But KN-hk-4 gas—that was truly the ultimate weapon. One sniff of the gas and the victim began to suffer instantly from any number of reactions—rage, paranoid states, depersonalization, loss of ego identity, and so-called "magical" thinking, a peculiar fragmentation of thought and progressive loss of insight.

Within an hour, a single pilot in a small plane could turn the entire population of New York City, or Detroit, or Los Angeles, or Chicago, into millions of raving lunatics!

That's why I am here in Hungary. That is why Merrit is here. That is why a small group of decent Hungarians is helping us, so that the Kn-hk-4 gas can be rendered harmless. Get the formula. Kill Meleter. Like hell I will! I'm going to kidnap the joker and fly him out to Austria. If he's at the castle. It's too bad that Skedfu and Barthory don't make their headquarters there. I'd put them both to sleep forever without thinking twice.

The mass ended with Cardinal Keslarka's turning to the assembled thousands and giving his final blessing.

Ray Merrit, wiping perspiration from his big face, half-turned and leaned closer to the Death Merchant. "Now is when we're going to need luck," he whispered.

81

"All our careful planning won't be worth a lava hill in hell if our cars aren't able to stay together."

"The men know what they must do," Camellion said. "Our transportation is parked fairly close. We saw to that when we first got here. Even after we get underway, if there's another car or two between our own vehicles, it won't make any difference. The plan won't go into effect until after we get to the shrine." The Death Merchant uttered a funny little laugh. "Have faith, Brother! I've been through much worse. The worst that can happen to us is that we'll all be killed. And dying is easy."

"Yeah, that may be so, but I'm not in any hurry to get to the other side!" Merrit said.

It took several hours for the hundreds of cars and buses to form into orderly movement and begin to drive northwest over the wide concrete road that twisted and turned slightly upward toward the Bakony Forest. The high-noon heat was steady and relentless, and progress, out of necessity, was slow, not only because of the several miles of moving vehicles, but also because many of the terminally ill could not be jostled about or moved too quickly.

It had required speed and expert maneuvering—and luck, too!—but the Death Merchant and his eleven men had managed to keep their four machines fairly close to each other. Of the four motorcars, the Volga was first, Frantisek Palfecky doing the driving. Three cars behind the Volga was the Pobeda, Janos Rosmartyi behind the wheel. Between the Pobeda and the Volkswagen minibus were a Russian GAO-12, or Zim, and a Hungarian Tourist IBUSZ bus. There was a car behind the minibus which was being driven by Father Nosbyti, and behind the car was the Trabant van, Brother Schmid sitting in the driver's seat. Father Csoki, who seemed strangely relaxed, sat beside him.

Behind the two men, in the rear of the van, the Death Merchant had opened the secret compartment beneath the floor and was preparing three olive-drab Kumfort Katahdin backpacks, filling them with squares of C-4 plastic explosive, P-T grenades, a dismantled Czech model vz/25

82

submachine gun for Father Csoki, the two Ingram machine pistols, and plenty of spare magazines for the three weapons. Camellion hoped that by now the men in the other three cars were preparing their own death-dealing equipment. They had better be! There was a tight schedule to keep.

Into his own pack Camellion put the dismantled crossbow and the arrows, barely managing to close the canvas top flap over the arrows, which he had shortened after Thomas Lakatos had brought them to the church from the sporting goods store in Budapest. Since there wasn't room for the L-14t detonators, Camellion stuffed them into his pants pockets. There wasn't room either for the two pairs of twin shoulder holsters, the four holsters filled with Kal pistols, neither his own nor Merrit's.

Well now! The Death Merchant was suddenly thankful that formality, in spite of heat, had demanded the wearing of coats at the mass; the festivities at the shrine would also require coats. Good deal. Camellion slipped on the twin shoulder holsters, buckled the strap in back, fastened the bottom of the holsters to his back, then put on his coat. Merrit could put on his holsters before he left the van.

Any hidden flaws? Once more Camellion went over the general plan. The shrine itself was situated on an enormous plateau, at an elevation of 1,250 feet. At the south end of the gigantic area was the highway, set in the long, gradual slope that merged into the forest. To the north was the shrine; behind the shrine was a wall of mountain. To the east and to the west of the shrine, stretching out for several miles on either side, were deep valleys dotted with trees and rocks and sliced at various angles by tiny ravines. Beyond the valleys, to the east and the west, were the Bakony Mountains, some as high as the American Rockies, with extremely steep slopes. There were isolated peaks bounded by escarpments and giant ledges marred by faults and erosion. In other places, between the peaks, there were huge slabs of granite thrown together as if by some giant hand and rearing up grotesquely at criss-cross angles.

Days earlier, Father Csoki had explained that during a

pilgrimage many amateur as well as professional climbers tried out their techniques on the Bakony Mountains.

As the police had explained, "It's not unusual to see groups of men and women leave the area of the shrine to go climbing. In fact, the Bakony Mountains are popular in this respect the year around."

The plan was simple but dangerous: the four vehicles would park together as closely as possible and as far away from the shrine as possible. The Death Merchant and the eleven fighters for freedom would leave the cars and, while Cardinal Keslarka was imploring Our Lady of Bakony to heal the sick and the dying, they would climb down the east side of the plateau to the valley below. Due east, perched on the side of a mountain, was Karolyi Castle, fronted by a rocky upland. Undoubtedly there would be other climbers in the area; there always were during the warm weather months—*so much the better for our side!* There would be AVO guards posted around the castle itself, and Hungarian army tankmen. Climbers, who were members of the Society of the Double Cross, had reported months earlier that no one could approach within a mile of the castle without being waved off by machine-gun-carrying AVOs.

Smoothing his coat down over the two Kal pistols snuggled against his sides, the Death Merchant had no illusions about the dangers involved. This was really a suicide raid, but there wasn't any other way.

All of us might as well have targets painted on our backs! Well, at least time helps make all reality an illusion. . . .

The long line of cars and buses began to move through the Bakony Forest, the abundance of fir and beech and thick stands of tall, slender pines furnishing a mantle of shade and giving some respite from the heat. The vehicles speeded up slightly, the road becoming smoother, the route more direct, until finally the Trabant was going forty miles per hour.

"After we pass through the forest and the road reaches the lowest part of the mountains, we'll slow down again because the road will begin to twist once more," Father

84

Csoki explained. He turned and looked at the Death Merchant, who was sitting behind him in a high bucket seat bolted to the floor. "I pray to God that we won't have to hurt any innocent people. You and Brother Schmid will be careful, won't you? There's something else. I wouldn't recognize your real names, but I'm still going to ask who both of you really are."

Merrit said, "I'm Brother Hugo Schmid, and he's Brother Helmut Krim. What more is there to know, Father?"

"I didn't think either of you would tell me," Father Csoki sighed. "I can't blame you for protecting your true identities. I understand that security is a part of your job."

Father Czoki's attitude did not surprise the Death Merchant, who had seen the signs before, many times—the open honesty, the frank confidentiality, the attempt at emotional closeness and unity. They were all symptoms of the death disease, shown by a man who expected to die very shortly.

"Father Csoki, we always try not to hurt innocent people," the Death Merchant said, his voice almost tender. "But very often fate decides otherwise and innocent people do get hurt. In case that should happen today, the only consolation I can give you is that God often works in very mysterious ways. The trouble is that humanity's conception of time makes it impossible for man to see any kind of pattern to tragedies and catastrophes."

Ray Merrit added solicitously, "It's like the guy who gets cancer. Right off, he asks, 'Why me?' He should be saying, 'Why not me?' He doesn't realize he's only one organism among billions, no better or worse than the guy next to him. But that's part of what keeps him going in this world, the idea that he's special and somehow different. Get what I'm saying?"

Father Csoki looked from Merrit back to the Death Merchant, admitting to himself that, although the two brothers were men of violence, they still made sense, even if they were anti-religious.

Father Csoki said to the Death Merchant, "I think your trouble is that when you mention time, it's from the standpoint of an atheist. The New Testament is very specific as to God's plan for humanity."

"Who said I was an atheist?" Camellion smiled ruefully.

"I had just assumed that you were," Father Csoki said, somewhat taken back. "I'm glad to know that you are not."

"I didn't say I wasn't! For practical purposes, let's say I'm an inhabitant of spaceship earth, who believes in a universal power, which you refer to as God and to which you attribute anthropological and anthropomorphic qualities."

"We'll be out of the forest before long," Merrit said. "I can see the road up ahead."

He turned the wheel slowly, taking the Trabant around a wide curve. An AVO man on a motorcycle roared past the van, but since AVOs were posted all along the route, the two brothers and Father Csoki didn't pay any particular attention to the man.

Father Csoki turned away from Camellion, leaned forward slightly, and peered through the front window of the van. The cars in front blocked the view directly ahead of the van; yet the three men could look to the left and see through the trees how the road, a mile ahead, twisted up the slope to the shrine.

Within half an hour the majority of the buses and cars, including the four vehicles of Camellion's party, had left the Bakony Forest and were in the foothills. Again the cars and buses had slowed. Not only did the road twist like a giant pretzel, but the incline, on either side of the highway, was becoming very steep. There was a two-foot concrete barrier on each side of the road; nevertheless, each driver knew that he would not be able to control his machine should it somehow leave the road, although this was impossible because the cars—all of them keeping to the right in single file—were moving no faster than fifteen miles per hour. On each side of the road were curiously eroded outcroppings of brightly colored sandstone, rearing upward in primitive grandeur like stone islands among the tops of pines and firs.

The circuitous road, as it neared the tabletop on which the shrine was located, seemed to fall into a series of patterns, each of which was either a giant *S* or an enormous *Z* with rounded corners.

The river of traffic continued to flow toward the top, and finally Merrit, Camellion, and Father Csoki saw a part of the actual shrine, when the van, moving on the top section of an *S*-curve, was a thousand feet to the west of, and six hundred and fifty feet below, the plateau. Because of the angle of perspective, they couldn't see the altar nor the top of the high rock mesa. They could only glimpse a part of Our Lady of Bacony: a forty-foot-high granite statue, glazed over and painted snow-white. The beautiful image glistened in the sun, its head bowed, its hands outstretched to the world.

"It won't be long now—like the farm boy said when he caught his arm in the feed grinder!" muttered Ray Merrit, and swung the Trabant onto the bottom section of the next and the last giant *S*.

The car ahead of the van, a four-door Polish Lubb filled with nuns, came to a dead stop.

Merrit braked the van and growled, "I wonder what the hold-up is?" He didn't honk at the Lubb. It would have been a waste of time. The entire chain of traffic ahead of the Lubb had halted. Now all the cars and buses behind the van had to stop.

"Let's have a look," the Death Merchant said. "We're sitting ducks out here on the road."

By putting their heads out the windows on the left side of the van and looking upward, they could see the top section of the *S*—four hundred and eighty feet away—which was just below the south end of the plateau. They saw that the very first car of the parade, the air-conditioned limousine in which Cardinal Keslarka and his aides were riding, was pointed east and had been stopped by two AVO patrol cars and a light armored car. There was a man standing in the turret behind the 7.92 mm machine gun mounted on the swivel ring. A group of AVO men were clustered around the long black limousine.

"Well now, would you look at that!" the Death Merchant said. "There's nothing at all miraculous about that armored car, and it didn't get there by any miracle either!"

He pulled his head back into the Trabant, and so did Merrit, who turned to Father Csoki. "A mess of AVOs at the top, blocking the Cardinal's car. We don't like the looks of it."

"Brother Schmid, I'm going to go outside and have a look," Camellion said. "Now's a good chance to put on your shoulder holsters."

The Death Merchant moved to the right door of the van, quick to notice the worried look that had dropped over Father Csoki's face.

The priest made the sign of the cross and muttered, "*Pater Noster qui es in Coelis...*"

"It's fine to pray, Father," Camellion advised, "but let's not forget one prime truth about good versus evil—the malice of the wicked is often reinforced by the weakness of the virtuous."

As Merrit moved to the back of the van, Camellion pushed open the door on the right-hand side and stepped out onto the pavement. Four feet in front of him was the concrete barrier on the side of the road. Beyond the small wall was the tree-studded declivity, the steep decline as battered as the surface of a battlefield recently blasted with high-explosive shells.

Camellion walked between the Trabant and the bus behind it and went to the other side of the road. The space to the left was wide enough to permit the passage of even a fairly large truck. Looking downward toward the south, he saw a mile and a half of traffic curled out on the zigzagging road behind him, hundreds of vehicles, parked like toys on the slope.

A mile below two armored cars, half a dozen AVO patrol cars, and several men on motorcycles were coming up the road. *Damn!*

Camellion turned and looked up in the opposite direction. Ray Merrit, now wearing a suit coat, had gotten out of the van and he, too, stared toward the north, grimacing as he saw the armored car move past Cardinal Keslarka's limousine and pick up speed. The armored car was coming down the slope.

The thought burned through the Death Merchant's brain:
A trap—and we've walked into it!

CHAPTER EIGHT

Raymond Merrit had turned and was staring at the AVO vehicles coming up the road from the lowlands below, his jaw set, his eyes mere slits behind the lenes of his sunglasses.

"A double approach by the AVO," he whispered to the Death Merchant. "It can't be sheer coincidence. Even if it is, we can't take the chance that it isn't. Camellion, we've had it!"

"Give the others the signal to put on their packs and to get back here to the van," Camellion said. "We'll have to go down the east slope. It's the only chance we have."

"I hope we can count on those priests to pull the trigger while they're praying," Merrit grumbled, then turned toward the van.

The Death Merchant was getting into the van behind Merrit when the driver of the bus behind stuck his head out the window and called out in poor Hungarian flavored with a strong German accent, "Hey, do you know what's going on?"

Camellion yelled back in German, "The AVOs are about to set off fireworks!"

Camellion stepped into the van and brushed past Merrit, who gave the horn a long three-second blast, followed by a pause, then another long blast. To show that they understood the signal, the drivers of the three other cars responded simultaneously with a similar signal, a blare of noise coming from the minibus, the Pobeda, and the Volga ahead.

Merrit rushed to the rear of the van, where Camellion had taken the two Ingram machine pistols from the Katahdin packs and loaded them. Camellion had slipped into his backpack and so had Father Csoki, who was com-

89

plaining that they should take the time for him to assemble the Czech submachine gun in his pack.

"Father, we haven't the time," the Death Merchant explained, helping Merrit into his pack. "Besides, we don't need your weapon up here on the road. Innocent people—remember?"

Merrit snapped the buckles of the Katahdin pack across his chest, then turned and took the Ingram machine pistol from Camellion. Holding the deadly little weapon below the bottom level of the front windshield, he stuck his head out the door and looked toward the north, along the sides of cars ahead. Father Deak, Father Nosbyti, Thomas Lakatos, and the other six men, weighted down with their packs, were trotting toward the Trabant van. Other people, impatient over the delay, had also left their vehicles and were looking up and down the road.

"Our people are coming," Merrit said happily. He pulled his head back into the van and glanced at Camellion. "Are we all set?"

"Tell you what, you get Father Csoki and the rest of them started down the side of the mountain," Camellion said, and moved to the open door on the left side of the van. "I'm going to toss sand in AVO oil."

"You're nuts!" growled Merrit. "Nine-mill stuff won't stop those armored jobs, and neither would grenades, even if you could use them. Anyhow, we have the whole damn line of traffic between us and the AVO. The AVO will have to stop and fire down over the barrier. More likely, they'll come after us."

"Get going. I'll join you in a few minutes." The Death Merchant pushed Father Csoki against Merrit, who sucked in his lower lip against his top teeth, a so-what-the-hell mannerism of his.

Too much of a realist to argue with the Death Merchant, Merrit said to Father Csoki, "Let's go, Father." He stepped out of the van onto the highway, no longer bothering to conceal the Ingram submachine gun. Several Catholic sisters had gotten out of the Lubb in front of the van, and one of them uttered a tiny cry of terror when she saw the machine pistol in Merrit's right hand.

90

"Back into your car, Sisters," Merrit called out. "There may be some shooting."

By then, the nine other members of the attack force had started to gather close to Merrit, who raked their nervous faces with a level stare and pointed down toward the east. "We're all going down the slope, and the faster the better."

"But we have only our pistols," Paul Tisza said mournfully. "Don't we have the time to put our machine guns together?"

"Assembly time comes later," Merrit said. "All we have time for now is to put distance between the barrier and ourselves—and don't worry about Brother Krim! He'll be along when he's finished pulling the tiger's tail."

In the meanwhile, the Death Merchant, holding his own Ingram under his coat, had left the van, stepped onto the left side of the road, and was looking toward the north. The armored car, which had been on the rock table above, was only a quarter of a mile away, the AVO crud still behind the heavy machine gun mounted on the turret.

Camellion swung around and stared toward the south. The two motorcycles, way out in front of the two armored cars, were less than two hundred feet away and roaring up fast.

"Poor Precambrian haploids!" the Death Merchant said tonelessly. He pulled out the Ingram and, holding the weapon with both hands, took careful aim and opened fire, the machine pistol sounding like a very short-playing record of an electric typewriter with the volume turned up.

A dozen nine-millimeter high-velocity projectiles stabbed out in a flat trajectory, slammed into the two AVO men on the motorcycles, and killed them instantly. The corpse on the motorcycle to the left of the Death Merchant tumbled backward and fell off, but his machine roared on for another dozen feet before it went out of control. The front wheel cut to the right and hit the concrete barrier on the side of the road. The rear end of the motorcycle jumped upward; the machine flipped over the wall, end over end, and crashed down the slope. The mo-

91

torcycle exploded into a fireball when it struck a boulder half the size of a pickup truck.

The corpse of the other AVO man flopped forward on its cycle and its arms turned the handlebars so sharply that the machine flipped over at once on its side and tossed off the corpse, which did a forward loop and landed on its head, popping open its skull on the concrete. The motorcycle skidded straight down the road for twenty feet, then came to a stop, amid shouts and screaming from men and women in the cars and buses who had witnessed the blast-out.

The Death Merchant, still standing in the middle of the road, again raised the Ingram and sighted in, this time at the first armored car that had been behind the two motorcycles. Reacting automatically, the driver of the armored car was slamming on the brakes in an effort not to run over the body of the AVO man who had fallen backward from his motorcycle. The shooting and the subsequent blowing up of the two AVO men had occurred so unexpectedly that the driver began thinking like a corkscrew. But it was his panic that saved his life. If the driver had been a quick thinker, he would have slowed down and let the wheels on the right side roll over the corpse. As it was, he slammed on the brakes at the same instant the Death Merchant pulled the trigger of the Ingram machine pistol. Instead of moving straight ahead, the front of the armored vehicle swerved to the driver's right, while the rear of the car, almost hitting the protective wall, cut to the left.

It was too late for Camellion to correct his aim. His stream of projectiles missed the open slot in front of the driver, hit the left side of the car, and ricocheted off with high-pitched melodies.

The skidding car had also bounced the gunner in the turret around like a rubber ball, almost knocking him to the floor of the turret well. Frantically the driver twisted the wheel, doing his best to prevent the front of the car from crashing into the side of one of the cars or buses. The driver succeeded in avoiding a head-on collision, but he couldn't prevent the left rear end of the car from crashing through the concrete wall. The terrified driver finally got lucky. He jammed on the brakes, and his effort, plus the wall, managed to stop the momentum of eleven tons. The armored car came to a complete stop, its huge left rear wheel and a section of the back compartment, sticking out through the smashed concrete, hanging in midair over the steep west slope.

With a screaming of brakes, the second armored car and the AVO patrol vehicles ground to a stop on the hot road, the second AVO car in line skidding sideways so that its right front fender crashed into the left front fender of a bus filled with Romanian school children. Although the damage was slight, it was enough to cause cries and screams of fear from the boys and girls aboard the bus. One of the sisters fainted.

The children and the four nuns were only half as terrified as the group of sixteen adults in the bus behind the Trabant van. The driver, a young man in his twenties, had been the first to see the Death Merchant raise the Ingram and begin firing.

"Get down!" Herman Schramburger had yelled at the other Germans in the bus, throwing himself from the driver's seat to the floor. "There's a maniac out there with a machine gun!"

Stunned, the men and woman hunched down on the floor between the seats, some even throwing themselves into the narrow aisle. There had been the popping, staccato chattering of the machine pistol, a short pause, then, down the road, the crashing and the skidding of motorcycles. Then there was another burst of gunfire, followed by the tortured screaming of rubber grinding against concrete. The sound of metal coming together, the shrieking of brakes, more rubber wearing itself hot and thin against hard concrete. Then silence, a long, terrible silence.

Shaking, Schramburger got to his knees and, wide-eyed, looked up over the dash. He was just in time to see the "maniac" with the machine gun climbing over the concrete barrier to the right of the road. A few seconds later and the man dropped from sight. Schramburger stared at the emptiness above the wall.

Mein Gott! How could all this happen at the shrine of Our Lady of Bakony?

CHAPTER NINE

Architecturally, the stronghold of Count Louis Sandor Vergevus Karolyi, built in the fourteenth century, was an extension of the architectural concepts of the twelveth century—the castle had been built for offense as well as defense.

With concentric fortification and immensely strong, Karolyi Castle had been built halfway up the side of a three-thousand-foot peak. Tons of stone had been taken from the mountain and the fortress erected partly on the face of the wall and partly on a large plateau dizzily overhanging a giant gorge.

In building the castle, the first step had been to substitute the less vulnerable round keep for the square keep which, when completed, was a linked strongwork of three semicircular towers, the three fat, tall towers on that part of the castle facing the open tableland. By furnishing the curtain walls with round towers of deep salient, the Hungarian designers enabled defenders to provide flanking fire; and since archers were very important in the Middle Ages, the builders also provided for three tiers of fire in the curtain wall. Lastly, Count Karolyi himself—a brilliant but brutal man with the temperament of a raging Adolf Hitler—had designed the concentric lines of defense, the inner lines dominating the outer.

Every attention had been given to detail, every military device exploited and improved. The curtain walls were liberally furnished with posterns to enable the garrison to play an offensive role, these posterns so placed that men fighting their way back to the shelter of the castle would expose only their left or shield side to the enemy. A determined enemy could come up from the gorge, or from the top of the mountain, or creep in from either side; thus, there was a dark basalt wall all around the outer rim of the plateau. To defend the main gate—always a point of weakness—the designers elaborated the bent-entrance.

To penetrate the area of the castle yard, attackers had to make any number of blind, right-angle turns, which effectively discouraged charges. The designers also reintroduced the long-forgotten Roman portcullis—an iron grating hung over the entrance and dropped during an attack. There was machicolation—a series of overhead apertures through which arrows or hot liquids could be dropped from the parapet onto attackers. The walls of the inner ward were strengthened by a massive talus, that is, tumbled masses of rock debris at the base of the walls. The only means to the inner ward was a vaulted passage, which contained more right-angle turns, or elbows, and was defended by machicolation and by a series of portcullises.

Yet in its day, Karolyi Castle had been as elegant as it was strong. Its Romanesque chapel, its traceried Gothic arcades, and the vaulted and pilastered chamber of the Grand Master embodied the genius of the medieval masons who built cathedrals of Austria and France.

Karolyi Castle was no longer elegant. It hardly even resembled a castle. For almost eleven years the AVO had used the castle, after it had sat lonely and empty for centuries, had used it as a secret base, first as an I-center, then as a combined intelligence center and laboratory.

Workers had removed the ruins of the outer wall. The main gate, the elbows to the castle yard, the vaulted passage to the inner ward, the inner ward itself—all were gone. The main part of the castle structure—five stories tall, excluding the three towers of the keep—had been repaired and reinforced with steel rods and modern structural I-beams. The foundations were strengthened, concrete having been poured to a depth of thirty feet in some places. Modern wells were drilled in the castle yard, out on the plateau. Two pumping stations were erected. A generating station was built on the west side of the yard.

The entire interior of the castle was completely renovated, new walls installed, along with elevators, plumbing, and electricity. When the work was completed, there were comfortable barracks for the regular AVO and soldiers of the Hungarian army units, living quarters for officers, and even modern apartments for visiting high-ranking officials.

In addition, there were offices, work and storage rooms, and even a small hospital.

The entire top floor of the keep and its three towers were turned into a vast laboratory. One section of the top floor was partitioned off and reserved for the communications center. Directly above the lab was the rebuilt roof of the castle, now perfectly flat and a quarter of a block square. After the specialists completed their work, the roof contained a radio tower, a television antenna, six air-conditioning units and four roofed-over entrances to the laboratory below.

To the north of the roof was the ragged wall of the mountain, rising 1,234 feet like a giant granite gravestone—a marred tombstone because there was a radar station built on top of the mountain.

To the east, the west, and the south, there was only the emptiness of space and the clear mountain air. In the distance, across the valleys to the east and the west and across the gorge to the south, were more mountains, isolated in their splendor, magnificient in their glory.

To the east of the castle the AVO had built a garage, repair shops, and a storage depot for fuel, the latter contained in four long tanks placed horizontally on concrete pillars. Over the garage and shops and tanks, they had built a triangular-shaped landing pad large enough to accommodate freight-hauling helicopters. There was, however, a limit to the weight a 'copter could lift. To compensate for this technological deficiency, the AVO had a road built from the rocky gorge below, a twisting ribbon of concrete that meandered up the mountain until it ended on the east side of the castle yard. A road from the gorge necessitated the building of a road to the gorge, and so a spur was laid out from the highway that led to the shrine of Our Lady of Bakony, a road that was closed to ordinary traffic and was guarded day and night by crack units of the uniformed AVO.

Other improvements were made at the castle. Three concrete watchtowers were built on the south side of the plateau. Twenty-five feet high, the towers overlooked the gorge. A weather tower, also of concrete, was positioned next to the center tower.

It took three years, four months, and two weeks to complete the giant project. General Bela Skedfu and Lieutenant General Sigismund Barthory congratulated each other, confident that Karolyi Castle had been transformed from a pile of historic stones into a modern, impregnable installation, safe from any attack, with the exception of a thermonuclear bomb. Yes, the castle was one hundred percent secure.

Now, at 4:30 in the afternoon, General Skedfu and Lieutenant General Barthory were not so sure. Boris Lysemki and the two other KGB officials with him were even more dubious. The most doubtful of all was Doctor Imre Meleter, who, even as a boy, had been a timid soul, shrinking from any kind of violence.

From where they sat at the table, on the south side of the laboratory, the three Hungarians and three Russians could look through the long window and see the three guard towers, the weather station, and the dim, foggy haze drifting over the mountains across the gorge. It was all so idyllic, so calm and peaceful. And so deceptive! As if they were sitting on a hidden time bomb, waiting for it to go off.

"General, what do you intend to do, now that the quarry has eluded your trap?" Boris Lysemki asked, his voice carefully indifferent.

Sitting at the head of the glass-topped table, General Skedfu regarded the red-haired Russian with unblinking eyes. He had never liked the tall but not muscular Lysemki who, while holding the official title of agricultural attaché at the Soviet Union's embassy in Budapest, was actually the chief of all the KGB in Hungary. Officially, the KGB was not in Hungary; unofficially, the KGB was there to give "advice"—to make sure the Hungarian Communist government remained loyal to the Soviet Union.

General Skedfu said firmly, "It's only been an hour. There are only twelve of them. They are in the mountains and have nowhere to go. It may take a few hours, but the helicopters will find them."

Sitting at the table to the right of Skedfu, Lieutenant General Barthory presented an odd, sideways smile to Lysemki, who was at the end of the conference table.

"Not even the incredible Death Merchant can fight the entire AVO and win," he said, his voice rich with confidence, "although I understand that the Death Merchant has made the KGB look more than stupid on any number of occasions."

Dr. Imre Meleter, who was next to Barthory, looked down at the table and cleared his throat uncomfortably. The biochemist was a florid, big-framed man, sixty or thereabouts, with a pot belly and shrunken legs, but with a kind of youthful vitality that belied his years.

Across the table from Meleter and Barthory were the two KGB lieutenants: Gleb Ezhov, a fleshy, rawboned man with an enormous nose and ill-fitting clothes which accentuated his corpulence; and Rostislav Grusha, a muscular, cocksure young man, who had a face like a fat, yellow pug dog.

Both Russians glared in silent disdain at Lieutenant General Barthory, whom they considered an inferior, a fumbler whose pathetic intelligence service was riddled with KGB infiltrators. The two Russians thought of an old Hungarian expression they always used in private when referring to Skedfu and Barthory—*hazatlan bitangok*. The two Hungarians were that all right—outlaws without a true fatherland.

Barthory's intended insult was difficult for Lysemki to ignore; yet he had no intention of losing his temper in front of the Hungarians, and, worse, in front of Ezhov and Grusha.

"I suggest, Lieutenant General Barthory, that you and General Skedfu stop making fools of yourselves by pretending to be experts in security," Lysemki said almost affectionately, faking a half-smile of sympathy. "This morning you both said that Section 4-D had linked George Rakoczi and his cell to another underground member whom you suspect of having contact with Paul Tisza. You could have made Rakoczi confess a lot more if your dumbox interrogators hadn't beaten him to death! What a botched-up job."

"I also suspect that the food poisoning was not an accident," Barthory went on stubbornly, "particularly since Father Redlich is one of my agents."

98

Gleb Ezhov said in his thick, nasal voice, "How can you deny what the doctors at the hospital said? They affirmed that the three priests had been stricken with a true form of staphylococcal food poisoning and explained that such poisoning does not have to affect all who partake of the same meal."

"It's all academic and a waste of time to discuss the poisoning at this moment," snorted Barthory. He stabbed Ezhov with a furious gaze, then turned to Boris Lysemki, the very image of shrewd calculation.

"None of you can deny that General Skedfu and I were correct in our suspicions," he said. "They've convicted themselves by their own murderous acts, by shooting at and murdering our men." Barthory scratched the side of his nose and sighed with a sort of broken-spirited incredulity. "I must confess that I am perplexed as to how they suspected we were onto them. No doubt it was their own fear of discovery that forced them to act in such murderous haste."

"Comrade, I must also confess—that my faith in you and in General Skedfu is at rock bottom!" Lysemki said in disgust. He pushed back his chair and crossed his legs. "I warned you and General Skedfu to close in fast and not to let all of them run loose. But no! You two were convinced that if you let Tisza run free and watched him, he'd lead you to the others. He sure did! All eleven of them, including those two who are supposed to be Catholic brothers from West Germany. I was in favor of arresting the whole bunch at Fonyod, anyone that Tisza spoke to, especially those priests and the two brothers, since Tisza is a member of Saint Matthias parish and is so friendly with Father Csoki. But, Comrade Barthory, you and General Skedfu were foolish enough to believe that they'd make contact with more Society members after they reached the shrine. Well, damn it! Ten of your men are already dead because of your stupidity!"

Lieutenant General Barthory glowered, but said nothing, wanting to control his temper before he spoke. He was finding it difficult to do so.

At the head of the table, General Skedfu leaned back, folded his arms across his chest, and digested what Boris

Lysemki had said. There was a lot of merit in the Russian son-of-a-bitch's words, but he was still making too much of a simple miscalculation. He was also forgetting, very conveniently, that the attempted arrest had been made on the road and not at the shrine.

A natural stalker, Skedfu studied Lysemki, who was tall, hard-eyed, and thin-lipped. His shoulders were wide and bony, and he had a ball player's swing of the arms; but he was so lean in the loins that, during winter, his greatcoat blew voluminously about him. He was forty-one, had a head of thick, carefully combed red hair parted on the left, and his habitual gait was indolent. Nonetheless, he was capable of great activity when he wished. And he was clever, very clever. He held a high rank in the KGB, because even visiting Soviet army generals treated him with respect.

Skedfu rolled his chair forward and put his hands at on the table, looking as mournful as a condemned criminal being led to the chopping block. "Comrade Lysemki, I find it difficult to believe that you should have such a faulty memory," the general said with sudden, disarming candor, all the while watching the KGB official. "Or have you deliberately refrained from mentioning that we didn't wait for the four vehicles to reach the shrine on the top before attempting the arrest? I'm sure it must have been an oversight on your part, Comrade. . . ."

There was a long silence, unbroken except for the steady blowing of cool air through the air-conditioner ducts.

Lysemki shifted uneasily, surveyed Skedfu somberly, and skillfully extricated himself from the general's verbal trap. "No, General. I did not forget," he said politely. "I merely saw no reason to repeat my previous statement that the whole damn pack of traitors should have been surrounded and arrested at Fonyod. As things stand now, we don't know what those twelve are up to. We only know that all of them are somewhere"—he waved a hand toward the long window—"out there."

"We know more than that," volunteered Lieutenant General Barthory, his voice silky. "We know that the secret of the NK-hk-4 gas is no longer a secret!"

Dr. Imre Meleter looked up and down the table with owlish dignity, then said querulously, "Gentlemen, I'm not interested in why an arrest wasn't made at such and such a place at such and such a time. I want to know what has been done about providing extra security for this laboratory. My assistants are getting nervous. In a week, as soon as the new elements are processed, the complete gas will be ready for testing on prisoners from Recsk prison. At this point, I can't tolerate any interference. And I think we're in agreement that this laboratory is the target of those revolutionaries." The scientist turned and focused his watery eyes on Lieutenant General Barthory and General Skedfu, then swung around and blinked at Comrade Lysemki.

Rostislav Grusha began to tap the tabletop rhythmically with the long fingers of his left hand. "Doctor, we can't be positive they ever intended to come to this castle," he said. "That is only a guess. There is no actual evidence."

"Don't be foolish, Comrade," Barthory mocked, sneering at Grusha with his jet-black eyes and moving his medium-sized body sideways on the chair. "Why else are those twelve murderers out there? What else but this castle could interest them?"

"They certainly didn't bring automatic weapons to help them pray to the Virgin Mary," General Skedfu pronounced solemnly. He glanced in annoyance at Grusha, who was still tapping the tabletop.

"And I wouldn't consider backpacks items of worship!" Barthory said truculently. He felt happy when he noticed Boris Lysemki's Adam's apple jumping up and down. Good! He and Bela were getting to the Russian son of a worm!

Barthory continued, "Simple deduction informs us that they intended to go to the shrine and slip away with other mountain climbers. If they had succeeded, it's possible they could have reached the base of the mountain. Now that they have been discovered, they haven't any chance. We'll have them all within a matter of hours, at least by nightfall."

"But surely they must have had an original plan!" Dr.

101

Meleter said in a nervous voice. "This mountain isn't difficult to climb. You don't even need climbing equipment, except for the south face over the gorge and the south side overlooking the castle. There is the possibility of catastrophe. Suppose those murderous madmen get past the AVOs and—"

"And climb to the castle?" interrupted Barthory, his black eyes pouncing on Dr. Meleter. "As you have said, Doctor, it's possible for them to climb the mountain, but only under normal circumstances. Now that we know who they are, I assure you, it's not possible for them to even get near this castle, much less the laboratory."

Boris Lysemki grunted in disagreement. "I heard the same story this morning," he smiled. "Then, too, Comrade, you were bubbling with confidence."

Barthory nodded, as if at a certainty. "To climb any side of the mountain in the daytime is impossible for them. To attempt such a climb at night would be far too dangerous. I think their plan was to slip down to the supply road in the gorge and hijack one of the trucks coming along. They would then drive up to the castle. But now they realize their opportunity is gone. They can only be concocting some crazy scheme of escape. I doubt if we take any of them alive."

Dr. Meleter was not convinced, if for no other reason than because by nature he was a pessimist. Under ordinary circumstances, he would have remained silent. He didn't care about the Russians, who were paying for the development of the gas. He cared even less about the AVO. All the secret police in Hungary could not harm him; he was far too valuable to the Hungarian scientific community. But on this day the stupid AVO and the ridiculous Russians had invaded his world, his own private domain of pure research!

The scientist turned in his chair, an angry expression on his ruddy face. "Lieutenant General, the extra AVO guards posted at the elevators and at the doors to the stairs in the lab lead me to believe that a great deal of your confidence is sugar-coated. I noticed the new men just before we came into the meeting room. I might add that you should have your operatives dress in less drab

102

clothes. And it would help if they'd smile once in a while. Even my assistants can spot a Section 4-DII agent! They always look like they're waiting for something to happen!"

Lieutenant General Bathory flashed his teeth in a broad smile, reached out, and patted the biochemist on the shoulder.

"My dear Doctor, the guards are not there to keep the enemy out. They have been placed there to keep you and your assistants in—to prevent any of you from making the fatal mistake of going to the floor below the laboratory."

"Fatal mistake?" Dr. Meleter's mouth remained half-open in surprise. The expressions of the three Russians changed to interest.

Sigismund Barthory smiled again, his intense black eyes darting briefly to Boris Lysemki, who was looking at him with frank suspicion.

"You see, Doctor," explained Barthory, "the entire floor below this one is being subjected to intense microwave radiation. I don't want to risk you or any of your assistants absent-mindedly wandering down there by mistake before one of my men can turn off the radiation."

"How many angstroms?" asked Dr. Meleter, his scientific curiosity aroused.

"Almost eighty-six thousand."

It was Doctor Meleter's turn to grin, and he did—for the first time since the meeting had begun. Microwaves are electromagnetic waves located in the portion of the radio spectrum having wavelengths between 1 mm and 30 cm, corresponding to frequencies between 300,000 Mc and 1,000 Mc. Longer wavelengths (lower frequencies) are known as VHF and UHF (very high and ultra-high frequencies).

Wavelengths shorter than 1 mm are in the infrared region.

Very short ultraviolet wavelengths, below 2,200 angstroms, are highly toxic for animal and plant cells. In the intermediate range, the greatest killing effectiveness on cells is at about 2,600 angstroms. Go higher, concentrate the infrared, and it becomes possible to cook a thick steak in several minutes—a microwave oven.

That was what Lieutenant General Barthory had turned the entire fourth floor into—*a giant microwave oven.*

Doctor Meleter almost began to hope that the twelve revolutionaries would somehow reach the castle and succeed in penetrating the fourth floor. Eighty-six thousand angstroms of infrared microwave radiation would kill a human being within seconds, would char the very bones inside the body. . . .

CHAPTER TEN

When Richard Camellion went over the barrier on the right side of the highway, he was not a happy man. He had every right to be sad. The AVOs had gotten wise to the whole setup. The whole damn plan had gone to pot—*so far!* And if the secret police had not been wise up there on the road, if they had just been coming along from two directions at once by sheer coincidence—*they sure know by now something is not quite kosher!*

But Camellion wasn't despondent enough to linger and wring his hands in sorrow. After he let his body drop the eight feet beyond the wall, he began to move as fast as he could over the steep slope, his hard, lean body topheavy from the pack on his back. The secret, as he had learned from experience, was to rear backward with each step and make sure your feet didn't slide on any loose shale, to balance yourself each second as your eyes and brain compute where you should put your feet next. All the while as you flee down the incline, tearing between trees and boulders, you move at an obtuse angle, not only to confuse the enemy above, but to keep the heavy pack from making you topple forward.

Panting, his clothing soaked with sweat, the Death Merchant was several hundred feet down the side of the mountain when the armored car, which had roared down

104

from the plateau, ground to a halt by the side of the Trabant van. The man in the turret couldn't fire the machine gun because the van was in the way. If the van hadn't been parked between the armored car and the slope, the AVO man still couldn't have fired. The machine gun couldn't be depressed to such a steep angle.

A few minutes later, several green AVO patrol cars screeched to a halt behind the armored car and three officers and AVO troopers got out. An officer and the troopers ran between the rear of the Tribant van and the bus behind it, the troopers carrying Kiraly automatic rifles and Zel submachine guns. They moved to the right side of the road and raked the slope with several hundred 7.62mm and 9mm projectiles, the vicious storm of lead cutting through leaves and foliage and zipping dully off granite boulders and streaked basalt outcroppings.

Captain Cyril Szigip, a big, blue-black NV-Budapesti pistol in his left hand, barked an order, and four of the troopers started lobbing hand grenades out off the slope. The grenades tore up a lot of rock and tore off a lot of branches, the echoes of the explosions thundering back and forth throughout the mountains.

Meanwhile, two AVO officers questioned Herman Schramburger, who explained to them what he had seen. Down the road, AVOs from the southern column removed the two corpses from the highway and debated what to do about the armored car, whose left rear wheel had crashed through the barrier and was hanging out in space over the decline. A hundred feet below, on the same left slope, the wreckage of the motorcycle continued to burn, clouds of black smoke boiling up into the air.

To the right of the highway, Captain Szigip and the nine troopers crawled over the small concrete barrier and, keeping in a long, parallel line, began to move down the slope.

None of the hand grenades had harmed the Death Merchant. When the grenades had exploded, he had been too far down the incline for any of the shrapnel to reach him. Just after the last grenade roared off, he had made contact with Ray Merrit, who had lingered behind the other ten in case of pursuit. Together, Merrit and Camellion had taken positions behind boulders and had waited. Five minutes later, Captain Szigip and his men came down the side of the mountain, creeping toward their own executions without knowing it. Caught in a vicious crossfire, the officer and the troopers died—jumping as if wearing electric trusses when 9mm slugs from the two Ingram machine pistols tore into their bodies. They jerked and fell all over the place, not a single man uttering a cry of either surprise or pain.

Camellion and Merrit jumped up and moved down the slope, careful to keep the fir and pine trees between them and the highway above, although the Death Merchant and the brawny CIA agent were not in any immediate danger. The slope was so thick with trees and uneven masses of rock that it was impossible for anyone above on the road to see them.

"Have any of them pulled a panic act?" Camellion asked as he and Merrit moved over the rough terrain.

"They're more disgusted than frightened," Merrit said, "but how they'll react in a fire-fight is a moot question. They have the nerve, sure. But where's the experience?"

Soon they reached the spot where Merrit had stashed the other members of the attack force to rush back up the slope to help the Death Merchant. The ten men were in a small cave below a flat overhang of basalt that jutted straight out from the slope like a flat piece of wood.

Camellion had seen more hope in a cemetery. Sitting on their heels, the four priests had the mournful appearance of pallbearers who had lost the casket. The six other freedom fighters appeared to be equally as tortured by hopelessness. Their feelings were obvious to the Death Merchant; he knew they felt cheated. He felt sympathy for them and for all the brave men and women who had ever put their lives on the line—anywhere—for liberty.

The men stood up and looked at Camellion and Merrit.

"What do we do now?" Tibor Arpad asked, his bushy eyebrows making him look as if someone had painted a big, black V on his forehead.

"The only thing we *can* do," the Death Merchant said crisply. "We keep out of sight the best way we can and

106

continue to move toward the castle. If we can keep ourselves alive until dark, we'll have a chance."

The men were dumbfounded, finding it difficult to accept the idea that Brother Krim was apparently determined to execute the original plan.

"But the AVOs will be waiting for us at the castle!" Mihaly Szechenyi regarded Camellion with extreme skepticism. "They know we're down here in the valley. They must have guessed, along with everything else, that our objective is Karolyi Castle."

"I'd like to know how the AVOs got wise to us in the first place," Frantisek Palfecky muttered, as if talking to himself. "George Rakoczi must have known something we didn't know, and the AVOs tortured it out of him." The physician's long, whimsical face reflected puzzlement, his wintry blue eyes two pools of concentration; but before anyone could answer him, Szechenyi said fiercely, "I think we should face facts and admit that we've failed. All we can do right now is try to save our lives."

A man with a harsh, pale face, a bottle nose, and a sandy cowlick, Szechenyi looked around him at the circle of faces.

The Death Merchant half-smiled and winked at Brother Schmid, who sighed and slowly shook his head from side to side.

"Tell us, Mihaly. What would you propose? What would you have us do?" Father Csoki, his brown eyes glaring at Szechenyi, gripped his Czech vs/25 submachine gun tightly with both hands. "I'm a priest, but only God can perform miracles."

"I'll tell you, Father. We could try to get down to the side road that leads to the gorge," Szechenyi offered. He glanced again at the two brothers. "That makes more sense than trying to get to the castle. The AVO is sure to send troops in here by helicopter, and it doesn't take an expert to know that the AVO will be on double alert at the castle. Let's be practical. Our chances of reaching the lab are nil."

To almost everyone's surprise, Father Lido Nanasi agreed with Szechenyi, saying in his high voice, "I for one think we have a better chance with a truck on the road. It

107

shouldn't be difficult to grab a truck and its two AVO drivers."

"Too dangerous," Ray Merrit commented, speaking as if he weren't the least bit interested. "Far, far too dangerous."

The Death Merchant, still not speaking, sized up Father Nanasi, who was small, but wiry. The priest's backpack looked extra large on his thin body. In fleeing down the slope, he had torn his left pants leg, had also fallen a few times, and his hiking clothes were dusty and smeared with crushed plant juice. He looked exhausted.

Janos Rosmartyi sat down on his heels and looked up when he spoke. "It seems to me that the AVO will be expecting us to show up on the road more than they will be expecting us at the castle. I can't feature the AVO thinking we're crazy enough to head for the castle. And suppose we did get a truck? Where would we go? Drive all the way back to Fonyod? Without being stopped once by the AVO? My God, if we did get back to Budapest, where would we go? What would we do?"

Thomas Lakatos took a pack of cigarettes from his shirt pocket. He quickly changed his mind about smoking when the Death Merchant said quietly, but firmly, "No smoking—any of you. In this quiet air, the smell of tobacco smoke will carry a mile or more."

Suddenly Camellion cocked his head to one side. With the exception of Merrit, the other men tensed at the faint *thum-thum-thum-thum*, the sound growing constantly louder.

A helicopter!

"Everyone stay under the ledge," Camellion ordered.

Finally the sound was very loud, the huge blades of the rotor chopping the air. Then there was a roar, and the men could tell that the craft was passing directly overhead.

As quickly as it had come, the helicopter was gone, the sound fading toward the west.

"Damn it, they're looking for us already," Paul Tisza said in a funereal voice. His burning eyes swept the dismal faces of the other men. "If it makes any difference, I'm all for trying to get to the castle. The AVOs can't do

108

any more than kill us. I've had enough of Communism. I'd rather be dead. I'll never surrender to the AVOs. I'll kill myself first."

"Paul, suicide is a dry rot of the soul," Father Csoki said angrily, his leathery face dripping sweat. "To kill oneself is to hurl the soul back into the face of God with a curse."

Ray Merrit assumed his best undertaker's smile. "I recall reading that in the United States it used to be the law that any person found guilty of an attempt upon his own life was guilty of a felony and could be sent to prison or fined, or both. Only when it dawned upon the stupid lawmakers that this statute was setting a premium upon truly effective attempts at suicide was the article repealed. It was practicaly saying to the hesitant: 'Make a good job of it or you will be punished.' "

"Brother Schmid, I'll tell you this: you had damn well better make a good job if it, if there's no other way to escape being captured by the AVOs," Tiza said grimly. "If there is any hell in this world, it's at the AVO main prison on Fo Street in Budapest. When the experts get through with you, I tell you, Brother, you'll wish you were dead! You'll wish then that you had killed yourself."

"Paul," Father Csoki began severely. "I won't have this kind of blasphemous talk. To even think of self-destruction is unnatural and a violation of the Sixth Commandment. It's—"

"Father, you're free to believe what you want!" Tisza spoke sharply, cutting off the surprised priest, who was disturbed by the behavior of his old friend. Father Csoki was more horrified as Tisza made angry motions with his skinny hands and practically shouted, "I've been in an AVO prison! You haven't. You spend three years at the Korzo Compound and you'll damn soon get a different opinion of a suicide!"

Shocked into speechlessness, Father Csoki stood in frozen, stunned silence. He could only gape open-mouthed at Tisza, who, shaking in anger, looked away from Csoki and the embarrassed stares of the other Hungarians and made an effort to control himself. There was a short, bewildered silence; then Tisza inclined his head toward Merrit and Camellion.

"Ask those two," he said bitterly. "All of us know that they're intelligence agents, no doubt working for the American CIA. They'll tell you that suicide is preferable to capture. No doubt they each have a poison pill or capsule. They'd have to kill themselves. They have too many secrets the Communists could use."

Tisza addressed himself directly to Ray Merrit. "I am positive that you were not born and reared in Germany. Your German is excellent, but I have spoken German all my life, and I can detect those minute differences in pronunciation. Deny it, if you can."

Merrit, his face expressionless, remained silent.

Richard Camellion said in a patient tone of voice, "Who we might be doesn't matter. Nor can we lecture on instant morality. I myself recognize no categorical imperative to *live,* but rather to live *well.* Everybody get ready. We're moving out."

"To Karolyi Castle?" asked Tibor Arpad gruffly.

The Death Merchant nodded slowly. "Our only option is the castle," he said without emotion. He reached up to the low overhang roof of basalt and put his hand against a rock jutting downward like a crooked stalactite.

Camellion's iceberg eyes ripped into Mihaly Szechenyi, and the Hungarian suddenly felt chills sliding up and down his spine. "Szechenyi, you admonished us to face facts. I am doing precisely that. The fact is that if we want to go on living, we must get to those helicopters at the castle. If we don't, we're dead."

"Brother Krim, or whatever your name is, you're telling us that we've got to do the impossible!" Janos Rosmartyi protested. A physical therapist by profession, Rosmartyi was a swarthy man with a blue grained chin and eyebrows that met across the bridge of his nose. "If we're lucky, we'll reach the mountain before midnight. But there's no way in this world that we can climb in the dark."

Rosmartyi looked pleasantly surprised when Brother Schmid agreed with him. "He's right, you know," Merrit said in a relaxed manner. "If we tried to climb after dark, it would be like looking for a needle in a haystack at the bottom of an unlighted mineshaft."

"You're right, it would be," Camellion said, and removed his hand from the rock in the roof. "What we must do is make the AVO think we're trying to get to the road that moves through the gorge to the castle."

"You mean we're going to try for a truck?" Thomas Lakatos said. "But I thought—you said—"

"I said we're going to make the AVO *think* we're trying to get to the road. Whoever is in charge is going to send in troopers, and the only way those men can get down here is by helicopter."

Merrit rubbed his chin and frowned. "Which only means that we'll have to kill them before they kill us. So what else is new?"

"It makes no sense to climb a mountain when we can fly back to Karolyi Castle," the Death Merchant said with a slight smile.

CHAPTER ELEVEN

The single-file formation is often the most practical way of crossing difficult terrain. This formation is easy to keep in line, but the commander has the problem of controlling the men in front of and behind him. The Death Merchant solved this problem in a very simple way. He was the first man in the single-file formation. Ray Merrit was the last. Between them were the ten Hungarians. The formation was vulnerable to fire from the front, but not from the side. Although extremely cautious, Camellion wasn't worried about meeting any of the enemy coming up the incline.

The Death Merchant choosing the route, one that kept the men underneath the trees or close to overhangs, the small force picked its way down the slope to the valley below. Until they reached the valley and were headed south toward the castle road, it was vitally necessary that they remain hidden from low-flying helicopters searching the area.

Camellion was gambling that whoever was in charge of the search wouldn't waste manpower and land troopers just anywhere, in the hope that they might stumble across the band of traitors. Such a freewheeling tactic would incur the very serious risk of an ambush. The wise thing to do would be to wait until one of the choppers spotted the group and then land men in an area closest to that position. Camellion was counting on the AVO commander to do the really intelligent thing: land two groups of troopers—one behind and one in front of the revolutionaries. The troopers could then form a giant ring and close in.

Paratroopers? Not very likely. The rocky and heavily forested countryside excluded an air drop. A troop-carrying helicopter would have to land in an open area; and that was why the Death Merchant hurried down the slope: he was anxious to reach the valley, turn south, find a clearing, and then let one of the spotter puddle-jumpers see him and his men.

There were problems. The first was the pilot of the troop-carrying whirlybird and the co-pilot next to him at the dual controls. If the pilot landed the craft and shut off the rotor, there would be no problem. Camellion or Merrit would put a bullet through the heads of the pilot and the co-pilot—shots that wouldn't be too difficult for experts.

The real danger was that the pilot would hover the craft and that the troopers would jump the few feet to the ground—in which case the situation would be as tricky as playing baseball with a blowtorch in a fireworks factory! Camellion or Merrit could still blow up the two men at the controls, but if the sudden shock of instant annihilation caused either pilot or co-pilot to jerk against the pitch stick or move the cyclic control, the big flying eggbeater could zoom up, swing sideways, then crash. Or it might set itself down without any harm. It was a fifty/fifty chance. But it was their only chance. To capture the craft and then fly to the castle would not only take the AVO at the castle off guard, but would eliminate the

112

necessity of blowing up the Soviet tanks parked on the plateau.

Another danger was that not all of the enemy troops could be whacked out fast enough after they left the helicopter. An AVO trooper or Hungarian army man might manage to kill two or three or more of the freedom fighters if given three-fourths of a chance to use an automatic weapon. There were any number of dangers and dreadful possibilities. Yet the Death Merchant and his men, hemmed in as they were by the AVOs, considered themselves already half-dead. They had nothing to lose, nothing but the other fifty percent of their lives. . . .

Because of Paul Tisza's bad leg, it took the force another hour and a half to reach the valley. Twice, while the men had been stumbling down the slope (and the four priests had been praying silently to all the saints in heaven), a Soviet Bratukhin B-10 military observation puddle-jumper had flown over—the second time so low that its landing wheels had almost touched the tops of the tallest trees. Both times, hearing the noisy approach of the eggbeater, the men had hidden. The first time they had flattened themselves against the trunks of leafy trees; the second time they had made themselves invisible under masses of gray shale jutting out from a partial hillock. The Bratukhin had not seen them. Neither time had the pilot swung back to take a second look.

They moved due south. Five more times the Bratukhin flew over, and each time the Death Merchant and his group scrambled for cover. It was almost dusk, and they had covered only two miles, their slow progress caused not by Tisza's game leg nor the ruggedness of the land, but by the caution Camellion was forced to take. It was not inconceivable that a troop-carrying helicopter had landed beyond their range of sight and hearing. Circumspection had to be the order of advance. To go charging ahead was to risk getting a dose of the same deadly medicine Camellion intended to give the AVOs—the lead toxicity of an ambush. . . .

Then they found the clearing. Relatively large, the clearing was free of large rocks and surrounded by elm and pine trees, the wind making the short grass ripple like flowing, green waves. There was more than enough room for a large helicopter to land, and the area surrounding the clearing offered numerous places suitable for complete concealment.

Grouped together, the men studied the open space cloaked in shadows. The elm spread over the crouching force an opaque canopy of foliage, ink black, shutting off the early stars. Against the dying brightness of the west, an exquisite pattern of branches and feathery leaf sprays was sketched against a background of red and orange.

"I felt something dragging behind me." Merrit said to Camellion. "I looked around, and it was my butt. So what do you think?"

"About what?" the Death Merchant asked. "Your rear end or the clearing?"

"In a short while it will be pitch dark," Merrit said, playing the Devil's Advocate. "If a whirlybird flaps over, we can get its attention by firing at it. But what do we do if and when a troop-carrying deal comes down? If the pilot doesn't turn on the lights in the cockpit, we'll have only the instrument panel lights to use as markers. I figure the clearing is about three hundred feet in diameter. The bird will come down in the center. You're on one side of the clearing, and I'm on the other. We'll have about a hundred and fifty feet shooting range. I'm good, but smacking the guys in the cockpit at that distance, even using K-cartridges—I just don't know."

Father Josef Nosbyti, who was down on one knee on the other side of Merrit, said in a low, nervous voice, "Suppose two helicopters land? One here and the other one, say, a mile away. How do we stop the AVOs in the craft farthest from us from sending word back to the castle by radio? We can't fly faster than radio waves!"

Tibor Arpad frowned good-naturedly, then smiled at the young priest. "Don't be a pessimist, Father," he said. "As long as we're alive we have a chance. But I've been wondering about that myself."

The Death Merchant stood up and walked a few feet forward.

Overhearing Father Nosbyti and Arpad, Ray Merrit

114

provided the solution to their problem. "If we're spotted, the AVOs will think we're trying to get to the road, since we're south of where we were on the highway to the shrine," he explained. "If two troop jobs come after us, one will land here. The other will land in the first clearing south of here. If the one south of us doesn't lift off, we'll get it with explosives on our way to the castle."

"If we can see it, you mean," Arpad said dismally.

Merrit, who had dropped his pose as a West German, resorted to American slang. "Right, if we can see the bird. All we can do is play this game by ear and pick up the dice when they fall."

In the twilight, the Death Merchant turned and looked at Merrit.

"Brother Schmid, take five of the men and go to the right. I'll take the rest and we'll reconnoiter the area around the clearing on the left."

The two groups were soon moving in a semicircle around the northern edge of the clearing in a pincer movement. The Death Merchant had to be positive that the entire area around the clearing was enemy-free. Fifteen minutes later, the two groups merged into one again, twenty feet south of the large glade, which by then was shrouded in complete darkness. Once the sun had vanished behind the mountains, light had fled very quickly.

While moving around to the south of the clearing, the group had heard several helicopters in the distance, but the puddle-jumpers hadn't come within a mile of the large glade. Judging from the irritating sound of the rotors, one had been flying west, the other north.

High in the branches above, a summer locust cut loose with its whirring wings in a mounting series of lazy, rasping sounds, until it lapsed exhausted back into silence. Far to the south came the lonely sound of a screech owl.

There in the darkness, the men stood like statues, listening. All they heard was the owl and the dissonant symphony of insects.

Father Nanasi whispered in disgust, "Those helicopters might not come this way for hours."

"It's this waiting I hate," Frantisek Palfecky said resentfully. Exhaling noisily, he shouldered his Kiraly submachine gun by its narrow leather strap. "I've been waiting ever since I was a child. That's been my whole life—waiting."

"And now you're waiting to die. We all are," Paul Tisza commented. He sat down, placed his machine gun on the grass, and, with both hands, began to massage with vigor the lower part of his right leg.

"Not being able to smoke is what bothers me," muttered Thomas Lakatos. "I never thought I'd see the day that I'd be walking around with seven packs and yet not be able to smoke a single cigarette."

"There are worse things to hurt about, Little Thomas," Mihaly Szechenyi thrust out sullenly. "I've been hurting all my life, about one thing or another. You might just as well get used to it."

He sat down flat on the grass, leaned back, braced himself by putting his hands on the ground, and looked up through the branches at the sky. The blue ice of stars stared back at him. There was a yellow sliver of moon in the east, but it was hidden by a high row of peaks.

Still standing, the Death Merchant began to unstrap his Katahdin Kumfort pack. "We might be here for the next hour or for the remainder of the night. We might even die here. But for now, we might as well conserve our energy and eat what little food we have. No smoking and talk only in whispers."

He slipped out of his pack, sat down, and began to feel around in the pockets of his suit coat, secretly envying Father Nanasi, who was wearing tough, gray-colored hiking pants which matched his suit coat. Presently Camellion pulled a packet of crackers and a flat tin of canned beef from his left coat pocket. Then he reached for the canteen of cold vegetable juice fastened to the side of the backpack.

Merrit laughed in irony. "I haven't done this since I was a Boy Scout," he joked. No one laughed.

The other men began removing their packs, Father Csoki glancing down at the Death Merchant, who was opening the tin of beef with a small pocket can opener.

"Brother Krim, how do think you can shoot the pilot if you can't even see him?" the priest asked in sepulchral

116

tones. Carefully he placed his pack on the grass and sat down. "In this darkness I can barely see your face, and you're only six feet away."

The Death Merchant smiled, and Father Csoki had a slightly disconcerting sensation. Although it was dark, he could see that Camellion's whole face never smiled at the same time. His mouth smiled, but his eyes remained as cold as outer space. The priest wasn't sure, but did he detect a quality of luminosity in those eyes? Yes there was something about Brother Krim that made the priest afraid, that conjured strange images in his mind.

"Let's look at it this way, Father," Camellion said, opening the packet of soda crackers. "If we are seen, the AVOs won't expect us to wait around for troopers to land; and the helicopter that brings those troopers, or Hungarian soldiers, won't come down and land in the dark. It would be far too dangerous. Whether the craft lands completely or hovers above the ground, the lights will be on inside the craft when the troops get off. The cockpit lights should be on, too. If they're not, we'll have to judge by the lights of the instrument panel."

Chewing loudly, Janos Rosmartyi ruminated, his mind jumping to two or three obvious intermediate comments. Looking at Camellion, he finally asked, "How do you know which way the helicopter will land? I mean, how will you get a clear shot at the cockpit if the nose is pointed away from you?"

The Death Merchant, eating with a small folding spoon, thought of what a bunch of amateurs he and Merrit had become involved with. As he ate, he explained very patiently.

"It will take a few minutes or more for the helicopter to come down. We'll know at once the direction in which the cockpit is pointed. I'll be on one side of the clearing. Brother Schmid will be on the opposite side. One of us will have to get into position for a cockpit shot before the bird takes off. We should have the time; the open area isn't all that big. If we don't make the cockpit shot, if we can't"—the Death Merchant looked up, and Father Csoki decided there was a distinct glow in his eyes—"we'll all be dead before tomorrow night."

Ray Merrit broke a cracker in half. "Let's say it the way it is," he said with a half-laugh. "We might all be in heaven before dawn. Or the other place, where you can never get the shivers from cold weather."

The men continued to eat. Several times they heard the sound of helicopters, but the Soviet Bratukhins were always in the distance. Talking in subdued tones, they drank hot coffee laced with Palinka, the Hungarian national hard drink, and waited impatiently, convinced that the only luck they were going to have would be bad.

When the magic moment did arrive, they could hardly believe it was happening, just as they found it incredible that not one but two helicopters were approaching the area in which the clearing was located. They first heard the bird that was coming from the northeast. Moments later, they heard, very faintly, the rotor of the craft that was coming their way from the south. The men jumped to their feet and looked up at the sky, waiting, hoping. This time the helicopters did not swing away. The sound of the rotors grew in volume and intensity. Both helicopters were definitely on a course that would take them over the glade, or at least very close to the clearing.

"All of you wait here," hissed the Death Merchant. Camellion grabbed his Ingram machine pistol and started moving toward the clearing. His stride lengthened; then he was running.

The noise from both directions became very loud. But by the time Camellion reached the center of the clearing, the helicopter flying from the northeast swung off straight west. The eggbeater could not have been more than a fifth of a mile away. However, the copter approaching from the south continued straight on course. In another fifteen seconds the noise of the main rotor blade had become a terrific roar.

The Death Merchant spotted the bright white light through the trees to the south before he saw the dark shape of the helicopter outlined against the lighter sky. The beam was from a large spotlight mounted on the nose of the whirlybird, a beam that swung back and forth, searching, probing the ground below.

118

This is going to be more enjoyable than a sex life after death!

Camellion switched off the safety of the Ingram just as the column of light moved toward him through the trees and briefly touched the edge of the glade. At a height of eighty feet the Soviet Bratukhin roared over the clearing, the shaft of light splashing all over Camellion's body. For a split second, as he pointed the muzzle of the Ingram toward the sky, he was the star, standing in a ten-foot circle of brilliant light. A half-blind observer could have seen him.

The Death Merchant triggered the machine pistol, careful to make certain that his short burst of slugs would go wild and not strike the craft.

Yeah, they saw me! The Bratukhin soared upward; the pilot expertly manipulated the cyclic control to correct for dissymmetry of lift, and the craft swung off to Camellion's right, to the west. Camellion waited. The helicopter flew off in a wide semicircle, headed south for a quarter of a mile, then started to roar back to the clearing, this time at a height of about two hundred feet.

Once more it flew over the clearing, the long beam of bright light raking the ground, the white circle on the ground moving frantically back and forth, up and down, and from side to side. Again it found the Death Merchant, who, satisfied that the men in the bird had seen him, jumped back, raised the Ingram, and fired off a long burst, tiny tongues of red-orange flame flashing from the muzzle.

The spotlight very quickly found another form by the south edge of the glade—Ray Merrit, who also raised his machine pistol and pretended to fire a killing burst at the helicopter.

The Russian spotter-craft swung off to the left, to the east, rose higher, and soon was gone, the pounding of its rotor fading quickly.

The Death Merchant hurried over to Merrit, who was shoving a fresh magazine into his Ingram.

"I figured if there were two of us, we'd have a better chance of their spotting our beautiful forms," Merrit

119

cracked. "And they caught us both. They've got to be thinking we're headed for the road to the south."

Camellion motioned with his right hand. "Let's get the men in position," he said. "Since we've moved south, I estimate we're no more than seven and a half miles, maybe eight, from the castle. A big twenty-man-carrying bird can load up and be here in less than fifteen minutes. That chopper is probably giving our position by radio right now."

He turned and, taking long strides, hurried to the man beneath the trees on the other side of the clearing. Ray Merrit followed. Reaching the group, the Death Merchant became all business, telling the ten Hungarians to spread out and surround the clearing.

"But at all costs, don't open fire until all of the troopers are out of the bird and on the ground," Camellion said. "Another good thing to remember is that sub-guns tend to rise off target and twist to the left or right after about five rounds in a burst. When this happens, hold fire and get back on target. There's no need to brace yourself for the kick of a cannon. Just lean slightly more forward than you would to fire a single shot from a rifle and hang on tight. That's all there is to it."

Father Csoki's slight saw-edged laughter came as a surprise to Camellion and Merrit.

"Brother Krim, I assure you that we know how to use a submachine gun," the priest said lightly. He moved closer to the Death Merchant in the darkness. "It's like swimming or riding a bicycle. Once you learn how, you never forget."

"All of us took part in the uprising," Father Deak whispered. "All of us except Lakatos and Father Nosbyti. They were too young."

"There is something I'd like to know," asserted Janos Rosmartyi stoutly. "I think we all would. We've heard you and Brother Schmid mention K-cartridges. What are these K-cartridges? What do they do?"

The Death Merchant knew he'd lose less time by explaining; yet he was irritated. "K-cartridges are a special kind of ammunition," he said, his voice impatient. "All the ammo that was smuggled to us from Austria is K

120

stuff—and that includes the ammo for your vz/25, Father Csoki. A K-bullet is slightly heavier than a normal bullet, and it has a tungsten-carbide core. We're using K-cartridges on this job because they're made for precise shooting against long-range targets and also against protected targets. Another advantage is that tungsten-cored bullets have a greater range. We have about an extra hundred and fifty yards."

"At least we have something going for us," Tibor Arpad said and looked up at the sky. It was pitch dark, the stars intensely blue.

The Death Merchant went on swiftly. "Remember, keep about forty feet apart when you surround the clearing. Stay down, and don't fire until either Brother Schmid or I fire. Now split up into two groups and move out. Don't forget—*stay down.*"

Camellion and Merrit watched in silence as Father Csoki and four of the Hungarians went through the trees to the left, and Paul Tisza and the second group of four moved quickly to the right.

"I think that maybe we'll be able to depend on them," Merrit commented in a low voice. "Four men of God, they seem to be on friendly terms with the devil. Which side do you want?"

His head tilted at an odd angle, Camellion listened for the sound of rotors. He heard nothing. There was only the sky and the starwind.

"Take your choice," he said at length.

"I want the other side," Merrit replied lazily. "The girls are prettier on that side of the street—see ya."

The helicopters came ten minutes later. At first, there was only the faint sound of rotors, but very quickly, within minutes, the whisper turned to a scream. Then the helicopters were there, four of them: two Bratukhin observers and two Yak-24 "Hound" military assault transport helicopters.

Flying at an altitude of four hundred feet, a Bratukhin puddle-jumper and one of the Hounds passed very close to the clearing. They continued to fly south. The Death Merchant smiled in the darkness. *It's better than a license*

121

to steal! The AVO thinks we're trying to escape to the south. They're looking for a second clearing.

The second Hound and the other Bratukhin hovered over the glade, the large troop transport coming down to about a hundred and fifty feet and staying to one side while the Bratukhin observation bird began to come down in the center, its spotlight raking all around the edge of the glade. As the little craft got closer to the ground, the searching light played tic-tac-toe over the clearing itself. Once the beam came to within ten feet of the Death Merchant, who had buried himself in the grass, and, lying flat, was peering out between two young pines.

Satisfied that none of the traitors were around, the observation copter zoomed upward, then sideways, so that it was a hundred feet above the ground and a hundred feet opposite the Hound.

The roar of its twin rotors increasing, the Hound moved to the center of the air space above the clearing and began its descent by the light of two spots, one mounted on the nose, the other toward the middle of the starboard side.

Powered by two 1,750-hp ASh-82V radials, one four-section blade over the pilot housing, the other at the rear stabilizer, the Hound carried a crew of twenty-two combat men.

With the two beams of light remaining perpendicular, as if they were supporting the craft, the Hound slowly began to descend, coming down in a position that put its cockpit between Merrit and Camellion, and fifty to sixty feet away from them to the south.

The Death Merchant crawled backward on his hands and knees for a dozen feet; then he got to his feet and started through the darkness, moving south. His feet cracked twigs and, in his haste, he brushed against low branches; yet he knew that any sound he might make would be more than absorbed by the racket of the Hound's twin rotors.

The Death Merchant had covered maybe thirty feet when he heard a loud, curious whisper. "I'm down here. What's going on?" The husky voice belonged to Mihaly Szechenyi, who was hidden in the grass and weeds.

122

"Stay down," hissed Camellion. "I'm getting into a better position."

Richard's feet flew across the ground. Practically running, pushing aside branches with the Ingram machine pistol, Camellion crashed forward; and by the time the tricycle landing gear of the Hound touched the grass in the clearing, he was flat on his belly behind a clump of grass to the right side of a tall, stately elm.

The helicopter settled down, the pilot down-cycling the blades, which began to revolve more slowly in a neutral nonlift. Immediately a spotlight, mounted on top of the metal fuselage just behind the cockpit, was switched on. Camellion snuggled down and hoped the other men were doing the same.

Slowly the light began to revolve, the bright beam stabbing out at the edge of the glade. The enemy force was not going to take chance one. The searching circle of vivid radiance roamed over the ground, bathing vines, branches, and wild flowers in an eerie blue-white light. But the light did not find the Death Merchant or any of his men.

As abruptly as it had been switched on, the spotlight was clicked off. Lights inside the craft were turned on, the round windows becoming a row of big, yellow eyes. Faces appeared at the windows.

Damn it! Turn on the lights in the cockpit! However, there was a faint glow from the instrument panel, and Camellion could distinguish the forms of men in the control compartment. He looked up at the sky. The Bratukhin just hung there, waiting, off to one side, and the Death Merchant knew that now it was impossible to get to the castle without the AVO there expecting them. The moment the clearing exploded with gunfire, the Bratukhin would instantly notify headquarters at Karolyi Castle.

On each side of the Hound, in the center of the fuselage, was a door. These doors were now thrown open, and the first man, dressed in a camouflage suit and wearing full battle gear, appeared in the doorway on Camellion's side of the glade.

At the same time, the lights went on in the cockpit. The Death Merchant's heart skipped several beats when

123

he saw one of the two men—the one on Merrit's side—in the cockpit open a hatch above his head and stand up, pushing his head and torso through the opening, no doubt to watch the AVOs or Hungarian army soldiers get off. And get off they did—on either side of the craft, one by one going through the doorways and jumping lightly to the grass. Each man carried an automatic rifle, and the Death Merchant noticed that several of the men had infrared scopes mounted to their weapons. The AVO assault force had come well prepared. One man, an officer, started shouting for the men to hurry and not to worry about the revolving helicopter blades, which were too high to do them any harm.

The Death Merchant crawled backward, stood up, moved to the side of the elm, and raised the Ingram, bracing the deadly little machine gun against the side of the tree. Putting to sleep forever the dumbo half outside the cockpit would be as easy as hitting the side of a mountain with a blast from a 12-gauge shotgun. But smacking the joker still sitting down would require some extra effort. The Death Merchant could see that he was wearing headphones and leaning forward slightly. *He's reporting to the castle that the landing went well. I'm going to have bad news for that fellow!*

The problem was not impossible to solve. The thing to do was to first ice out the man who was seated. The high-velocity tungsten-cored projectiles would zip through the plexiglass the way a hot poker burns through toilet paper. There would be that few seconds' surprise lag-time with the man standing, and by the time he reacted and tried to drop down—*he'll be a corpse starting to grow cold!*

The Death Merchant aimed very carefully, centering the *V* of the sight on the head of the man seated in the control compartment. A split-hair of a second before Richard's finger touched the trigger, Ray Merrit's Ingram started its distinctive *duddle-duddle-duddle-duddle*.

Camellion's own machine pistol began chattering its final message as Merrit's stream of projectiles popped into the man who had thrust his head and shoulders up through the top hatch of the cockpit. The man dropped

124

into infinity at the same instant that Richard's line of slugs shattered the rear side panel of the cockpit housing, the plexiglass dissolving in a shower of ragged chips. And so did the head of the man wearing the headphones! It's difficult for a skull to stay intact when it's hit by five nine-millimeter Ingram projectiles.

A hell of roaring gunfire erupted from the entire edge of the glade, the ten Hungarians firing almost as one. And Camellion found himself in agreement with Merrit. *We can depend on them. They are doing a good job—as good as pros.*

Exposed as they were outside the Hound, the twenty battle-garbed men were cut to pieces, the thundering roar of nine Kiraly sub-guns and Father Csoki's vz/25 chatter-box drowning out even the sound of the Hound's twin rotors.

Within ten to fifteen seconds the massacre was complete, the dead bodies twisted in grotesque positions on either side of the helicopter. One man was even half-sprawled in the doorway of the Hound, whose rotor blades continued to move with monotonous regularity.

Very suddenly an unnatural stillness fell over the area, abnormal because even the insects had been frightened into silence. There was only the rolling echo of gunfire and the drifting blue haze of burnt gun powder. And the monotonous sound of the revolving rotor blades.

The body of one of the soldiers twitched several times. The man's right leg moved, then his left arm. The man tried to push himself up. To the right of the Death Merchant came a short burst of Kiraly fire, three more slugs thudding into the man, who fell flat on his face and lay still.

Richard looked up at the wide bowl of the sky, his head moving toward the sound of the Bratukhin observation helicopter. The pilot had cycled down his rotor. The puddle-jumper dropped fifty feet, swung out until it was dead center over the glade, then zoomed up and moved toward the left. Very quickly it was gone, flying northeast.

The Death Merchant moved toward the edge of the clearing and shouted, "Move in, but be very careful."

Camellion and Merrit and the ten Hungarians closed

in. Creeping from the trees, they moved to the Hound in a circle that grew smaller, each man alert for any corpse that might suddenly show signs of life. None did. Every single one of the enemy was stone dead.

The freedom fighters gathered by the south side of the Hound. None seemed to be upset or the least bit nervous, and Camellion felt rather foolish when Father Csoki looked him straight in the eye and said, "Brother Krim, I think by now you should be convinced that we know how to handle machine guns."

"Yes, I'm convinced." The Death Merchant looked out over the clearing, over the stage where death had just performed. "But I don't have the time to congratulate each of you personally. The spotter craft that just whizzed away reported what we did. We have to be out of here before the assault helicopter to the south of us can lift off and come calling. Some of you pick up those five Wal automatic rifles equipped with infrared scopes. We can use them."

Lakatos, Arped, and Father Deak moved out toward the corpses to pick up the A-Rs as Ray Merrit, who was inspecting the Hound, called out, "Brother Krim, come here and take a look." Paul Tisza grabbed the Death Merchant's attention with his grave-digger eyes.

"I was under the impression that we were going to try to destroy the second assault helicopter," Tisza said, sounding half-angry. "I mean, if we can find the one that must have landed south of here."

Camellion shook his head. "Negative. We don't have the time," he said, looking up at the sky. He saw only the stars, and beyond, the galactic emptiness. He looked at Tisza. "There isn't any sense in pressing our luck. Another factor is the number of troop assault helicopters the enemy might have at the castle. If there are only two, and we blow up the one south of us, that leaves only this one. When we land at the castle, we can expect to have this baby riddled."

"Brother Krim! Take a look at these bullet holes." Ray Merrit's voice was harsh and demanding.

The Death Merchant turned and hurried across the short space to the side of the large helicopter. Father

126

Csoki tagged along behind. Ray Merrit was standing a few feet to the right side of the open door, slowing moving the tip of one finger over bullet holes in the metal fuselage.

Camellion leaned closer and stared at the holes.

"I haven't checked inside," Merrit said gravely. "But I don't think these did us any harm." He indicated the two spinning blades of the twin rotors by jerking his head from left to right. "There's no change in pitch to the blades. Still, there's a chance that some of my slugs, or yours, might have hit a vital spot in the cockpit."

"We'll soon know," Camellion said, and turned to the rest of the men, who were standing in a half-circle, an expectant look on their sweaty faces. "Everybody get inside. But don't bunch up. Spread out so your weight is evenly distributed."

The Death Merchant swung around, put a foot into the rung that served as the single step, and pulled himself up through the door into the interior of the Hound, catching a brief sight of the lighted cabin—two metal benches bolted on each side of the fuselage—as he headed for the cockpit. Behind him, Merrit and the ten Hungarians climbed into the well-built Russian attack helicopter.

The cockpit was almost as bloody as the killing floor of a packing house. The airman who had stood up through the top hatch lay twisted in a grotesque grimace of death, his body half on the cushioned seat and half on the floor, his gray uniform shirt ripped, torn, and bloody from Merrit's 9mm projectiles. The man the Death Merchant had made inactive was headless, the body hanging sideways over the tiny space between the seats, the corpse imprisoned in its own seat by the safety belt. Drops of drying blood and slivers of skullbone decorated the floor, the sides of the seats, and the instrument panel. The air smelled sweet, very sweet, but the fragrance was not from the wild flowers in the glade. Camellion scratched the back of his neck. The man that Merrit had whacked out was the strangest-looking dead man the Death Merchant had ever seen. One eye of the corpse was open. The other eye was closed.

Merrit stuck his head into the cockpit and looked

127

around. "Tch, tch. What messy housekeepers they were." He stared down at the corpse of the man he had killed. "I'll be damned. He's winking at us!"

"Let's get them out of here and take off." Camellion started to unstrap the headless corpse. Beside him, Merrit moved into the compartment and tugged at the other corpse, which was already half-rigid with rigor mortis.

It required all of seven minutes for Camellion and Merrit to pull the two corpses from the cockpit, drag them to the door on the port side, and shove them out of the helicopter. Camellion sealed the door, glanced briefly at the Hungarians sitting on the two benches—they looked as happy as patients with two broken legs—then went back to the cockpit, where Merrit had already settled down in the left seat and was twisting the throttle of the collective pitch stick.

The wide-faced Company man glanced at Camellion and grinned.

"You or me, buddy?"

"You've put in more time with copters than I have," Camellion said. "Take her up and fly us to Karolyi Castle."

Merrit went to work on the primary controls. The revolutions of the two big blades increased, the two ASh-82V radial engines roared, and the white and green assault copter lifted straight up from the glade. To the men looking out the circular windows, the clearing simply dropped away, then vanished. There was only the star-dotted sky, and, in the east, the sliver of orange moon, which by now was higher. There was a bright glow to the northeast, a small patch of light that appeared to be suspended in the darkness, as if hanging in midair. None of the men had to be told that the brightness represented the end of their journey—Karolyi Castle, perched high on the side of Mount Zivatar.

There was no sign of the other assault chopper as Merrit swung the Yak-24 Hound to the northeast and continued to up-cycle the blades. He leveled off at 2,100 feet and headed the bird straight at the patch of light. He and Camellion both did a doubletake and stared at the instrument panel when the craft started to quiver slightly.

"Good God Girty! Look at the tachometer!" Merrit

128

said, genuine concern in his deep voice. "The front rotor
is losing revolutions."

"I see it," the Death Merchant said. The odor of cigarette smoke and burning pipe tobacco drifted to his nostrils. "One of our slugs must have hit something above the
cockpit, maybe the hub or the rotor or part of the gearbox."

Paul Tisza leaned into the cockpit, bracing himself in
the low, narrow doorway with his hands. "They're getting
nervous back there," he said, his piggy-shrewd eyes darting from Merrit to Camellion. "What is wrong?"

"Blade stall," Camellion said, watching the tachometer.

Tisza inhaled loudly in alarm. "What happens if the
blade quits altogether? Will we crash?"

The Death Merchant turned and looked at the dour-
faced Hungarian.

"We'll go down—and hard!"

The Hound quivered again, harder this time.

CHAPTER TWELVE

There wasn't anything that General Skedfu and Lieutenant General Barthory could do about the disguised verbal insults of the three Russians. As the late afternoon
quickened into twilight, the taunting innuendoes of Boris
Lysemki and his two KGB aides increased. It would take
only a few hours, General Skedfu had said, and the helicopters would find the revolutionaries. Only the three
Bratukhins hadn't found anyone, and now it was dark.

The bony, hard-eyed Lysemki had brought up the subject of Mr. and Mrs. Kobalinsky. Had Lieutenant General
Barthory made an investigation to ascertain why the two
Poles had not exhibited any symptoms of staphylococcal
food poisoning? Barthory had derived sadistic pleasure
from informing Lysemki that the Polish couple had not
eaten lunch that day at the priests' home. They had been
out exploring Budapest and hadn't returned to St. Matthias until nine o'clock that night.

129

The radio message from Captain Ifjusag, flying one of the Bratukhins, that he and his observation team had located the revolutionaries and that they were two and a half miles south of the point on the road where the two troopers on motorcycles had been murdered, proved not only that General Skedfu and Lieutenant General Barthory had been correct, but also that the members of the underground were attempting to escape by means of the gorge road. Now it was Skedfu and Barthory's turn to smirk. The three Russians reverted to their usual tactic of remaining silent. When in doubt, say nothing.

General Skedfu had called Major Edger Furdo, the AVO commander of the castle, and had instructed Major Furdo to come to the roof of the laboratory. Boris Lysemki had followed Skedfu and Barthory to the roof, where they and Major Furdo watched two of the Hound assault helicopters lift off from the pad and roar away toward the southwest.

The four men quickly walked to the west side of the broad roof and stared after the two Yak-24 military transport helicopters. All they could see were the red and green landing lights, and these, too, soon faded into nothingness, as did the sound of the rotors.

Skedfu and Barthory, luxuriating in new-found confidence, studied the region to the southwest through high-resolve, wide-angle binoculars. Boris Lysemki smoked a cigarette. Major Furdo, a heavy, dignified man with heavy-rimmed nose glasses, kept a respectful silence. He stood by the four-and-a-half-foot-high mesh fence that was built all around the edge of the roof. His hands around the top steel-pipe railing, he thought of how nice it would be if he could pick Lysemki up and throw him screaming over the railing to the side of the mountain below. Furdo was uncomfortable. Superstitious and believing in hunches, he had the feeling that some kind of monstrous disaster was about to happen.

"Tell me, Comrades. Do you actually think your field glasses will let you see the two Hounds land?" Lysemki said, the sneer in his voice clearly evident. "They won't. The distance is too great."

General Skedfu and Lieutenant General Barthory lowered their binoculars, the general smiling tolerantly at the KGB *Residentura.*

"The traitors are in a trap, Comrade Lysemki, and you know it," Skedfu said disdainfully.

"Let us hope so," Lysemki said reprovingly. He dropped his cigarette and crushed it out with the heel of his foot. "There is no need for this continued failure."

Thirty-five minutes later, Major Furdo's worst fears became a reality. The small walkie-talkie on General Skedfu's belt made a buzzing sound. Skedfu removed the device from his belt and switched it on.

"Yes, what is it?"

"General Skedfu, this is the radio room!" The voice was highly agitated and hesitant with disbelief. "Captain Ifjusag has just reported that Lieutenant Endras and his unit have been wiped out by the fugitives. Captain Ifjusag reports that the pilot and co-pilot are also dead."

It was several moments before General Skedfu could speak. "Did he say anything about the Hound?" Stunned, he was not successful in keeping his voice free from shock.

"The helicopter appears to be undamaged, Comrade General."

"Very well," choked Skedfu, and switched off the walkie-talkie. "It's—it's impossible!" he mumbled, then turned and looked at Sigismund Barthory, who stood transfixed, staring toward the southwest, a sick look on his shadowed face. General Skedfu's worried eyes leaped to an angry Boris Lysemki, who stood glaring at him, his thin lips pulled back over his teeth in a kind of snarl. "There are only twelve of them!" Skedfu protested. "How could twelve men kill an assault unit of AVO troops?"

Lieutenant General Barthory said tonelessly, "The revolutionaries will use that captured Hound to fly to Austria." As if some wound-up spring had triggered itself within him, he spun and faced Skedfu and Lysemki. "The fighter jets at Csepell!" he blurted out. "We could radio the airfield and have them send jets. It's possible they could intercept the Hound and force it to land or shoot it down before those twelve murderers escape in it to Austria!"

"The two of you are first-class idiots!" Lysemki said, emphasizing each word, his face a mask of chagrined rage. "It's perfectly clear that Lieutenant Endras and his unit dropped into a cleverly set ambush. If it's the Death Merchant leading the group, he could have done it with five men! And don't be so damn sure they'll try to fly to Austria. If it's the Merchant of Death we're fighting, I wouldn't be at all surprised if the son-of-a-bitch headed in our direction. That maniac never knows when to quit!"

"Here, to the castle?" exclaimed General Skedfu. "He wouldn't dare! He may be daring, but he's not crazy!"

Major Furdo asked in a timid voice, "Should I have the radio room contact the Csepel airfield? The Migs—"

"Forget those Migs," Lysemki said in weary patience. He thrust out his jaw toward General Skedfu, who became aware of a terrible fear overpowering him, a dread moving closer and closer to blind panic.

Boris Lysemki's tone was low and vicious. "Ask yourself, General: how would it look if we asked the air force to send Mig fighters to do the job we were supposed to do—to wipe out a mere handful of men?"

The Russian was so furious that he trembled, while his Adam's apple rolled up and down with the speed of a yoyo. "What would the central government in Budapest think of such inefficiency, especially since you and Barthory have employed two extra Hounds and two more smaller craft to protect the castle during the pilgrimage? No matter what action is taken, we have to be the ones who take it."

Skedfu, Barthory, and Furdo stared in helpless frustration at the Russian KGB expert. To make matters worse, they knew that Lysemki was right. But how could anyone plan rationally against the Death Merchant?

Lieutenant General Barthory said, with a perceptible tremor of agitation in his voice, "We can't just let them fly off to Austria! How do you think that would look to Kadar and the Council—and to your center in Moscow?"

For several seconds, the Russian stared through narrowed eyes at Barthory. He knew that they knew he was trying to protect himself, and that in covering for himself, he would have to cover for them, and vice-versa.

132

"If the revolutionaries fly toward Austria, we'll let them go," the Russian insisted in a very soft voice. "I can concoct a story that Moscow will believe. Between the three of us, we should be able to explain away the situation to Budapest. But can we trust him?" He nodded toward a surprised and now frightened Major Eger Furdo.

"He knows the proper route to advancement," General Skedfu said slyly. "Isn't that so, *Colonel* Furdo?"

Pleased, Furdo nodded mechanically. Just as mechanically, he said, "I am a soldier. I do what my superiors order me to do."

General Skedfu shoved his binoculars into the case hanging from his neck. "I think we had better hope that the swine down in the valley are crazy enough to attack the castle. It would not be easy to fool Budapest. There are too many AVOs who know the truth. We can't be sure they would never talk."

"We could black out the castle," suggested soon-to-be Colonel Furdo. "The revolutionaries might crash against the face of the mountain." A moment later Furdo wished he had kept his mouth shut.

Boris Lysemki showed his low opinion of Major Furdo by ignoring the man completely, not even bothering to glance in his direction.

"There are only three places where the Hound can land," Lysemki said, moving his hands for emphasis. "It can set down on the regular landing pad, or in front of the castle, or on this roof. We'll make it easy for the sons of bitches. We'll not turn off a single light. If the rotten traitors land in front, the tanks will have them. We'll ring the pad with men and keep them out of sight, so there's no problem there."

"Here on the roof we can place men with machine guns in the housings over the stair openings," General Skedfu commented, avoiding the Russian's eyes. He wondered how he and Sigismund might blame the entire fiasco on Lysemki and the other Russians. No, there was not any way. What he and Sigismund needed was time, Skedfu thought. But time was what they didn't have.

The right side of Boris Lysemki's face glowed dimly but briefly from the flash of one of the red strobe lights on the four-legged radio tower. The Russian's smile was almost pleasant, but his eyes remained as cunning as a weasel's.

"For once, General, you have said something intelligent. Now let's get to work. This night will see the end of the Death Merchant. His time has about run out. . . ."

CHAPTER THIRTEEN

The sky above, the blackness below! Between was the captured Yak-24 Hound assault helicopter, with twelve worried men aboard. Even the Death Merchant, in spite of his pragmatic philosophy of realism, didn't relish the thought of crashing into the trees or the mountains, although there wouldn't be a crack-up, as such, unless both rotors malfunctioned.

Every now and then the blade of the front rotor missed its synchronization cycle and the Hound shook violently. Each time the craft quivered, Richard Camellion and Ray Merrit knew that the 'copter had lost altitude and that it was impossible to regain the loss. Merrit could not climb back into the sky. By the time the Hound was halfway to Karolyi Castle, the needle of the altimeter read 1,983 feet.

Merrit handled the controls as though they were made of glass. He was alone in the cockpit. The Death Merchant was in the main part of the ship, preparing the Hungarians for the landing—or the crash—and readying his own equipment.

When Camellion returned to the cockpit, he had two Kal pistols strapped around his waist over his suit coat and a kit bag on each hip, the straps of the bags crisscrossing his back and chest. The only thing he lacked was the Ingram machine pistol and the extra magazines for the weapon. They were behind the cockpit in another shoulder bag, along with his Katahdin backpack.

Ray Merrit, making a tiny alteration in course, glanced

at the Death Merchant, who was looking at the instrument panel.

"I guess you attached the detonators to the ends of the arrows OK?"

Camellion nodded. "Yes. All I have to do is clip a packet of C-4 to each arrow and jam in the D-points. I distributed the C-4. I'm carrying most of it. I put two packs in your bag."

"If we manage to get to the castle in this bird, no matter where we land, they'll be waiting for us. I guess dropping down on the roof of the castle can be said to be the shortest distance between two points. We'll be right above the lab."

"Unless the intelligence service of the Society of the Double Cross goofed." The Death Merchant had fastened a blood-smeared cloth over the square opening to his right, where he had shot out the plexiglass window. But the wind had torn away the cloth, and he hadn't bothered to replace it. An eerie whistling issued from the opening, an unpleasant sound that Camellion ignored.

Camellion stared through the front plexiglass of the cockpit. Karolyi Castle was less than four miles ahead; however, the Hound was still too far away for Camellion and Merrit to distinguish the castle. They could only see a lot of intense light.

"Any special plans for the attack?" Merrit asked morosely. He tried to give a fraction more power to the front rotor, but his effort was useless. It was evident that the problem was not in the ASh-82V radial engine. It was at full power, and so was the engine in the rear. The trouble lay somewhere in the front rotor.

"We land, jump out on both sides, and pick it up from there," Camellion said. He almost had to shout to make himself heard above the roaring of the engine. He leaned sideways, moving closer to Merrit.

"Is there any chance that you can turn her around and make several passes over the roof? If you can, we can plaster the three front towers with C-4."

"No dice. I can't do it, buddy," Merrit said. "If I tried, the odds are that we'd get complete blade stall and rotor decay. We've already lost translational lift. It has to be a straight shot in and drop down. There's—"

A tremendous shuddering rippled through the craft, switching off Merrit's words. There was a long, grinding noise outside the helicopter, a few feet back from the cockpit. Both men had heard that kind of noise before. The main gear in the gearbox below the rotor was off balance.

The blade stalled, then stopped completely.

Frantically, Ray Merrit tried to adjust the cyclic control stick. Just as quickly he put the trim controls at half angle.

"It's the best I can do," he said in desperation. "We're going down. We might reach the castle, but don't make book on it."

The Death Merchant looked at the tachometer of the front rotor. The needle was on a big fat zero. He looked at the tachometer of the rear rotor. In an airplane the tachometer shows the revolutions of the engine alone. But in a helicopter, this one instrument provides the revolutions per minute of both the engine and the rotor on one clock face. This is accomplished by having two needles on the same shaft. One needle points to an inner scale on the face of the instrument with one set of numbers, while the other needle points to an outer scale with a different set of numbers; one needle indicates the rotor revolutions; the other shows the revolutions of the engine.

The tachometer showed that the speed of the rear rotor was 540 revolutions per minute, while the engine speed was approximately 3,200 revolutions. Camellion checked the altimeter—1,640 feet.

"We might reach the castle, but as far as landing goes . . . with one rotor out . . ." Merrit didn't finish the sentence. His implication was clear enough: to land with one rotor out of commission would be the same as trying to fly a kite in a hurricane.

Merrit switched off the front engine. Immediately there was a half-silence. The wind whistling through the opening next to Camellion seemed extra loud. Even the sky appeared unfriendly.

Camellion turned to Merrit. "We have one chance," he

136

said. "Shut off the rear engine, come down on autorotational descent, and hope we hit the castle roof, or at least some part of the plateau. Can you suggest anything better?"

"An A-D will give us a better chance than we have now," Merrit replied. He switched off the rear engine, and almost at once the silence became complete.

The autorotational descent of a helicopter, which has been compared to the glide of an airplane with a dead engine—a "dead stick landing"—is that process in which the blades will continue to turn and produce lift even though the power has been stopped entirely. The helicopter descends with the airflow coming up through the rotor from the front and below, rather than from above, as happens in normal powered flight. In autorotation the airflow meets the rotor blades at an angle of attack which induces a lift force inclined slightly forward, so that it serves to pull the blades around and thus keeps the rotor turning. And now, as the Hound headed for Karolyi Castle, that was how the helicopter was going down.

"I'll go tell the Hungarians the sad tale of woe," Camellion said. He got up from the seat and moved through the low doorway to face the ten Hungarians sitting on the two metal benches. They stared at him and exchanged glances among themselves as he gave them the grim facts of the present predicament, hanging on to the sides of the doorway for support.

Dr. Frantisek Palfecky looked up at Camellion, a tenseness on his long, horselike face. "Put another way, Brother Krim, you are saying that we'll either land on the roof of the castle or maybe somewhere on the plateau, like in front of the castle. If we don't, we'll either hit the side of the mountain or miss the castle completely and land in the east valley."

"Some choice!" laughed Mihaly Szechenyi; and they all knew his laugh was faked to keep up his courage and theirs.

"It's our only choice, men," the Death Merchant said. "Keep a watch on the windows and you'll know when we're coming in—and where!"

He swung back into the control compartment—*you*

137

might be able to see your own deaths approaching—and sat back down next to Merrit, who, out of habit, still had his hands on the collective and throttle and the cyclic control.

"This is it!" Merrit said, a breathless quality of awe to his harsh voice. "A few minutes more, and we'll know where this baby is going to hit."

They could see Karolyi Castle looming up not quite a quarter of a mile ahead—a gigantic mass of stone that seemed to rock from side to side, due to the motion of the helicopter. The helicopter drew closer to the castle, the wind, coming up from the front and below, keeping the two big blades revolving. Merrit and Camellion spotted the castle keep—the three round towers—and saw a series of lighted windows on the west side of the monstrous castle staring at them like slitted eyes. They caught a glimpse of the powerhouse, which was actually a booster station, and the heavy power lines leading from the building, across the ground, and down into the gorge. Strung out on towers, the power lines continued on to the south to the power station at Veszprem.

All Merrit and Camellion could do was sit there and trust to luck. There was a brief picture of the three concrete watchtowers on the rim of the precipitous gorge and, between the towers and the castle, a row of T-62 tanks with their 115mm cannons pointed toward the south, in the direction of the gorge. Then the broad roof of the castle, with its radio tower and television antenna, a half dozen stairway housings, and the building containing the air-conditioning equipment came into view.

The roof of the castle vanished!

The helicopter had dropped lower, and although Merrit and Camellion could not see the roof, they realized it was at a level that put it *above* the Hound.

"So much for the roof!" Merrit said matter-of-factly, shifting his unlit pipe to the other side of his mouth. "We're either going to hit the side of the goddamn mountain or sit down on the edge of the tabletop. Too bad prayer doesn't work. I'd be outpraying the Pope!"

"If prayer worked, we wouldn't be here!" Camellion replied.

138

Leaning sideways, he turned and yelled at the men in the rear, "Let yourselves hang loose. We're almost down. The second we land, get into your packs and grab your weapons."

By now it seemed that the entire west side of Karolyi Castle filled the area ahead of the cockpit, and for an instant the men had the horrible impression that the Hound was going to end its life—and theirs—against the thick stone wall. But before the notion had time to firmly establish itself, the castle rose quickly upward as the helicopter dropped downward.

And then, with a jar that made the men feel they were inside a vibrator, the helicopter landed heavily on the edge of the plateau west of the castle, which was a few hundred feet away. The Hound came down where the west side of the plateau inclined steeply for fifty feet before it terminated at the edge. Beyond the edge was a thousand-foot drop.

The landing gear wedged in the jagged rocks. The big helicopter shuddered once more and came to a creaking halt.

Almost total silence. There was only the constant crying of the wind and the deep humming of the transformers in the booster station.

"By God! Be damned if we didn't make it!" Merrit exclaimed, his tone indicating he might have begun believing in miracles. But he was talking to an empty seat. The Death Merchant was already moving through the cockpit doorway to the main cabin in back. Merrit scrambled out of the pilot's seat and was soon slipping into his own pack, along with Camellion and the other men, then jumping out of the side door to the rocky ground.

"Don't bunch up," Camellion said to the Hungarians. "We'll take positions at the top of the slope. Brother Schmid, stay with me."

Watching all sides, the Hungarians followed Camellion and Merrit across the pebbly ground, which, as it curved upward toward the level part of the land, became thick with flintlike boulders, none larger than a basketball. Other parts of the slope were filled with columnar structures of igneous rock and loose slabs of dark shale.

Spread out in a crooked line—Merrit and Camellion at the south end—the twelve-man force, charging up the incline, moved between rocks, sometimes slipping on loose shale, in their effort to reach the top.

Quite unexpectedly, a submachine gun opened fire from the west-side wall of the castle, as the men threw themselves down at the top of the slope and snuggled between boulders and slabs of shale and granite. Two more sub-guns joined the first, the three lines of hot projectiles striking the rocks in back of the men and screaming off in wild ricochets. However, the AVO troopers, who were firing from third-story windows, were at a disadvantage. Not only was much of the slope smothered in darkness, but, because of the location of the slope and the positions of Camellion and his companions on the slope, the AVOs had to fire downward at a left-sided angle. Even by leaning out the windows as far as they could, the AVOs couldn't get the angle that would give them clear shots at the group below.

Crouched just below the rim, Camellion and Merrit raised their heads and looked out. A hundred and fifty feet away, to the right, was the powerhouse. Farther to the right was the corner watchtower. East of the southwest tower was the second tower, and behind it, the weather station structure. Camellion could also see four Russian T-62 tanks and dozens of AVO troopers clustered around the armored monsters. The powerhouse obstructed Camellion and Merrit's view of the other tanks and the guardtower on the southeast side of the gigantic ledge. They could, however, see the front of the garage and repair shop, which was to the east of the castle, and the forward side of the helicopter pad above the building.

Once again the three Kiraly submachine guns chattered from the west castle wall, the high-velocity 9-millimeter slugs kicking up long lines of dust and rock. The AVO gunners realized that they couldn't hit any of the invaders, but at least they could keep them pinned down until the tanks moved in.

The Death Merchant turned and looked down the dark line, his eyes barely able to distinguish the Hungarians lying prone in the rocks.

140

"Some of you use the Wals to knock out those sub-guns!" he called out. "There's too much danger from ricochets."

Janos Rosmartyi and Tibor Arpad began worming their way north, each man carrying a Wal automatic rifle equipped with an infrared scope. Careful not to expose themselves above the rim, Arpad and Rosmartyi crawled at least fifty feet to a position that permitted them to fire straight up at the west wall of the castle; yet they were in terrible danger. By the same token, the AVOs could fire almost straight down at them—if the AVOs found them by using either a spotlight or an infrared scope.

Arpad and Rosmartyi moved closer to the rim, raised their Wal A-Rs, and began searching through the infrared scopes. An infrared device puts out a beam of light that has been filtered to eliminate all but infrared light, which is invisible to the human eye; the special scope catches the reflection of the infrared light and changes the image so that it can be seen by the person looking through the viewer.

Rosmartyi and Arpad soon found the three AVO troopers firing the submachine guns. Together they opened fire, Arpad killing one man, Rosmartyi slamming out the other two. Butchered by 7.63mm slugs, the first AVO fell back from the window. The second trooper, struck in the throat and chest, sagged to one side and disappeared. The third AVO died with his face erased by lead.

Arpad and Rosmartyi began to crawl back to their original positions. They were halfway to the rocks from which they had started when a spotlight came on, the long beam of bright white light stabbing down from a fifth-floor window on the southwest corner of the castle. The beam, moving in wide circles, raked the entire area in front of the slope. Finding nothing, the light searched the rim, but the men jerked their heads back and ducked down, hugging the rocks until the light had passed; and when the light attempted to search the slope itself, it could only—because of the angle—catch the outer edge that overlooked the gorge on one side and the deep valley

141

on the other. For a long time the light lingered on the helicopter.

Angered at the probing light, Father Josef Nosbyti, using a Wal and an infrared scope, sighted in on the man holding the light and killed him with a single short burst. The man fell back from the window. The spotlight and its battery smashed themselves on the ground far below.

Having assembled the crossbow, the Death Merchant, with the help of Ray Merrit, was preparing the arrows. The day before, Camellion had affixed the impact-contact L-14t detonators, each detonator requiring only seven pounds of pressure to trigger the contact that would send the spark to the one-pound package of C-4 explosive attached to the shaft of the arrow. Camellion and Ray Merrit finished with the last two arrows. They each clipped a packet of explosive to the shaft, then thrust the pointed lead wire through the oiled brown paper and into the putty-like substance of the C-4.

"If we try to get in the castle through the main gate, they'll make hamburger out of us," Merrit said. He still had his unlit pipe in his mouth.

"We're going to fly to the roof of the lab," Camellion said.

Both men pulled themselves back slightly as a spotlight on top of the watchtower in the southwest burst into bloom, its brilliant glow illuminating the front of the powerhouse, some of the glare spilling close to the rim of the slope.

"Hear that?" Camellion tilted his head toward Merrit. "We're getting company."

There was the faint sound of rotors to the west. The other assault helicopter was returning to Karolyi Castle, its approach giving birth to the possibility that it might hover above the men and hose them with sub-gun and A-R fire.

If the approaching Hound wasn't enough to cause gray hair, the Russian tanks were. Three of the T-62s had turned around so that their 115mm cannons were pointed in the direction of the slope. However, the Death Merchant was not worried about the big guns of the tanks. The 115mm deals could not be depressed enough to fire at the slope. An HE shell would only arc over and explode hundreds of feet down in the valley.

Camellion placed an explosive arrow on the bed of the crossbow, inserted the steel bowstring into the notched groove at the end of the shaft, and switched on the trigger-lock safety. He pulled the fiberglass bow to maximum and flipped the plate over the rear of the arrow. The arrow was now set to leave the bed with ninety pounds of thrust.

The Death Merchant ducked closer to the ground, and so did Merrit and the ten Hungarians down the line. The beam of the spotlight on the watchtower began probing the top edge of the slope. Thomas Lakatos didn't pull back fast enough, and the white light caught his face for a split second. The AVOs in the watchtower depressed their slugs cut into the rocks only a few feet in front of them, KPV heavy machine gun and began chopping the rim with a vicious fire.

Camellion and his men hugged the rocks while 14.5mm showering them with dust and rock chips. The beam began to probe and explore the slope itself. But again, the angle and the position of the slope, in relation to the position of the watchtower, prevented the round circle-end of the beam from reaching the men. Five feet to their rear was as close as the light could get. Even so, five feet was too close for comfort, for it meant that the Death Merchant & Company were pinned down to just below the top edge of the slope.

As if to remind them of their predicament, the beam moved back and forth over the helicopter imprisoned in the rocks not far from the edge overlooking the valley. Another KPV heavy machine gun roared from the watchtower, this one using 14.5mm tracers, which slammed into the Hound, boring through the fuselage and into the twin rotors and engines. The rear ASh-82V radial exploded with a loud *whoooshhhhh*. There was a flash of orange fire that formed into a tumbling fireball; then the entire helicopter began to burn, the fire and dark oil smoke crawling at crazy angles toward the sky and casting grotesquely flickering shadows over the men crouched on the steep hillside. The beam of the spotlight once more started to probe the rim of the slope.

To the right and in front, two of the tanks began to rev up their engines. Behind and up, the rotor noise of the incoming Hound became louder.

Ray Merrit whispered, "I have the feeling we're not going to make it home for Christmas!"

"We won't even get there for Thanksgiving at the rate we're going!" The Death Merchant looked up at the dark sky. He could hear the approaching Hound, but it was still too far away to be a danger. He could see its red and green navigation lights.

"Pass the word to the men that they should use the Wal A-Rs and concentrate on the cockpit area if that Hound comes in to attack," Camellion said to Merrit. "I'm going farther south. You stay here and stop the Hungarians if they try to get crazy-brave."

To the roaring of the KPV machine gun, which again had begun peppering the rim with 14.5mm projectiles, Camellion inched his body downward a few feet before he turned to his right and began to crawl through the rocks toward the south. After he had estimated that he had moved from fifty to sixty feet and was past the powerhouse, he moved toward the rim, handling the crossbow very carefully, and ever so cautiously looked out over the area in front of him.

Fudge! Now that the powerhouse no longer obstructed his view, he could see that there were eight T-62 tanks, the last four in line facing the castle. The tanks wouldn't use their 115mm guns, but the machine guns in their turrets could set up a fire that a flea wouldn't be able to fly through. The spotlights on the middle and the southeast watchtowers were on, but they weren't raking the rim of the slope because of the intervening powerhouse. There were several dozen Hungarian army soldiers around the far guardtower, standing around jeeps and smoking. Several AVO officers were with them.

The Death Merchant didn't feel like Robin Hood as he reached behind him and pulled one of the arrows from the Katahdin pack strapped to his back and placed it next to him. He thought for a moment, then took the remain-

144

ing arrows from the pack, trying to decide what he should blow up first. The closest watchtower was a mere 125 feet away. On the other hand, the first T-62 tank had begun clanking toward the northside slope, AVO troops trotting behind the metal monster.

They won't be there for long!

Camellion placed the cherry-stained hardwood stock against his right shoulder, pushed off the trigger-lock safety, and, while his left hand supported the weapon underneath the bow, curled his right hand around the checkered pistol grip, his finger moving toward the trigger. He sighted in through the front and rear sights, moving the tip of the arrow to a point where the turret revolved on the body of the tank.

Bye, bye, boys. Camellion pulled the trigger. Without any noise, the arrow left the crossbow, zipped across the open space, and struck the side of the tank, the L-14t detonator sparking the C-4 explosive clipped to the middle of the shaft.

The Death Merchant didn't see the flash of flame. Positive of his aim, he ducked down the second he pulled the trigger. He did hear the explosion. God must have heard the blast, which was the equivalent of a hundred sticks of dynamite. The terrible force lifted the turret and its 115mm cannon ten feet from the rest of the tank, pitched them to the ground, and sent ripped pieces of equipment and jagged chunks of steel flying outward like giant shrapnel from a giant hand grenade. The AVO trooper who had been standing behind the machine gun mounted in front of the commander's cupola was blown apart. His arms and legs soared off in one direction, while his head and torso sailed away in another. All eighteen AVO troopers died, either from concussion or from flying pieces of steel. Their corpses lay scattered around the area, torn and bloody.

The barrel of the ranging machine gun—which should have been sticking out the front of the turret—flew over Camellion's head. The turret's searchlight fell back down from the sky, hit the ground, bounced, and came to a stop close to the head of the man who had been behind the turret's machine gun. The head lay on its side, its open

145

eyes staring straight at the Death Merchant, who had already loaded the crossbow with another C-4 arrow and was aiming at the southwest watchtower. Smiling slightly, the Death Merchant pulled the trigger of the crossbow, then dropped and buried his face in the rocks.

Whhhhooommmmmmmm! A giant flash of red flame! The square 8' x 8' top section of the watchtower vanished, and so did the four AVO troopers inside, pieces of their bodies raining down in a spray of blood, along with chunks of concrete and steel bracing.

The Death Merchant chuckled. What were good friends for?

He quit smiling. There was an insufferable stench in his nostrils: the sweet stink of death, mixed with the odor of burning tank and burnt TNT from the C-4. For the time being, he had the advantage of surprise. When fired, the crossbow made no sound; there was no telltale muzzle flash. And who among the AVOs would suspect an enemy of using arrows carrying one-pound packs of C-4 plastic explosive? Nonetheless, the laboratory and the secret of the NK-hk-4 gas were still a universe away.

Camellion looked up at the sky. The enemy Hound had flown in over the castle, as if to land on the large triangular pad over the repair shops. Only it had swung a hundred feet to the south, had turned on its two searchlights, and was headed west, approaching the hillside that concealed Camellion's men.

Would he be able to hit the helicopter with an arrow? Probably not, but it was worth a try. Camellion aimed ten feet ahead of the helicopter and pulled the trigger of the crossbow.

I shot an arrow into the air. It—

At the same time that the Death Merchant pulled the trigger of the crossbow, the Hungarians opened fire on the Hound with the Wal A-Rs, using the infrared scopes to zero in on the plexiglass-covered cockpit. Several hundred projectiles dissolved the housing and killed the pilot and co-pilot instantly. Out of control, the huge aircraft dropped down and swung to the south, the blade of the front rotor striking the Death Merchant's incoming arrow and setting off the C-4. There was a monstrous *wwooooommmmm,* a bursting ball of bright red fire, and the blade, rotor, and helicopter dissolved into useless junk. The blazing wreckage crashed to the ground with a loud roar, the AVO troopers, turned into torches, screaming hideously, but only for a very short while. The helicopter fell apart when it hit the ground between the castle and the powerhouse, and the burning bodies spilled out.

It didn't fall to earth! It smacked into a helicopter!

Keeping very low, the Death Merchant stared ahead at the confusion.

The searchlights on the middle and the southeast watchtowers were moving all over the place, their beams frantically probing the area. Several times, as the beams came close to Camellion, he ducked, and the lights missed him. The tank Camellion had blown up burned with fiery red flames licking around its steel hull, while velvety, coal-black smoke poured upward toward the night sky. On the southeast side the Hungarian soldiers were clustered around the last two tanks, the AVO officers with them uncertain of what to do. Their orders were to remain in position, and remain they would.

Camellion wasn't at all cheerful about the situation. Searchlights had been turned on in the tall, foreboding towers of the castle keep, and they kept sweeping the forward section of the plateau. The beam from the searchlight in the southwest tower was the most dangerous because, moving along the rim of the slope, it kept Merrit and the ten Hungarians pinned down most of the time. At times the AVOs lobbed grenades from the windows of the west castle wall, but, because of the distance involved, the grenades always exploded short of the target.

With cold gaze and narrowed eyes, the Death Merchant went to work on the remaining tanks. Part of the demolished watchtower had fallen across two of the T-62 mastodons closest to Camellion, and their crews and the soldiers who had been clustered around the tanks had retreated to the east side; but Camellion still killed the tanks with two arrows.

The explosions were beautiful. The ends of the arrows hit the bottom of the turrets; the contact detonators sparked the plastic C-4, and there were tremendous

147

wwhhoommmmmmsssss! The tanks seemed to shrink and exploded, turret, cannon, and hot metal flying through the air. Then came colossal flames, the metal rubble burning furiously.

The searchlight on the middle watchtower, which overlooked the gorge, was swinging in Camellion's direction when his arrow struck and the top part of the tower vanished in a ball of bright red flame, two bodies flying outward over the gorge.

In quick succession, Camellion blasted the fourth, fifth, and sixth tanks, the tremendous explosions shaking the entire area—or so it seemed.

By the time Camellion reloaded the crossbow and was aiming at the seventh tank, the soldiers, the AVO officers with them, and the AVO guards from the last watchtower were in full retreat, running toward the repair shops to the north. They didn't know what the explosions were, or how they were being caused, but they had seen the two watchtowers and the six tanks dissolve in flaming destruction. Why wait for their turn?

At the same moment that Camellion pulled the trigger of the crossbow and sent the arrow on its way, the last T-62 tank in line roared into life. Its broad track links clanking, the monster headed north, its low, gray body obscured for a second as the C-4 arrow exploded the seventh tank. The driver put on speed, and by the time Camellion had put another arrow on the bed of the crossbow, the fleeing tank was in a position that placed the powerhouse between it and the Death Merchant.

Just for the hell of it, Camellion scattered the last watchtower all over the gorge. But this time he was slow in ducking, and the searchlight beam from the southwest keep tower struck him full in the face, momentarily blinding him.

Camellion dropped down and moved a few feet back down the slope, in time to escape the rain of 14.5mm bullets from a heavy KPV machine gun being fired from the southwest keep tower, the copper-covered slugs digging into the dirt and rocks so close to Richard that he was showered with dust and marginal residue.

Clutching the crossbow, Camellion crawled back

148

toward Ray Merrit and the ten Hungarians, all of whom were pinned down by the heavy KPV, which continued to rake the fringe of the slope with lines of 14.5mm projectiles. To the left of the machine gun was the searchlight, acting as a scout for the weapon.

Camellion, weighed down by kit bags of grenades, spare ammo, and other equipment, reached Merrit, who lay on his belly, the top of the level ground a foot above his head. Father Lido Nanasi was down on the other side of Merrit, who said to the Death Merchant, "That KPV can keep us pinned down indefinitely. And that last T-62 that escaped—it's looking right down our throats."

The Death Merchant waited until the *zip-zip-zip* of slugs striking the ground went past, then reared up for a quick look. The powerhouse, which was now to his right, no longer obstructed his view, and he saw the T-62 parked in front of the repair shops and garage. The hell with the 115mm cannon: they wouldn't it at such close range. But the hull and turret machine guns would be able to stop an army!

Merrit turned over on his left side, pushed back his sun-visor cap, and gave Camellion a worried look. "It's close to three hundred feet to the top of that corner tower where the searchlight and KPV are."

"Yes, and you're right." Camellion was way ahead of Merrit. "An arrow with a pound of C-4 could never reach that height, not straight up. The pull of gravity would be too strong."

Father Nanasi said in a small voice, "Brother Krim, it would be possible for you to destroy the tank from one corner of the powerhouse."

Camellion felt like telling the priest to go away. Instead, he pushed himself up, looked at the corner tower of the keep, and saw why the Hungarians had not been able to shoot out the searchlight, even with the Wal A-Rs. Not only did the searchlight have direction shutters sticking out all around the edge of its lens, but a pinnacle was on one side of the light, the tall, pointed buttress acting as protective armor against small-arms fire. A row of corbels, projecting from the wall underneath the mount of the light, also protected the light from slugs from below.

The Death Merchant removed the cross-strapped hip bags and unsnapped the Ingram machine pistol from the cartridge belt around his waist.

Merrit removed the unlit pipe from his mouth. "Need some help?"

Camellion, who had reached into his backpack with his left hand and was checking the C-4 weighed arrows, picked up the crossbow with his right and licked his lips. "One man can do as well as two on this deal. There's no need for both of us to tempt Old Rattle Bones."

Merrit lazily scratched the side of his cheek and drawled, "The only time a man isn't taking a chance of some kind is before he's born and after he's dead; and if there isn't another Hound on that pad, we'll all be eating breakfast in hell. You'd better watch that KPV."

The shaft of light stabbed out, and again the Russian-made Kintovka Prazets Vitomaticheskaia machine gun, high up on the corner keep tower, roared, and scores of 14.5mm slugs peppered the rim from north to south, the passage of the high-velocity projectiles marked by a series of muffled *zip, zip, zip*s and foot-high sprouts of dust and gravel.

The Death Merchant, reacting with a speed that was incredible, jumped up to level ground and began racing to the southwest corner of the powerhouse. He was halfway across the clearing by the time the circle of light and the 14.5mm slugs following it started moving back from the south to the north. But when the light and chain of slugs raked across the center of the opening, he was out of sight, creeping toward the southeast corner of the power-house.

CHAPTER FOURTEEN

The ten Hungarians and Raymond Merrit had never been witnesses to such a carnival of death. The entire southern margin of the plateau was a huge rim of leaping red flames and tar-black smoke from the wreckage of the tanks. Fanning the flames, the stiff mountain wind did more than accelerate the burning: it blew smoke and the stink of blazing metal and rubber, plastic and wood, fuel and flesh across the area.

Still burning, too, was the helicopter that had crashed between the front of the castle and the rear of the power-house. It had become a skeleton, the blackened ribs of its framework showing. Around the twisted frame and the blades lay blackened mounds—some still burning—with arms and legs.

The searchlight beam and the hot chain of KPV 14.5mm slugs darted past Ray Merrit and Father Nanasi, and the two men dared to look up over the edge. Down the line, Father Nosbyti, Tibor Arpad, and Paul Tisza sprayed the front of the castle with long bursts of Wal automatic rifle fire. Janos Rosmartyi flung up his Wal and sent a long burst at the searchlight, and all his 7.65mm projectiles struck either the tall pinnacle or the corbels jutting out from the ledge on which the light and its mount rested.

Their eyes on the Russian tank in front of the repair shop building, Merrit and Father Nanasi saw the metal behemoth suddenly explode. There was a roar, a bright flash of flame, and turret and cannon rose eight feet up, then crashed straight back down. Fire and smoke poured from the tank.

Neither Merrit nor Nanasi could see the Death Merchant, who, crouched by the southeast corner of the powerhouse, was feeling very satisfied; yet he knew that before the night was over, many in his group would be dead.

Merrit and the Hungarians were surprised when the Death Merchant sent an explosive arrow to the front of the castle and the explosion ripped a ten-foot hole in the wall of the ground story, huge stones flying outward, broken glass falling from windows of the upper floors.

The second explosion, toward the southeast end of the castle, pitched more stones crashing outward, the concussion so severe it loosened a section of machicolation from the front of the middle keep tower. Half a dozen enormous stones crashed to the ground and bounced toward the smoldering wreck of the helicopter.

The searchlight from the end tower speared out and began to rake the area from east to west, then back again. The Death Merchant, in a wild, zig-zagging run, raced back to the hillside and dove into the rocks beside Merrit, who had rolled over on his belly and was watching the front of the repair shop.

Camellion slipped on his kit bags, checked his other equipment, leaned closer to Merrit, and said very calmly, "Pass the word. We're going to move out as soon as I put the searchlight out of commission."

"The helicopter pad is forty feet above the repair shops." Merrit didn't sound very enthused; his mouth wrinkled in distaste. "A covered crosswalk connects the pad to the castle."

"We're going to grab one of the wind-flappers on the pad and fly to the roof of the lab," Camellion said firmly.

Merrit turned over on his side, aversion on his wide face, protest in his low voice. "If we try to reach the pad by using the stairway on the outside, AVO shooters on the east side of the castle will kill every one of us."

Snuggled down on his right side, Camellion edged up closer to the top of the hill. He held the crossbow in his left hand, his fingers wrapped around the pistol grip of the stock. "There's a freight elevator and a passenger elevator inside the repair shop," he said, "and stairs that go to the helicopter pad. We'll use the stairs."

"Automatic relays will turn on battery power for emergency lighting after you knock out the powerhouse," Merrit said resignedly. He sucked in his lower lip. "It will be enough power to keep that searchlight on."

"So what? We'll be flush against the front of the castle. The searchlight won't be able to find us, and neither will the AVOs in the upper stories. By the time they wise up, we'll be at the garage and repair shops." The Death Merchant's smoke-smudged face was as hard as the rocks on which he lay. "Merrit, start getting the men into position, so that we can head straight east. Tell them we're going to use only sub-guns and no grenades once we're inside the garage."

152

Merrit smiled a tiny, bitter smile. "The fuel tanks behind the garage! If they blow, pad and helicopters will go with them. Hell, we might as well be wearing handcuffs and a ball and chain."

He rolled away from the Death Merchant, nudged Father Nanasi, and whispered to the priest. Both men then began to crawl clumsily through the rocks, moving to the north.

Camellion, pondering the problem of how to handle the three towers of the castle's keep, adjusted the zippered, six-pocket belt pack that he wore across his chest like a bandoleer, squirmed up the side of the slope another foot, raised his head, and looked out. The KPV heavy gun had quit firing. The searchlight was moving slowly over the burning tanks at the edge of the precipice. In front of the repair shops, the blasted T-62 burned like a torch dipped in pitch.

Time to go to work! A sour taste in his mouth, Camellion put the stock of the crossbow to his shoulder, lined up the center of the powerhouse in the front and the rear sights, and squeezed the trigger. He then jerked back and dropped down below the top of the slope.

Weeeerrrrrrooooommmmmmmmmmm! The colossal explosion demolished the west wall of the powerhouse, caved in the flat roof, and ripped the cables and breakers from the seven heavy-duty transformers.

The searchlight in the keep tower went out. The entire castle and the garage and repair shops were plunged into darkness. Smiling a smile that was half a snarl, the Death Merchant unbolted the bow from the stock and bed and put the dismantled crossbow into his backpack. He unsnapped the Ingram machine pistol from his cartridge belt, got to his feet and, hunched over like a cripple, moved north to the area on the slope where Ray Merrit had assembled the force of ten Hungarians. One glance told Camellion that they were as ready to die as they would ever be.

"Fire only when you're sure of hitting the enemy," he ordered, "and don't use grenades inside the garage."

In the darkness he raced up the slope, the kit bags flapping against the holstered Kal pistols on his hips, the canvas ammo holder, at the back of the right Kal, annoyingly heavy. Behind him, carrying an Ingram sub-gun, pounded Merrit, followed by the ten Hungarians, their hands clutching Kiraly submachine guns. However, Father Csoki carried a Czech-made vz/25 sub-gun.

The Death Merchant passed the southwest corner of the castle and raced east across the front of the dark wall. For a moment he glanced up, his eyes glimpsing the full five stories and the soaring height of the middle tower silhouetted ominously against the star-dotted sky. In that hair of a second, Camellion had the impression that tower and castle wall were toppling over on him. He lowered his eyes, reoriented himself, and saw how the light from the burning tank ahead, flickering over him and the other men, cast their bodies into long, parallel shadows that moved grotesquely all the way to the rim of the plateau.

Yes, it was a gamble, a calculated risk. But Camellion hadn't expected any enemy fire from the ground floor, his reasoning based on years of past experience. Only fools fight in a burning house. The AVOs were not fools. Nor was the first story burning. Nonetheless, the AVOs would expect more explosives to rip open the front of the building. Why stand by the windows and wait for the explosions?

His long, powerful legs leaping over broken stones and rubble, the Death Merchant ran past the first gaping hole blasted from the castle by the powerful C-4 plastic nitro-celocene. The cavity yawned like an obscene mouth ... an open mouth filled with blackness and broken teeth of stone. But no high-powered slugs slammed out of the opening; death had moved to another position.

The Death Merchant and the men behind him tore past the second hole in the front wall, raced to the right of the burning tank in front of the garage, then turned and rushed toward the building's twenty-foot-wide entrance.

Not expecting a handful of revolutionaries to actually attack the castle, the AVOs had not closed the electrically controlled double doors. General Skedfu had also made a serious mistake. Once Skedfu had seen the Hound assault helicopter make a dead-stick landing west of the castle, he had ordered the AVO troopers guarding the helicopters

154

pad to assemble by the tanks on the southeast side of the plateau. The AVO, unable to cope with explosions coming out of nowhere, had retreated to the garage. They were milling around by the light of flashlights, privately thinking that General Skedfu had greatly underestimated the capability of the Society of the Double Cross, when the Death Merchant and his men stormed into the building and dove for cover.

Eight feet inside the doorway was an armored car resting on blocks, its six wheels stacked to one side of the car. Six large tires made a neat, round column next to the wheels.

In the middle of the building, two Russian T-62 tanks were parked side by side underneath a bridge-type hoist. One of the tanks was partially naked: its side bazooka plates, exhaust silencer, and transmission louvre grill had been removed. The commander's hatch, the loader's hatch, and the hull gunner's hatch were all open.

The glacis plate and the front mud shields of the second tank had been removed, and one could look straight into the driver's compartment and the hull gunner's section and see the controls, the gearbox, and the two seats.

The Death Merchant made a dive to the right and snuggled down by the side of a tall, twelve-drawer mechanic's chest, which was on rollers.

The ceiling lights came on as Merrit and the Hungarians sought the cover of the armored car, which was already singing from the whine of ricochets.

Camellion leaned out from behind the tool chest and fired a long, sweeping burst with the Ingram, the 9mm slugs stabbing one AVO trooper in the chest, cutting a second man across the midriff, and hitting a third, who was about to stand up, in the forehead.

Angered at the deaths of their comrades, other AVOs triggered off a veritable hurricane of lead at the invaders, the 9mm Kiraly and the 7.62mm Zel submachine gun slugs buzzing around the Death Merchant and his men like swarms of maniacal hornets.

Father Lido Nanasi got stung. He had fired off a short burst, killing two AVOs crawling between the two tanks, but he had not pulled back to the front of the armored car in time to prevent another trooper from hitting him. A 7.62mm slug struck Father Nanasi in his right side, bored through his gall baldder, and lodged against his spine. Two more Zel sub-gun bullets struck him on the right side of the chest, the hollow-nosed projectiles flattening out on impact to blobs of lead and copper almost an inch in diameter. Choking and gurgling on his own blood, the priest dropped to the concrete floor and lost consciousness from shock. He was dying, but the three other priests by the wheelless armored car couldn't take time out to give him the last rites.

The big garage and repair shop became a shooting gallery, the air thick with fumes, the racket of exploding cartridges stabbing at the center of the men's brains, the echoes jumping back and forth from wall to wall.

The back of the mechanic's tool chest, protecting Camellion, was quickly riddled with jagged holes, the slugs making ringing sounds as they struck and were stopped by wrenches and other tools inside the drawers. However, some bullets did bypass the tools and bore through the front of the drawers. One nine-millimeter projectile sped only a few inches to the left of Camellion's neck. A second bullet zipped through the lower compartment of the chest and cut through his right pants leg, the slug barely missing his ankle. Other bullets, on their way through the drawers, lost much of their momentum by glancing off tools, so they only dented the front of the drawers, making the metal bulge outward where they had hit. But some bullets split the metal and were protruding through the openings.

Zingggg! Zinggggg! Zingggggg! More slugs whined off a tap and die set on top of the chest, and the Death Merchant's coldly professional assessment of the situation told him that unless he moved, he would eventually catch a bullet. The situation was not hopeless, although at present it seemed to be a Mexican standoff. Since the two T-62 tanks were being worked on, their fuel tanks would be drained and their ammo and HE shells removed. There weren't any fuel or oil drums around the tanks or toward the rear of the repair shop. The danger of fire spreading to the fuel tanks behind the repair shop was unlikely. The floor of the building was concrete, the walls and roof made of corrugated iron. And according to the intelligence reports of the Society, the ends of the four fuel tanks were twenty-five feet away from the rear wall of the repair shop. Anyhow, desperate situations called for desperate and dangerous solutions.

Camellion switched on the safety of the Ingram machine pistol and fastened the weapon to the belt-pack across his chest by pushing the trigger guard through a spring snap on one of the pockets. Putting his hands on the pull knobs of one of the drawers, he began to roll the chest to his left. A few minutes later he was only a few feet to the right of Raymond Merrit, who was down behind the square metal cabinet of an AC arc welder. Slightly ahead of the arc welder, and ten feet to its left, was the Lluch armored car, the length of its steel body horizontal to the two Russian tanks which, thirty feet ahead, were facing the attackers. The three priests were at the rear end of the armored vehicle. Frantisek Palfecky and Thomas Lakatos were at the other end. Mihaly Szechenyi had opened the side hatch of the armored car, crawled into the car, and was firing from the turret. Janos Rosmartyi had crawled to the driver's compartment and was firing through the side pistol port. Paul Tisza was crouched behind the stack of six wheels, Tibor Arpad behind the stacked heavy-duty tires of the Lluch. Both men were slightly ahead of Merrit and to his left.

His face dripping sweat, Merrit turned and looked at Camellion. "Some of the enemy are in the tanks—did you notice? I think the rest of them—at least most of them—are behind the tanks. Any ideas?"

"I'm going to push this chest close enough to use a P-T grenade," Richard said. "A bath of phosphorus-thermite should make them cry uncle." He wrinkled his nose. The smell of burnt powder was overwhelming. "Let's just hope there are helicopters on the pad above, or we will have done all this for nothing."

If Merrit shared the Death Merchant's optimism, his sweat-stained face didn't show it. "Make damn sure you get far enough away, or you'll be caught in the back splash. I'll signal the priests to hold their fire until you get the job done."

The Death Merchant nodded, pulled in his shoulders, and began to push the mechanic's tool chest straight toward the T-62 from which the mud guards and glacis had been removed.

Merrit picked up a small bolt from the floor and got Tibor Arpad's attention by tossing it at him. Tibor turned. Merrit held up his Ingram, shook his head, waved his hand back and forth, then pointed to the group by the side of the armored car, indicating he wanted Arpad to pass along the word. Arpad complied. The priests and all the other Hungarians stopped firing—all except Mihaly Szechenyi and Janos Rosmartyi. From their positions inside the Lluch armored fortress, they had a clear range of fire at the two tanks. And the two Hungarians made the most of it.

An AVO sergeant reared up from the commander's hatch of the tank without the bazooka plates over its wheels and tracks links and attempted to fire his Zel submachine gun. A trooper bobbed up from the hull gunner's hatch. Other AVOs, in back of the tank, sent a storm of slugs at the Lluch armored car. AVOs in back of the tank that Camellion was approaching leaned around the side and fired at the mechanic's tool cabinet, which, as if it had a life of its own, was slowly advancing. Two AVO troopers were in the turret, one looking out through the gunner's periscope, the other crouching on the turret floor, firing around through the opening leading to the driver's compartment.

Szechenyi, firing through a slit in the turret, killed the AVO sergeant with a short burst of Kiraly sub-gun slugs, the hot, cutting lead shearing off the top of the man's head like the top of a boiled egg. Brains, bone chips, and a thick spray of blood splattered the AVO troopers behind the tank at about the same time that Janos Rosmartyi fired through the pistol port and blew up the AVO man trying to toss slugs from the forward gunner's position. Four 9mm K-cartridges tore away the AVO man's face, flesh and bone exploding. Looking like a nightmare from leftover Halloween, the faceless corpse slid back into the tank.

Four bullets had bored all the way through the tool chest. Two had ripped across Camellion's side, raking his skin. A third bullet had struck the buckle of a cross-strap on his chest and bounced off. The fourth tiny mass of lead had smacked the side of the Ingram dangling from the spring-snap of the belt-pack, and it, too, had ricocheted.

The Death Merchant stopped pushing against the mechanic's chest. He estimated that he was not more than twenty feet from the front of the two tanks, and that was as close as he wanted to get. Too close, if he misjudged the distance and the grenade went off on the side of the tanks facing him.

Camellion took a P-T grenade from one of the hip bags and judged the distance to the tank farthest to his left. He pulled the pin, threw the grenade, hunched down behind the mechanic's chest, and waited. Five seconds later he heard the loud *whoosh* of the deadly grenade, a sound as if someone had swished a large cloth through the air; and he heard the screams, the high-pitched shrieks of agony, of men who suddenly found themselves in the midst of hell.

The P-T grenade had exploded behind the two tanks, the white-hot liquid fire bursting in the center of the troopers. The fire splashed over them, and instantly the terrible mixture of phosphorus-thermite began to melt flesh from bones.

Insane with agony, the screaming AVO troopers, now blazing torches, staggered around like drunks. Some fell and began rolling back and forth on the floor. Most of the troopers, in their wild efforts to extinguish the flames, exposed themselves, and the Death Merchant's men began cutting them down with short blasts of machine-gun slugs.

Some of the P-T mixture had splashed into the turret of one tank, but the two men inside were already dead and didn't mind. The two AVOs inside the turret of the tank in front of Camellion were unharmed. The P-T had not reached the two open hatches of the turret, although some of the liquid fire had doused the rear of the tank, splashing through the engine grill and the transmission louvers. Black smoke began pouring through the two grills, and the air became thick with the smell of burning oil.

The two AVO troopers inside the tank didn't know what to do. They could hear screaming and gunfire, and they knew that their companions were being slaughtered by the revolutionaries. How soon would their turn come?

Paul Nege, a young AVO trooper with a long mustache, whispered to Jeno Stepzo, who was down on his knees by the forward turret opening.

"Don't make a sound. They might miss us."

The Death Merchant hadn't forgotten the AVO men. He leaped from the protection of the mechanic's tool chest, zig-zagged to the tank, and fired almost a full magazine through the round opening between the driver's compartment and the turret. At such close range—he was standing in front of the driver's compartment—he wouldn't have to hit the AVO troopers to kill them. Bullet splash would do the job.

When a K-cartridge hits the outside of armor, it flattens and squeezes out its tungsten-carbide core in a splash which radiates in a circular pattern. Under the force of the impact, the lead becomes semiliquid and spreads out with almost explosive velocity. This is especially true when K-cartridges are fired at close range.

The 9mm K-cartridges, striking the steel floor of the turret well, flattened out, and semiliquid metal splashed all over Paul Nege and Jeno Stepzo, flooding them into the endless depths of infinity.

The Death Merchant moved with caution to the right of the tank. To his left, Raymond Merrit and the nine Hungarians raced forward. They spread out and, moving through smoke and the stink of burning flesh and cloth, took the long way around to avoid the several dozen blackened corpses, tiny puddles of burning phosphorus-thermite, and cartridges exploding in the burning belts of the dead men.

"M-My God!" Tibor Arpad stared in awe at the AVO corpses, a few of which had already been reduced to partial skeletons.

"Damus vitam et sanguinem," Father Csoki said in Latin. " 'We give our life and blood.' And they gave theirs, but for a cause born in hell."

The other men remained tight-lipped. Father Deak and Father Nosbyti crossed themselves and turned toward the Death Merchant, who was coming around behind the second tank.

"Brother Schmid, watch the front doors until we get to the stairs," Camellion said, reloading the Ingram machine pistol. "The AVOs in the castle must have wised up by now."

Merrit grinned, touched the bill of cap with his fingers, then ran back to the Lluch armored car and took a position toward the front of the blue-painted vehicle. The Death Merchant and the Hungarians ran to the steel stairs fifty feet to the rear of the two Russian tanks. The stairs, located in the back section of the shop, angled to the left for twenty-two feet and opened onto the roof. Forty feet above the roof was the landing pad, its weight supported by massive concrete pillars reinforced with steel cross-rod meshing.

The fluorescent lights hanging from the ceiling flickered for a few moments but stayed on. At the bottom of the stairs, the Death Merchant and the Hungarians looked up at the square, walk-through opening in the roof. A wooden housing has been built over and around the stairway opening. The door of the housing was open, and Camellion and the Hungarians could see stars. But there were no reflections of bright lights. Apparently, battery power was reserved only for vital areas.

Against the west wall of the shop was the freight elevator that serviced the pad; its shaft was four perpendicular steel beams, the eight rollers on the corner sides of the boxlike car securely attached to the four Z-beams. Next to the freight elevator was the passenger elevator.

"This is going to be easy," Thomas Lakatos said. He hooked a thumb over the sling-strap of the Wal A-R, shifting the weight of the weapon on his right shoulder. The sudden, high-pitched chatter of Ray Merrit's Ingram submachine gun served to remind Lakatos of how wrong he was.

161

AVO troops from the castle were attacking at the front of the repair shop. Merrit had already riddled seven of the troopers, who lay sprawled out, dead and dying, in the wide doorway. Camellion and the Hungarians with him started to move along the west wall toward the front of the building. They were wasting their time. Merrit didn't need their help. The big man first tossed two hand grenades, one to either side of the wide doorway. The instant the grenades exploded, Merrit presented the AVOs with phosphorus-thermite burn bombs. One! Two! Three! They landed in the center and at each end of the long entrance. Instantly, a wall of brilliant white fire leaped all the way across the entrance, the hissing accompanied by the shrieks of AVO troopers unlucky enough to have been splashed by streams of liquefied fire.

Down low, almost on his hands and knees, Merrit raced back to the Death Merchant and the group of freedom fighters. Soon all of them had returned to the bottom of the stairs.

"I'll go first," Merrit said severely, looking up the flight of stairs. He pulled a full magazine from his ammo bag, shoved it into the Ingram, jerked back the cocking knob on top of the small sub-gun, and laughed obscenely. "If we're lucky, we might save the whole damn human race from hallucinogen gas, although I can't think of one single good reason why such a murderous species should be saved."

Camellion said with feeling, "The east side of the castle is not more than a hundred feet from the pad. Our good friends will use heavy stuff." He looked at Thomas Lakatos and Tibor Arpad. They were the only two who still carried Wal automatic rifles. The other Hungarians had run out of ammo for the Wals and had left the A-Rs behind on the west slope. "You two can use your infrared scopes. The Wals are the best defense we have at present."

The Hungarians jumped slightly in surprise as Merrit raised his Ingram and fired a six-round blast through the square opening in the roof, the projectiles zipping out through the open door of the housing and shooting up toward the stars.

His ruthless eyes watching the opening in the ceiling

and the doorway of the housing, Merrit moved quickly up the stairs, the Hungarians right behind him. The Death Merchant, waiting at the bottom of the stairs, took one final look around. The whole damn place was indeed a tribute to the Cosmic Lord of Death. Corpses filled the center of the shop and were scattered across the long entrance. The air was blue with powder smoke and black with soot from burnt bodies and tank engine oil.

Camellion moved up the stairs, saw the last man—Frantisek Palfecky—move through the square opening in the roof, and shook his head in disgust at the annoying racket of gunfire—Kiralys and Wal A-Rs from the roof, Automat Kalashnikovs from the east end of the castle. Damn it! Russian AKs were deadly. Gas-operated, and with selective fire, an AK used an intermediate-sized cartridge with a bullet diameter of 7.62mm and was an extremely accurate weapon. Richard knew he was taking an enormous chance, gambling with all their lives. Yet, as he viewed the situation, there wasn't any other way to get the job done. But once more the question persisted in his mind: *suppose there are no helicopters on the pad?* What then? He didn't like the inevitable answer: *in that case it will be die-time!*

The Death Merchant drew close to the top of the stairs. He turned and carefully placed the Ingram on a step. Nonchalantly he removed an M57 demolition grenade from one of his hip bags, pulled the pin, but kept his hand tight on the clamp. With his other hand he took a second grenade from the bag, hooked the ring through the spring-snap on his belt-pack, then jerked on the grenade, pulled the pin, and kept his fingers tight on the clamp. Carefully he measured the distance. Just as carefully, he threw the two grenades. One rolled into the passenger elevator; the other tumbled into the freight elevator. Camellion grabbed the Ingram machine pistol, his feet pounded the steel steps, and he rushed through the opening in the roof and moved into the cover-housing, which was about three times the size of a telephone booth. Behind him the two demolition grenades exploded with a roar, making both elevators inoperative. Hunched down in the darkness, Camellion pulled a P-T burn bomb from a hip bag, activated the fuse, and flipped the round object down the stairs. It hit the concrete floor, exploded on impact, and flooded the area with a ring of white fire. If any AVOs tried to come up the stairs, they'd get a hot foot doing it.

On his hands and knees Camellion crawled through the doorway onto the roof. He dropped to his belly and wriggled to the other side of the stairway housing, which had been riddled with slugs.

Ahead, slightly over 125 feet away, was the east side of Karolyi Castle, the dark, grim slab of stones filling the horizon, as high as a small mountain and just as broad. There were few windows. Those that did exist were dark, except for occasional flashes of red accompanied by a staccato roaring—AKs, a KPV heavy machine gun, and, unless Richard's ears were lying to him, a Russian DPM light machine gun.

Twenty feet to Camellion's right were the four sections of steps that led up to the helicopter pad. A ten-foot flight angled to the left and ended at a small platform; then a ten-foot section went to the right and another platform. Again, a section to the left. A platform. The final flight to the right, then the top of the pad.

Ray Merrit and the nine Hungarians were down behind round metal ventilators and four square concrete columns to the east.

"I'm over here, Brother!" Merrit called out to Camellion in an even voice. Turning, Camellion saw that Merrit was only fifteen feet to his right, lying flat on his belly behind, and in line with, an aluminum ventilator.

For a brief moment there was silence, a strange, terrible silence. Then once again the KPV roared its loud symphony of death, a chain of 14.5mm projectiles *zip-zip-zip-zipping* through the sheet-metal roof. Many of the large slugs bored through the ventilators and struck the entire row of concrete supports. Other pieces of lead ricocheted from the sections of stairs between roof and helicopter pad. And before the firing ended, there were two loud *pingggs-pingggs* a foot above the Death Merchant's head. Two bullets had blasted through the black wall of the housing over the repair-shop steps. From the sound of

164

the firing, Camellion estimated that the KPV, as well as the AKs and the DPM light job, were being fired from windows on the third level of the castle. It didn't really make a lot of difference; the guns still had the group pinned down.

Camellion, his eyes adjusted to the darkness, turned and looked at "Brother Schmid." There was no particular expression on Merrit's face, but for some indefinable reason, he appeared to be oddly defenseless.

"Arpad and Lakatos," Camellion said tiredly. "Did they get bored with playing and take their marbles and go home?"

The DPM light machine gun started snarling, and 7.62mm projectiles struck the roof, zinged from the sections of stairs, and dug chips from a dozen concrete supports.

Merrit waited until the DPM ceased firing before he spoke.

"They're both behind one of the posts in back of me," he said in clipped tones. "When I saw how heavy the firing was, I told all of them to scatter and keep down, that the thing to do was wait for you and your trusty crossbow. I guess you know that the AVOs are firing from the third floor?"

The Death Merchant didn't reply. Merrit smiled in satisfaction as he watched Camellion pull the two sections of the crossbow from his Katahdin pack and attach the fiberglass bow to the bed and stock. Camellion pulled an arrow from the pack, inserted the tip of the detonator circuit wire into the C-4 package attached to the middle of the shaft, placed the arrow on the bed, and drew the steel bowstring into the back groove. On his knees, Camellion was leaning to the right of the housing at the same time that several AKs and the KPV started throwing 7.62mm and 14.5mm projectiles at the roof, the streams of hot slugs from the AK assault rifles moving from north to south, the lines of KPV tracers swinging from south to north, a terrible hail of high-velocity lead that zipped and wanged and zinged, not only through the sheet-steel roof, but bounced from the four sections of stairs and cut more holes through the tall ventilators. All Camellion's men could do was hug the roof and pray.

Several projectiles cut through the back wall of the housing and burned the air close to the Death Merchant. He waited until the lines of fire were away from him, then leaned to the right of the housing and caught a very brief glance of red and orange flashes 125 feet ahead. He raised the crossbow to his shoulder, snap-aimed, and gently squeezed the trigger.

There was a blinding flash of fire against the east wall of Karolyi Castle, a thundering explosion, and a wave of concussion that even touched Camellion as he pulled another arrow from the backpack.

The automatic weapons of the enemy stopped firing.

Merrit, his voice anxious, called over, "I'll get them started for the stairs."

"Wait!" Camellion pushed the end of the wire into the C-4, placed the arrow in position on the crossbow, leaned around the side of the housing, and saw that the explosion had blown an enormous hole in the wall, a monstrously ugly cavity that, against a background of smoke and yellow light from the interior, was rimmed with broken and jagged blocks of stone. Richard couldn't be certain, but he thought he detected moving shapes through the smoke filling the hole.

He raised the crossbow, aimed to the left of the hole, and pulled the trigger. "Get them started!" he yelled at Merrit.

The second explosion, more devastating than the first, not only created another immense hollow in the wall, but started a fire of no small proportions.

A few minutes later the third big blast tore off the northeast corner of the third floor and sent several tons of stone blocks crashing to the ground.

Not taking time to dismantle the crossbow, the Death Merchant jumped up and ran across the roof after Ray Merrit and the Hungarians, who were racing for the stairs on the north side. Mihaly Szechenyi was the first man to reach the stairs. He started up the first section, taking two steps at a time. The rest of the men followed.

The nine Hungarians were spaced out on the stairs,

Merrit on one of the platforms, and the Death Merchant on the first section when two AK assault rifles began firing. Janos Rosmartyi, on the last top section of stairs, jerked and cried out in pain. His head fell awkwardly to one side, and his body twisted heavily against Father Deak, blood spurting from his neck, dyeing Father Deak's full beard a deep scarlet.

"Keep moving! Keep moving!" Merrit and the Death Merchant both yelled. "It's our only chance!"

Horrified, Father Deak jumped to one side and allowed the corpse of Rosmartyi to slide down the steps. The priest was amazed at the force of the jumping blood, and, with a sickening sensation, he realized that each spurt came from a still-pumping heart. He hurried up the stairs, a vivid impression of Rosmartyi's wide-open eyes searing his brain. *Our Father, which art in heaven, hallowed be thy name....*

A few minutes more, and Mihaly Szechenyi was rushing through the entrance at the top of the last section. He jumped out onto the metal landing pad, threw himself down, and rolled to one side. Thomas Lakatos was next on the pad; behind him came the rest of the men. They all felt like targets at the end of a shooting gallery, 7.62mm lead hissing all around them, either zipping by or striking the steps or the guardrails, then ricocheting and screaming off into space at crazy angles.

A blob of lead hit the stairs ahead of Ray Merrit, glanced off, and missed the left side of his head by a scant quarter of an inch. Another ricochet—this one from one of the steps—smacked into a handrail, glanced off, hit the barrel of Father Csoki's Czech vz/25 submachine gun, then rocketed off into space.

Father Josef Nosbyti—on the small platform between the third and fourth sections of stairs—lost every bit of his luck. A bullet struck the young priest between the shoulder blades. A second 7.62mm projectile speared him in the base of the spine, severing the cord. The impact of the slugs knocked the dying priest forward. His body struck and pitched over the handrail to the roof below.

Paul Tisza, his bum leg paining him, flung himself through the top opening to the pad. Merrit was next to

167

reach the helicopter landing pad, then a wheezing Tibor Arpad, his bushy eyebrows dripping sweat.

The Death Merchant, his long legs eating up the steps, tore up the last ten-foot flight to the right, slugs slashing the smoky night air all around him. A bullet ripped through the canvas flap of his left hip bag, the one containing demolition grenades. Another hunk of lead cut through the cloth of his coat and shirt, raked the skin of his left shoulder like a dull razor, and hit the step in front of him. *Zzinggggggg!* And the slug had bounced and was tearing off into space. A third AK bullet passed so close to his right ear that he could hear the damn thing hissing at him. The fourth 7.62mm semi-Spitzer projectile didn't come as close, but it did more damage. It bored sideways through the varnished hardwood stock of the crossbow, almost tearing the weapon from Camellion's hand.

At last! The Death Merchant reached the entrance at the top of the stairs, jumped through the opening, and threw himself to the cold metal of the pad. He looked around him, not at all surprised that he was unharmed. He had a firm agreement with death. The time had not yet come. . . .

A big, black bowl of sky filled with bright blue stars. A pathetic-looking moon high in the east. To the west of the pad rose Karolyi Castle—the Castle of the Hawk—the great pile of stone rising upward into the sky like some monstrous thing alive, an eyrie of evil perched smugly on solid rock. In front were the three forbidding towers of the keep: proud guardians supremely confident of their impregnability, daring anyone to attack.

Richard Camellion had dared. The Death Merchant had started the job of destruction—the third floor on the east side was burning, the fire out of control—and he intended to finish it.

Camellion looked to the north. Behind the castle was the straight-up dark rock face of Mount Zivatar, its cone-shaped summit, bathed in moonlight, outlined sharply in stark lines.

The Death Merchant's mouth showed a slight smile. It was a perfect night for death to ride the starwind and

168

earthbound souls to lose themselves in forests of moonbeams.

His gleaming blue eyes swept the pad. Close by were the seven Hungarians and a brutal-faced Ray Merrit, all of them panting from physical effort and flattened on the pad, the majority of them looking toward the Death Merchant for orders and here-and-now salvation. Father Csoki and Father Deak might be able to save their immortal souls in the next world, but only Richard Camellion could save their bodies in this one.

Camellion grinned with all the enthusiasm of a gorgon as he looked around the pad. He saw that he and the others were close to the base, or bottom, of the pad, which was built in the shape of an isosceles triangle. There, toward the tip or apex, rested a beautiful Yak-24 Hound military assault helicopter. Farther back from the Hound, to the right, were two Bratukhin B-10 observation puddle-jumpers. A third Bratukhin was in the center of the pad. Toward the base of the triangle, to the left, or on the east side of the pad, were two more helicopters, the silver fuselages marked with the black eagle of the Hungarian air force.

Camellion recognized each helicopter as being an all-purpose craft, which the NATO identification system called "Hoplite," although the official Hungarian designation was MIL Mi-2. Built by the WSK-Swidnik works in Poland, the Hoplite had an eight-passenger cabin and a main rotor of three blades. Both the main rotor and the smaller tail rotor were powered by Isotov turboshaft engines mounted above the cabin of the large fuselage.

The Death Merchant crawled closer to Raymond Merrit. "The AVOs are afraid of blowing up these copters," he said, "or they would have opened fire by now. Just the same, we had better do some fast moving."

He looked at the tense Hungarians, his eyes moving from face to face. "Which one of you can use a crossbow?"

Camellion's question surprised Merrit as well as the seven Hungarians. Camellion quickly cleared up the confusion.

"We're not going to use the Hound. There's going to be

169

a lot of shooting. If the Hound is whacked out, our transportation out of here to Austria will have gone bye-bye."

"The two Hoplites!" Merrit, quick to perceive Camellion's plan, smiled in triumph.

Paul Tisza said, "I can use a crossbow. I used to hunt with one."

The Death Merchant nodded to Tisza and said to Merrit, "I'll take Paul and Father Csoki and Father Deak. You can take the others in the second bird. We've got to smash those towers before we can land on the roof of the lab. Otherwise, the AVOs will machine-gun us to pieces."

"It's going to be a tough job," Merrit said seriously.

"We can do it because we have to," Camellion said.

Father Csoki's lips moved in barely audible prayer.

Father Deak and the other five Hungarians were too frightened to even mumble a quick Hail Mary to Our Lady of Bakony.

CHAPTER FIFTEEN

It is only half true that when four or five people agree on everything, one of them is doing all the thinking. General Bela Skedfu and Lieutenant General Sigismund Barthory were in perfect agreement with Boris Lysemki, Gleb Ezhov, and Rostislav Grusha that the revolutionaries were not only defying all efforts to capture them, but were literally destroying Karolyi Castle. Where to place the blame—and on whom—was the only area of disagreement between the two Hungarians and the three Russians. The incongruity was that the very rules by which the five men lived made it impossible for either side to accept a single particle of blame for the failure to protect the castle. In the Communist world, one of the prime rules for remaining on top was never to accept responsibility for a decision if one could possibly avoid it. All five men were experts at passing the buck; yet each man knew that there wasn't any way to shift the blame for a disaster of this magnitude. In fact, there was no one to blame—except each other! The Hungarian Prime Minister and the Politburo, or council, of the Hungarian Socialist Workers' Party would demand an explanation from General Skedfu and Lieutenant General Barthory. Failure always speaks for itself. How does one explain it? The KGB chairman himself would place the blame squarely on the shoulders of Boris Lysemki, who held the rank of colonel in Special Services II—the counterintelligence service—of the KGB's First Chief Directorate. Lysemki felt that he'd be lucky if he ended up as a private beyond the Arctic Circle in Siberia. But now was not the time to worry about the future. Staying alive in the present was the problem.

Stunned over the loss of the tanks on the south side of the plateau, Colonel Lysemki, his two aides, and the two chiefs of the AVO had been in the communications center when Major Furdo had reported from the third-floor command post that the criminal fugitives had attacked the garage and repair shops. Worse, they had murdered not only the AVOs who had been in the garage, but also the score of AVOs that Furdo had sent in as reinforcements.

Forced to accept this new defeat, Skedfu, Barthory, and the three KG officials had waited impatiently for further developments, news of which had soon come. The revolutionaries had blown out sections of the east side castle wall, the explosions causing a fire that was soon raging beyond control, the flames spreading outward and upward.

A short time later, the gangsters fighting for capitalism had reached the landing pad and lifted off in two MIL Mi-2 helicopters. Now they were tearing the three towers apart with explosives, the terrific concussions ripping out huge sections of rocks, which crashed through the metal roof and fell to the floor of the laboratory. Jagged masses of stone from the east side of the southwest tower destroyed the communications center, burying the sensitive radio equipment and the three operators. Blocks the size of Volkswagens demolished the meeting room. More rubble, twisted reinforcement rods, and the broken and bloody bodies of two AVO men—they had been part of a KPV crew in the middle tower—buried the records room, crushing the metal filing cabinets as flat as tissue paper. Broken masonry was falling into the exercise and recreation area as Skedfu, Barthory, and the three Russians ran into the hall and looked around them. The air was so filled with dust that they could hardly see, and so filled with smoke that they had difficulty breathing. Twenty-five feet ahead, just before the entrance to the lab, was the stairway to the fourth level of the castle. The door at the bottom of the stairs was locked; yet dark smoke poured upward from underneath the door, and with the smoke, the smell of burning wood and rubber, paint and plastic, metal and other material.

"We're trapped!" Gleb Ezhov's voice bordered on panic. "But I don't understand how the fire could have reached the fourth floor with such speed." He looked at Colonel Lysemki for some kind of reassurance.

Lysemki, his face as austere as the broken stones scattered around him, brushed gray powder from his red hair, turned, and stared at the elevators on the other side of the hall.

General Skedfu said hoarsely, "Fire or not, we couldn't go to the fourth floor because of the microwave screen." He turned his head toward Lysemki. "And forget the elevators, Comrade Lysemki. Those two explosions on the ground level fifteen minutes ago not only wrecked the elevator motors, but some jammed the microwave circuits. We must face it: we're trapped up here."

"We won't burn to death," Lieutenant General Barthory said quickly. "The floors and the roof above are metal. They'll get hot but won't burn. We can climb the radio tower and wait it out."

"That's right! We'll wait until we can get one of the MIL helicopters," General Skedfu intoned solemnly. He looked around the hallway, peering through the dust and smoke. "Is Dr. Meleter in the lab?"

"With his assistants," Barthory said. "They're in the special test chamber. That chamber is the safest place up here."

Rostislav Grusha, a Soviet Stechkin machine pistol in each hand, looked up fearfully at the ceiling in front of the double lab doors, sweat dripping from his jaw, which was shaped like a bull terrier's. A mass of rock had fallen on the roof and ripped the metal, a sawlike projection of granite protruding through the ragged gash.

Colonel Lysemki swung around and stared at General Skedfu and Lieutenant General Barthory, his gaze compounded of rage and sheer disbelief. "You're both a couple of idiots!" the Russian almost screamed. He stepped closer to the two Hungarians, his fists tightly closed. "How in hell do you think we're going to get our hands on one of those helicopters? Those—"

The five men ducked down involuntarily when a helicopter roared overhead, going from the south to the north.

"Those maniacs up there are going to blow up this entire castle, piece by piece!" Lysemki raged on, once more standing up straight. "Do you think they're going to land and present us with a helicopter?"

"Both of you are crazy!" Gleb Ezhov's eyes bulged in astonishment. "There's only six or seven of the murderers left, but they're not going to come down here and commit suicide. I don't care if the Death Merchant is the leader. He doesn't want to die any more than we do!"

General Skedfu's neat mustache, gray with dust, twitched like the little wings of a dying bird, and his sad eyes flared with an anger rushing out of control. He opened his mouth and inhaled noisily. But before he could reply to the Russians, there was another shattering explosion—this one from the keep tower on the southeast corner of the castle. Moments later, several enormous blocks of sandstone, edged with bent steel reinforcing mesh, crashed through the ceiling at the end of the hall and bounced against the wall of the guard room. Smaller masses of stone and rubble followed.

"Let's get out of here!" shouted Rostislav Grusha.

The five men rushed down the hall to the laboratory, three of them convinced that their careers, and maybe their lives, were coming to a rapid end.

"Suppose some of the gas escapes?" panted Gleb Ezhov as they ran past AVO troopers who had Zel subguns and AKs trained on the four stairways that led to the roof.

173

"There's no danger," yelled Sigismund Barthory. "The gas is only dangerous when the various elements are mixed."

Seventy-five feet behind and overhead there was another thundering explosion.

His firm hands expertly working the controls, Richard Camellion swung the MIL Mi-2 around in a wide circle over the deep gorge and headed the Hoplite back toward the burning castle. Above the roar of the rotor, he yelled at Paul Tisza in the seat next to him, "This time I'm going to take us between the left corner tower and the middle tower. Aim for the top of the center tower. The pressure from the rotor blade will carry the arrow to the center of the tower. All of you hang on. Ahead is the only game in town and we're playing to win."

Nodding, Tisza carefully placed another C-4-packed arrow on the bed of the crossbow. "I've only two left," he yelled back at Camellion.

"More than enough!" the Death Merchant shouted. "The three towers are almost finished. Once the machine-gun nest in the center tower is destroyed, we can land."

Land? Tisza was afraid to ask how they would land. Mihaly Szechenyi, crouched by one window, and Tibor Arpad, beside the other window, also wondered about the landing. Kiraly submachine guns in their hands, the two men, sitting behind Camellion and Tisza, were badly frightened. Nonetheless, they were determined to do their share. And to die if they had to, fighting for freedom. Only slaves were willing to live on their knees.

The Hoplite, like some prehistoric bird of prey, closed in on the Castle of the Hawk. Five hundred feet below the onrushing helicopter, the south edge of the granite plateau flashed by, the burned-out Russian tanks glowing cherry red, the hot hulks sending up tiny, lazy drifts of dirty smoke.

Very briefly, the Death Merchant spotted the still-smoldering wreck of the Hound, which had crashed and burned between the castle and the powerhouse. There, far to his right, was the fire-consumed tank in front of the ga-

174

rage and repair shops. Some P-T stuff continued to burn in the wide doorway of the building.

For a grain of time, Camellion glimpsed the castle. The darkened first level was not burning, but part of the second floor and all of the third story were masses of flames colored with smoke, rolling clouds of gray and black smoke that were slapped by the stiff mountain wind.

He saw the three keep towers, that is, what was left of the tall structures. The southeast corner tower was practically destroyed. Ray Merrit and his group, using C-4 packs with contact fuses, had just finished demolishing the lower section of the tower, part of which had fallen and smashed a large hole in the roof. Now, to the north, Merrit was up-cycling the Hoplite, swinging the helicopter wildly to the west, the craft barely visible against the grim face of Mount Zivatar.

Only half of the southwest corner tower was standing. It reminded the Death Merchant of a hideous gray tooth that had been snapped off by a pair of giant pliers. Only the center tower remained intact, except for several bartizans—small overhanging structures built on the side of the tower—which had crashed to the roof. Behind the battlements, at the very top of the tower, frantic AVO troopers began firing a DshKM tripod-mounted machine gun through a wide crenel. It was all an enormous exercise in futility and a waste of ammunition. The Death Merchant had dropped the Hoplite to a lower altitude, and the helicopter was flying in below the angle of fire. The barrel of the DshKM could not be cranked down toward the roaring aircraft. The stream of 12.7mm patron 034g projectiles passed six feet over the hub of the rotor. A moment later it was too late for the AVO troopers on the tower. The Hoplite was screaming between the southwest tower and the center tower. In that split second, while the center tower seemed to be only ten feet ahead, to his right, and the rounded side so close he felt he could reach out and touch it, Paul Tisza pulled the trigger of the crossbow, aiming for the battlements. Air pressure from the spinning rotor blades drove the arrow downward, but it wasn't strong enough to overcome the draw-power of the crossbow. The contact-fused tip of the arrow

175

struck the west center-side of the tower, just below the two slits of a cross-shaped crenel.

Tisza, Camellion, and the two other men didn't see the giant flash of fire. The Hoplite was sixty feet to the north when the C-4 exploded. They did hear the explosion and feel the concussion, the pressure wave pushing against the helicopter as Camellion began taking the craft up, and Tibor Arpad and Mihaly Szechenyi raked the roof with 9mm Kiraly sub-gun fire. Most of the slugs whined off the metal roof and from several of the square air-conditioning units. But other projectiles found and killed three AVOs who didn't duck in time.

The tower in the center of the keep had been demolished. The C-4 had blown a gigantic hole in the west side of the tower and had loosened the rest of the stones. The tremendous weight above the huge cavity, now unevenly distributed, did the rest. There were loud ripping sounds and a low rumble. The tower fell inward, the AVO troopers screaming in terror as they and the stones crashed downward and vanished in clouds of dust and tons of granite blocks and rubble.

The face of Mount Zivatar glared at the Death Merchant for a second; then the mountain was gone and the Hoplite was streaking upward and due west. Within half a minute, the Castle of the Hawk was six hundred feet below and almost a thousand feet to the east, the giant structure, illuminated by crawling and twisting tongues of flame, casting gigantic shadows over the east and west valleys and the south face of the gorge.

Heading out over the west valley, Camellion moved the bird to the vicinity where Merrit and his group of four Hungarians were hovering at two thousand feet between the stars and the black valley.

Camellion switched on the radio, contacted Merrit, and yelled into the throat mike, "I'm going in. Watch us and set your baby down when we land."

Richard, switching off the radio before Merrit could reply, removed the headphones and the throat mike, swung the Hoplite around in a tight circle, and yelled loudly at Tisza, Arpad, and Szechenyi, "I'm going to fly over the

176

roof again. This time use P-T burn bombs and try to bottle up the stairway openings."

Tisza turned and stared at Camellion. "But how are we going to get into the laboratory?"

"The way they don't expect us to come," Camellion said. Grinning like a demon, he hunched down and sent the helicopter on a northeast course while the three Hungarians dug into their kit bags for P-T grenades.

Again Mount Zivatar loomed threateningly in front of the egg-beater growing larger and larger, finally so huge that the three Hungarians wanted to cringe. When it seemed that the Hoplite would have to splatter itself and its four occupants on the face of the mountain, Camellion swung the craft around to the south, straight south and down, cutting slightly to his left, to the east, to avoid the sixty-foot radio tower.

The roof of the castle, previously as tiny as a postage stamp, grew rapidly. And then the roof was as large as a meadow made of metal, and the helicopter, now only fifty feet above the area, was roaring over, slightly to the right of the four housings that covered the roof openings of the stairways from the laboratory.

One-two-three-four-five P-T grenades fell from the sides of the Hoplite, smacked the roof, and bloomed into magnificent white flowers of liquid fire. One P-T bomb fell short and hit an air-conditioning unit. Two fell on target, six to eight feet in front of two stairway openings. The fourth hit the top of a housing, and its molten fire began dripping over the front onto the stairs. The fifth burn bomb fell exactly in front of the fourth housing. Within a second the entire doorway was a mass of liquid, white flame.

The Hoplite soared up, shot out across the south edge of the roof, and was soon past the black gorge. With his right hand Richard dug into one of his kits and took out two brown packs of C-4 nitrocelocene. A round, shiny object, three times the size of a sewing thimble, was attached to the side of each package. On top of each shiny Polymer fuse was a blue plastic pull-tab.

The Death Merchant, swinging the helicopter around to the north, told Paul Tisza what he wanted him to do:

"Just pull off the tab when I tell you to and drop each pack out the window when I tell you to."

To the north roared the Hoplite. A tight swing-about in front of the mountain, and the bird was screaming down to the south, the Death Merchant quickly measuring the roof, his mind computing the distance.

"Pull the tab!" he yelled at Tisza, who instantly pulled the blue plastic tab and put his arm out the window.

Five seconds later—"Drop it!"

The Death Merchant instantly pulled the Hoplite upward, its resounding rotor failing to blot out the sound of the stupendous explosion on the roof. Camellion headed south, noticing that Merrit had moved in and was hovering his Hoplite five hundred feet up and five hundred feet to the west.

Very quickly the Death Merchant turned, moved north, skidded the bird on air in front of the moon-bathed mountain, and once more flew down toward the roof. He saw that the first C-4 pack had blown a huge section out of the roof, a ragged, smoking hole at least twenty-five feet in diameter.

Good! One more should do it!

"Pull the tab!"

One-two-three-four!

"Drop it!"

Tisza's hand opened, and the C-4 package fell toward the roof as Camellion clawed for altitude and the wave of concussion from the brain-crushing explosion pushed against the whirlybird. Camellion was more than a little happy when he noticed that the phosphorus-thermite had turned the four stairway entrances into roaring furnaces of flames. Satan himself would have gotten a fried butt.

Four minutes later, and the Death Merchant had turned the craft, flown back north, reversed at the face of the mountain, and was again approaching the roof, this time with the intention of setting the Hoplite down. Seeing what had happened, he quickly changed his mind.

The second C-4 blast had ripped off more of the roof and had created another hole, this one merging with the first. There was more than enough room to set the helicopter down through the hole and directly into the lab.

178

The only thing wrong was that the two explosions had greatly weakened the north end of the roof, to the extent that it could no longer bear the weight of the radio tower, located in the northwest corner. The bottom part of the tower had fallen straight down through the roof, the sudden tilt snapping off the top section, which had fallen partially over the huge hole.

Fudge! This is enough to make a man turn politician!

Tibor Arpad leaned forward from the rear of the Hoplite and shouted, "What do we do now?"

Moving the Hoplite to the south, Camellion shouted back, "We do it again. Tisza, get another C-4 deal out of my kit. We'll employ the same procedure. Pull and drop only when I say so."

Camellion made the run. This last drop had to be just right. If the C-4 dropped into the hole, it would explode and demolish part of the floor on the fifth level, in which case the Hoplite would never be able to land. There was only one way, just one: the C-4 had to detonate to one side of the hole.

Eyes, don't fail me!

"Drop!"

Paul Tisza dropped the package; it fell straight down. Camellion sent the craft to new heights and headed south. Minutes later, the Hoplite had reversed course, turned at Mount Zivatar, and was approaching the roof for what the Death Merchant hoped was the last time.

The Three Hungarians let out yells of victory when they saw that they had succeeded. The last package of C-4 had fallen ten feet to the west of the hole, exploded, and sent the twisted mass of tower girders flying. Not only was the original hole clear; it was much bigger.

"Make sure your weapons are fully loaded!" Camellion yelled. "We're going in and finish the job."

Or die in the attempt!

CHAPTER SIXTEEN

The dynamics of death often make reality difficult to accept. General Skedfu, Lieutenant General Barthory, and the three sons of Mother Russia were tough, clever individuals unaccustomed to failure. And now that total disaster was raging all around them, they were completely unprepared for it. Crouched down behind complicated apparatuses, the five men couldn't even decide on the best course of action to save their own lives. They couldn't because they had never considered such a possibility, not here at Karolyi Castle. It would take a modern army to invade the impenetrable fortress; yet by some extraordinary necromancy, a traitorous crew of revolutionaries had accomplished the impossible.

The five men did feel that the special chamber, used to bring the elements of the NK-hk-4 gas together, was the most secure section of the long laboratory. The special chamber had a double-strength ceiling and floor and triple windows of Finsen glass. But the Finsen glass, not having been created to withstand the concussion of close-by explosives, had shattered when the three explosions, a hundred and fifty feet to the north, had ripped apart the ceiling, tore up lab equipment, and sent pieces of metal flying outward. Some of the broken equipment killed four AVO troopers. A lot more of it crashed through the broken windows of the special chamber.

Bela Skedfu and Sigismund Barthory, although utterly ruthless, were not cowards. Neither were Boris Lysemki, Gleb Ezhov, and Rostislav Grusha. Ignoring Dr. Imre Meleter and his four assistants cowering in one corner on the debris-littered floor, the two Hungarians and three Russians waited for the attack, submachine guns in their hands, Skedfu cursing now and then over their lack of hand grenades. But the guard room, in which the grenades were stored, had been buried under tons of rock from the wrecked southeast tower.

180

Another impossibility became stark, naked reality! The five men, looking over the bottom edges of the broken windows, heard the loud *woom-woom-woom-woom* of a helicopter, and from the sound they could tell that the craft was coming down. And it was! The Hoplite was descending through the enormous hole in the ceiling, coming right down through the smoke into the laboratory itself, the big blade of the main overhead rotor throwing up clouds of dust from the rubble on the floor. Close behind, but still above the roof, was the *woom-woom-woom-woom* of another helicopter coming in for a landing. The Hungarians and the Russians ducked down to avoid streams of submachine gun slugs that started pouring from the side windows of the helicopter.

Sigismund Barthory pulled back the cocking bolt of the Zel sub-gun and said in a voice that was surprisingly calm, "Now we can kill the murderous bastards, including the Death Merchant if he's leading them."

It suddenly occurred to Barthory and to the other four men that no one knew what the Death Merchant looked like.

Richard Camellion, leaning sideways to avoid any bullet that might come tearing through the front glass, set the copter down. Because of wrecked equipment and broken metal furniture, the Hoplite landed unevenly, tilting to the right, then sliding three feet forward as the rear wheel bounced off part of a desk. The bird leaned heavily, then actually fell several feet to the right. The right wheel of the landing gear had broken through the metal floor. A surge of fear ran through Camellion, the fear that the floor might collapse from the weight of the helicopter, in which case the Hoplite would fall through the ceiling of the fourth level. Nothing of the sort happened. To the noisy tunes of the Hungarians' Kiraly music boxes, the helicopter sagged and settled into a final position. Richard switched off both rotors, picked up his Ingram sub-gun, dropped behind the control panel, pushed open the door on the left, and jumped out. On the other side and behind him, Tisza, Arpad, and Szechenyi piled out of the Hoplite, and, like Camellion, tried to see through the settling clouds of stone and mortar dust, tried to find the AVO troopers, who, also trying to find them, began firing in the general direction of the helicopter.

"Tisza, keep an eye on the roof above us," Camellion called out. Hearing the loud whine of glancing slugs, Richard dropped down behind a half-overturned Monostat pump while the three Hungarians snuggled behind wreckage close by, Paul Tisza in a position that enabled him to watch the edges of the roof over the slanted Hoplite.

"Give them grenades but no P-T stuff," Camellion called out. "We'll stay put until Brother Schmid and the others get here."

He pulled two grenades from a hip bag, pulled the pin on one, and pitched it forward, trying for a thirty-foot range. There was a violent explosion, a scream, several loud shouts, and the sound of objects crashing to the floor. Altogether, Camellion, Arpad, and Szechenyi tossed six grenades, spreading them in a wide-front semicircle.

Although the dust had settled around the helicopter, the smoke coming from the lower levels still made it difficult to see and to breathe. The hole in the roof had created an updraft, and the gray smoke drifted lazily toward the enormous opening, bringing to Camellion all kinds of smells—the odor of burning wood and metal, chemicals and cloth, and even the sickeningly sweet stink of roasted flesh.

Paul Tisza shouted, "Brother Schmid and the others are here. I just saw Dr. Palfecky looking down from the roof." Then, his eyes wide, Tisza dropped lower. A bullet had hit a piece of metal several feet from his head and had zinged off with a loud wail of failure.

Half a dozen canisters of KC103 signal smoke dropped from the roof around the Hoplite. Moments later, the dye and coolants ignited, thick red smoke began pouring from the tins, and Merrit and his group of four began dropping down to the cabin top of the helicopter. Luckily, all five men managed to slide down the sides of the craft without stopping any slugs. Quickly then, they moved behind torn-apart furniture and various kinds of chemical equipment, Merrit crawling up beside the Death Merchant,

182

who noticed that the big man was sucking on the stem of his unlit pipe.

"We're all safe," Merrit said, and turned over on his right side. "Any special ideas on how to do it? Oh, yeah, the garage to the east is on fire."

"This is one of those deals that can't be planned," Camellion replied. "All we can do is attack and hope we get lucky." He turned and gave Merrit a piercing stare. "How bad is the fire?"

Checking his Ingram machine pistol, Merrit spoke from around the pipe stem. "It's hard to say. All we could see was a lot of smoke. But the landing pad was clear. But you know what will happen if the fuel depot goes up? We can kiss the other Hound goodbye."

Merrit raised himself up slightly and looked around the right side of the Monostat pump. Hell stared back at him and the Death Merchant.

Through the drifting smoke and fumes, all seven men saw that the huge laboratory was devastated and lay in ruins, falling stones and concussion from C-4 explosions having done their job of destruction; and the anti-Communist fighters sensed that, interwoven with the ruins, was a putrescence they would remember for the rest of their lives. The four stairs to the roof were deserted, their steps, at the top, filled with liquid P-T fire. To the southeast, at the opposite end of the lab, two doors had been torn from their hinges by crashing tower stones. Beyond the opening, the hallway was completely filled with broken granite and enormous chunks of sandstone. Now and then, the Death Merchant and his people could see a green, peaked cap pop up and an AVO trooper take a quick look around. Toward the rear of the lab, 150 feet to the southwest, was an inner room, a square room made of metal, with thick walls, if the thickness of the broken window frames was an indication. Various pipes from the side of one wall of the large cube-room moved to numerous tanks spread out over the laboratory floor. It was only too apparent to the seven men that if they were going to obtain the secret of the NK-hk-4 gas, they would have to do it within the 200-foot area ahead.

Camellion's face was without expression. "Merrit, if we

both get iced, there will be no one available to fly the helicopters," he said. "Take three or four of the boys and go up along the east side. I'll take the west side. Sing out when you're all set, and take your cue from me. One more thing—if we get out of this alive, I want you to do me a favor."

"What?"

"Light that damn thing in your mouth."

The muscular Company man smiled and shifted the pipe to the other side of his mouth. "Yeah, I'll do that. Count on it, Brother Krim."

Merrit moved back, started to crawl on his hands and knees past the Death Merchant, then stopped and looked around at Camellion. "Have you noticed how hot the floor is getting?" His voice was deadly serious. "The metal in spots is more than merely warm."

Camellion turned and nodded. "I've noticed. I have the feeling that if we don't get this job done in a hurry, we'll all end up frying in the skillet."

With greater effort, Merrit crawled to the left, toward where the two priests, Tom Lakatos, and Dr. Palfecky were safe behind a row of vapor condensers resting on a long, steel-enclosed stand.

Noticing that Mihay Szechenyi was eight feet behind him, and that Arpad and Tisza were across from the big-nosed Hungarian, Camellion said in a voice that wasn't too loud, "Move when I move. Follow the route I take, but don't stay close together. If somebody stops a bullet, don't stop to help him. That's rough, but it's the only way to stay alive."

The three men slowly nodded, their grimy faces looking strangely unreal as the final fog of red signal smoke drifted over them. The Death Merchant resumed his watching of the forward area. There was no firing. The AVOs, playing it smart as they waited, weren't wasting ammo shooting at shadows. They couldn't see any better than Camellion and his men could, not only because of the smoke, which was constantly getting thicker, but because half the lights in the ceiling had been knocked out.

As soon as he heard Merrit's loud "Yo-oh!" ring out, Camellion removed a grenade from his kit bag, pulled the pin, and, with as much strength as he could muster, threw the grenade to the area in front of him. Six seconds later, five seconds after the grenade detonated and further wrecked the wreckage, Camellion jumped up from behind the Monostat pump and raced forward, on a course that zig-zagged him to the right. He expected slugs and got what he expected, just as four grenades exploded in succession far to his left.

Only twenty feet ahead, two AVOs stepped out from the protection of a tall machine that had two Klystron tubes mounted on its front. The tall man hip-fired a Zel submachine gun; simultaneously, his shorter comrade triggered a Russian Automat Kalashnikov. Almost with the speed of light, Camellion jerked his body to the right in time to avoid the wave of searing 7.62mm slugs and fired the Ingram, swinging the machine pistol slightly from side to side as he went down on one knee. At the same moment, above the sounds of K-cartridges exploding in the firing chamber of the Ingram, Richard heard a short scream behind him and spotted two more AVO agents thirty feet to his right.

The tall AVO with the Zel caught two 9mm slugs in the chest and one in the stomach. Moaning "Uhh!," he looked extremely surprised and fell backward, only a few seconds before Short-and-Fat with the AK assault rifle found out that while dying can be very swift, it can also be very messy. A 9mm K-cartridge projectile blew apart his Adam's apple, tore out the back of his throat, and ripped a hole in his neck the size of a silver dollar. A second blob of lead streaked through his open mouth and left another big hole in back of his neck. The third smacked him in the forehead, smashed his skull, and switched off his brain forever.

But the two dead AVOs had not been entirely unsuccessful. Their storm of slugs, while missing the Death Merchant, had accidentally found Mihaly Szechenyi, seventeen 7.62mm slugs slashing him from nose to navel. Made a corpse as quickly as if he had been struck by lightning, Szechenyi crashed down in a shower of blood. Seeing him fall, Tibor Arpad wanted to vomit. He charged forward, wondering where Tisza was.

Richard Camellion dropped to the floor and, almost flat, swung the Ingram to the right and fired half a second after twin streams of Kiraly nine-millimeter projectiles passed several feet over his prone body. *Dominus lucis vobiscum*—and Camellion smiled when he saw his own cloud of special K lead consume one of the AVO men, tiny green pieces of cloth jumping outward from the man's chest from the impact of the flattened-out slugs.

The second man was an old pro. During that tenth of a mini-moment, Cyril Lamoski realized he didn't have time to adjust his aim and fire, even though such action would take no more than three seconds. If he tried it, during those three seconds, the other man would riddle him. Lamoski did the next best thing: he tried to drop behind the overturned desk that he and his now-dead companion had used as a shield. He almost succeeded. Camellion exploded Lamoski's head, sending face, flesh, bone, and uniform cap flying, when the AVO agent was only a foot above the edge of the desktop.

With the impersonal scrutiny of a stargazer, Camellion studied the area to the right for a moment, then eye-raked the area ahead. He quickly reloaded the Ingram, got to his feet, turned, looked behind him and to the left, and saw that several of the enemy—forty feet to the east— were about to cut down Tibor Arpad with AKs. Arpad was moving south, at the moment stumbling over several hooded fluorescent fixtures that had fallen from the ceiling.

"Arpad—fall!" Camellion yelled. He then threw his own body to the floor and crawled underneath a table, whose top was filled with Balsam bottles, pyrex retorts, Squibb separatory funnels, test tubes in long racks, and other kinds of small lab equipment. There was a thick layer of stone dust on the table, but miraculously none of the items had been smashed. Camellion, for the moment, was safe, protected from the west and the south by a vacuum shelf drier installation in front of him and a Zaremba horizontal tube evaporator to his left. He could observe most of the east side by crouching down behind an intermittent still, used in the distillation and separation of liquid mixtures.

As for Arpad, instead of throwing himself down, he turned and stared in Camellion's direction. Yet his hesitation didn't cost him his life. Paul Tisza, who had been concealed behind a V-shaped contraption to Arpad's right, moved surprisingly fast for a man with a weak leg. He leaped out, grabbed Arpad around the waist, and pulled him down. Even if neither man had moved, Arpad still would not have died. Before the AVOs could fire, Father Csoki stitched the two men with lines of vz/25 subgun fire. The priest then dodged to one side in fear as double-cored Zel slugs burned the air around him. He dropped to the security of a tall steel tank, catching a glimpse of Dr. Palfecky, Thomas Lakatos, and Father Deak machine-gunning eight AVOs, who had become crazy-brave in desperation and had attempted a charge. The eight men went down, cut to pieces by lead, falling all over each other in their hurry to get to hell.

Father Stephen Deak followed the dead Hungarians into eternity (his soul traveling in the opposite direction). Over-confidence overcame caution; victory subdued wariness. Father Deak jumped up and ran ahead six feet, his sudden move exposing him to Lieutenant Sandor Gordesyi, who, ten seconds earlier, had fired at Father Csoki. This time Gordesyi didn't miss, his short burst of slugs catching Father Deak high in the right side. A 7.62mm projectile cut through Deak's beard and continued on to the east, burying itself in the wall. A second bullet knifed through the priest's neck, cutting apart the right external jugular. A third bullet smashed Father Deak in the center of his long sideburn and went all the way through his head, exploding out on the other side. The priest twisted slowly to the floor and fell forward on his face, while Father Csoki, Thomas Lakatos, and Dr. Palfecky found cover.

"What do you think Brother Schmid is doing?" Thomas Lakatos whispered to Father Csoki, who was with him. He tried hard not to cough, but it was difficult. The smoke was getting thicker, the floor hotter.

"Be quiet, Thomas," Father Csoki replied, his voice skating on the brink of hysteria. "We will know soon enough. Now let us say a silent prayer for Father Deak's soul." The priest began coughing in an effort to clear the smoke from his lungs.

Five minutes earlier, Ray Merrit had wormed himself to the east wall of the lab, moved thirty feet to the south, and now found himself in the position he wanted, a perfect ambush point. He tried desperately not to hack, and he thought that the AVOs had been damned dumb not to have posted any guards on the east perimeter. Shifting the pipe to the right side of his mouth, Merrit looked cautiously around the left side of a large deaerator, a machine that removes oxygen and carbon dioxide from dissolving water by a process called deaeration.

Merrit stared, doing his best to see through the smoke. By God! It was almost too good to be true. Thirty to forty feet ahead, to the west, a dozen or more AVO troopers were waiting behind metal furniture and piles of overturned or demolished equipment. Furthermore, now and then through the drifting smoke, he could see the tops of green caps behind other machines. Why, damn it! The area was crawling with the green cockroaches. Good! As far as Merrit was concerned, their ass was grass—*and I'm the lawn mower!* Hmmmmm! But why cut grass when you can burn it off? Brother Krim and his guys were far to the west; the others were far enough to the north to escape the deadly fire. And the square metal office! It too was far enough away. It was that inner room that was important. Intuition told Merrit that if the secret of the gas was to be obtained, it would be found in that square room.

Wondering who Brother Krim really was, Merrit reached into his kit and took out four P-T grenades—*I'm convinced he's the Death Merchant, but I'm not going to make a fool of myself and ask him!*

Carefully he stood up, calculated the distance, pulled the plastic-coated pin from the first P-T bomb, and threw it. In quick succession he tossed the remaining three P-T grenades, spacing them in the area ahead.

Hell exploded in the area in front of Merrit. The P-T bombs burst within seconds of each other, the liquid petals of the blooming fire flowers washing over the trapped AVO troopers, their shrieks of agony an ear-piercing cre-

188

scendo of doom that every man in the laboratory heard. This included General Bela Skedfu and his group, who had seen the southeast section of the lab explode with brilliant white heat.

"Damn them to hell!" General Skedfu roared. His dark eyes took on the paranoid stare of a madman.

"It would seem that your AVO men have been damned to hell!" Boris Lysemki said drily. "They're certainly being roasted." The KGB officer had fully retained his professional calm, in spite of the heat and the smoke and the inescapable fact that the revolutionaries were winning. A realist, Lysemki felt their chances for living were almost non-existent.

"Fogd be a budos pofadat!" Skedfu screamed in Hungarian, telling Lysemki to shut his stinking mouth. Catching himself, Skedfu switched back to Russian. "We'll settle our differences later, my Russian comrade. But if we stay in here, we'll never do anything. The enemy will fry us. Besides us, there's only Major Furdo and maybe a dozen of his men."

Skedfu turned away and began to crawl to the door. Lieutenant General Barthory followed him. Boris Lysemki and the other two Russians crawled after Barthory.

Ray Merrit looked around the side of the deaerator. He had seen a lot of death in his life, a lot of pain and suffering, but even he recoiled at the hideous spectacle of the dancing human torches, who were attacking the air and themselves with burning arms and legs. The smell of burning cloth and leather was intense. The stink of flesh being roasted was a purgatory in itself.

What a barbeque! Merrit, who had been a U.S. narcotics agent before joining the CIA, saw the face of a man, who was jumping around like a flaming Mexican jumping bean. The crepe-suzetted creep looked like an addict soaring on cocaine. Yes, sir. A coke joker flying high on nose candy!

The AVO man stopped his horrible screaming. He was dead. The flesh of the face of the corpse started falling from its cheekbones, and, as the dead man fell, the body began to melt the way a wax dummy dissolves in a blazing waxworks.

Merrit moved back because of the intense heat and to protect himself from cartridges that had begun exploding in the cartridge belts and the weapons of the burning corpses.

After a short fit of coughing and hacking, he crawled north. The thing to do now was to get the others, signal "Brother Krim," and move in for the quick-kill.

All of a sudden there was a *pingggggg!* Feeling a hard tug on the pipe, Merrit jumped and fell sideways. A bullet had exploded. Its lead projectile had ricocheted and had broken the bowl of his pipe!

In the meantime, the Death Merchant, seeing the intense flare of P-T mixture, put together what had happened. And so did Lieutenant Sandor Gordesyi, who realized he was all alone out front and without a backup. Sweat poured down his face and neck, trickled down his spine, and ran down his legs. The best course now, the only course, was to retreat to the west and link up with Major Furdo and his group, who were on the west side, fifty feet in front of the special chamber.

Dodging, bent over, Gordesyi went as quickly as he could, coughing as he stepped over wreckage and eased himself between various machines, so anxious to reach Major Furdo that he never realized when his entire skull exploded and parts of his brain splattered against a gismo that resembled a fishtank turned upside down. The Death Merchant, preparing to move south, had expertly placed four K-cartridge projectiles into his head.

Richard looked behind him, saw Arpad and Tisza thirty feet to the north, staring in his direction, and motioned them forward with a wave of his hand. He tried to look above the vacuum shelf drier machine, whose top was only a few inches higher than the table, but there wasn't enough space between the machine and the end of the table. Instead, Camellion crawled out from underneath the table, halfway stood, and moved around the right side of the Zaremba horizontal tube evaporator, his body as taut as a wound-up spring. He took several more steps, stopping and listening when his foot crunched on broken glass. Nothing. Almost total silence. Only the hissing of air from far to the south and the slight crackling of P-T flames. Twenty feet ahead was a Houdry catalytic cracking machine, the tanks and pipes and tubes mounted on a metal platform. Next to it, to Camellion's right, was a Dubbs Thermofor catalytic cracking machine, and it, too, was resting on a metal platform.

Camellion was instantly suspicious when he saw that a metal table had been placed against the north side platform of the Houdry machine. The table was too even, propped up too securely. Intuition, made razor-sharp by experience, did the rest: the Death Merchant jumped far to the right, swung up the Ingram, and fired the weapon in a sweeping arc as he did so.

The exact same instant that the Death Merchant rocketed to the right, Major Furdo and three of his men jumped up from the other side of the Houdry machine and its platform and fired, the roar of the four Zel submachine guns a screaming racket that shook the glass test tubes and other items on the table that had protected Camellion.

A few minutes before, Major Furdo and his pack of killers had estimated the Death Merchant's position from the snarling of his machine pistol as he had put Lieutenant Gordesyi to sleep. The clever Furdo and his crew had used extreme caution: they had remained concealed, listened to the barely perceptible noise made by Camellion as he moved, and then leaped up to fire after they had calculated that he was straight in front of them. How could they have known the incredible speed with which he could move?

Every single AVO slug missed the Death Merchant, although one 7.62mm projectile came very close, passing his left shoulder by less than half an inch. The rest of the lethal lead smashed the tubing of the vacuum shelf drier and smashed the test tubes, Balsam bottles, retorts, and other glass containers on the long table into a thousand pieces.

The Death Merchant's stream of hot 9mm projectiles sprayed all over Major Furdo and the other three men.

The slugs tore into their chests, ripped off chunks of green shirts, and rendered their hearts and lungs totally useless. More of the 9mm K-C projectiles blew apart the Flash Dephlegmator and pressure distillate condenser of the Houdry machine.

Another AVO had been about to rear up and fire but was knocked back by Major Furdo's bloody corpse. Five other troopers, crouching on the floor, did their best to avoid the three other corpses pitching backward. They had not stood up to fire because there hadn't been room by the side of the Houdry machine platform. However, Rudolph Jor, the round-faced agent knocked down by the dead Major Furdo, went to the floor in such a manner that he fell on his left shoulder beyond the east end of the Houdry machine platform. As chance would have it, Jor saw Tibor Arpad and Paul Tisza running forward in an effort to catch up with the Death Merchant, who was also racing ahead.

Jor brought up the Zel sub-gun in his right hand and fired a long burst at Tisza and Arpad, who had spotted him a few moments before he squeezed the trigger. Both Tisza and Arpad made a dive to their right to escape the hot rain of lead death. Arpad succeeded. He managed to dive behind a large steel tank. Tisza would have reached the same tank if four of Jor's 7.62mm slugs hadn't smashed into him—two into his left hip, one into the side of his left thigh, and one just above his left knee. One of the hip slugs severed both the left external iliac vein and the right external iliac vein, and Tisza, knocked unconscious by shock, was dying. Pitched sideways by the power of the slugs, he fell to the floor and lay still.

Satisfied with his work, Jor was getting to his feet when he died from half a dozen 9mm Kiraly slugs that popped him in the right side, the projectiles put there by Thomas Lakatos, who was charging toward the southwest corner of the lab with Brother Schmid, Dr. Palfecky, and Father Csoki. None of them knew it at the time, but they were on a collision course with General Skedfu, Lieutenant General Barthory, and the three KGB officials. All five were concealed behind a machine and other equipment that made synthetic ammonia. Merrit and his group found out moments later when General Skedfu, Barthory, and the Russians opened fire. But it was a mistake. They fired too quickly, at the first sight of Lakatos, and their hurricane of slugs found only him. Almost butchered by the tidal wave of lead, Lakatos pitched backward, his clothes practically shredded from his cut-up body. The only part of him that had not been touched by lead was his face, which now had the calm, drained look of youth after death pulls down the final curtain over the veil of freshness.

Merrit, Father Csoki, and Dr. Palfecky jumped, listening to the screams of glancing projectiles.

"Damn it, we're pinned down," Merrit growled. "We either stay here or go back. We can't go south through the P-T fire."

To the west, the five AVOs behind the Houdry apparatus had seen Rudolph Jor by the big one. They had then heard a wild blast of submachine-gun fire. Three of the men jumped up and prepared to meet this new threat. They were confused as to who was shooting at whom, but Jor was dead. It was therefore obvious that the enemy had spotted them. Two men on the floor remained down on one knee while they shoved fresh magazines into their Zel sub-guns.

The world exploded in the faces of the five! The three who were standing were turning to face the east when the Death Merchant streaked in through the space between the Houdry device and the Dubbs Thermofor machine. The Ingram machine pistol was in his right hand, a Model 48 Kal pistol in his left.

The three standing AVOs swung around but were lifeless before they could raise their Zels and fire. A 7.62mm slug from the Kal automatic smashed one of the AVOs in the hollow of the throat. He jumped and fell sideways. The Ingram M-P took direct action against the other two men who were standing. They crashed to the floor, each man heavier from the 9mm slugs in his chest. The two AVOs still down on the floor tried to rear up and fire. Camellion kicked the Zel sub-gun from the hands of one man at the same time that he put a Kal-pistol bullet into

193

the face of the second man. The first AVO only had time to open his mouth in horror, and then he, too, was dead, his head a hideous mess from two nine-millimeter Ingram slugs.

"Brother Krim!"

The Death Merchant swung around and stared at Tibor Arpad. The bushy-browed, heavyset man was so grimy he looked as though he had crawled from a sewer.

"Tisza and Szechenyi are dead," Arpad said in a shaky voice.

"We'll go to the south," Camellion said brusquely. "From the sound of the Zels, I think the AVOs—what's left of them—have Brother Schmid and the others in a bind on the east side."

Carefully they picked their way ahead through the smoke, stopping at times to cough. It was their coughing that kept warning General Skedfu and his group. But it was a two-way street. The hacking of Skedfu, Barthory, and the three KGB agents gave Camellion and Arpad, as well as Merrit and his group, a general idea of where they were located. Merrit, Father Csoki, and Dr. Palfecky couldn't advance, but neither could the two commanders of the AVO and the three Russians.

By no means had Camellion forgotten the special chamber; and when Dr. Meleter and two of his assistants finally found the courage to poke AKs through the shot-out windows and fire, their projectiles hit only equipment that was already useless junk.

From fifty feet away Camellion and Arpad stitched several rows of neat holes in the north wall of the special chamber. The lead didn't go completely through the three metal walls, but it did give Imre Meleter and his two assistants second thoughts. They threw down their AKs, ran back to a corner of the chamber, and hunched down with the two other cowards.

At the sound of Camellion and Arpad's roaring weapons, Sigismund Barthory leaned out around one tank of the ammonia-making apparatus, caught a brief glimpse of the Death Merchant, and fired a stream of Kiraly slugs at him. However, in that fraction of a second Camellion jerked back, and Barthory's projectiles went to waste.

Gleb Ezhov and Boris Lysemki, firing their Kiralys, joined in to help Barthory, the three men hoping their slugs would cut all the way through the metal cabinet and kill whomever was hiding behind it. Nothing of the sort happened. The projectiles did bore through the thin steel of the doors; then they screamed in protest when they hit tools and other objects and ricocheted back and forth inside the cabinet.

Arpad whispered fearfully, "What are we going to do?" He didn't like Camellion's answer. "I don't know," the Death Merchant said.

Camellion didn't dare throw a grenade directly across from where he and Arpad were crouching. Although he knew the enemy was east of him, he had no idea where Merrit and his men were.

On the other hand, I can throw a grenade to the other side if I throw it to the south of the AVOs. The explosion should confuse them long enough for me to attack.

"Arpad, stay here and watch the metal room ahead," Camellion said. He took a grenade from a bag on his hip pulled the pin, and threw the grenade over the top of the cabinet in a wide arc to the southeast. A mini-moment after the grenade exploded, Camellion leaped around the cabinet and started across the enormous room, spraying the east area ahead of him with a chain of Ingram M-P projectiles.

The explosion of the grenade—in back of the two Hungarians and the three Russians—had caught all five men off guard, and the Death Merchant's chain of hot slugs further increased their surprise and apprehension.

But the exploding grenade and the snarling of Camellion's machine pistol were the chance Ray Merrit had been waiting for. On the assumption that Brother Krim and whoever was with him were attacking the AVOs up front, Merrit, Father Csoki, and Dr. Palfecky charged forward, their own weapons roaring.

The two-pronged attack might have succeeded if it hadn't been for the smoke gagging the Death Merchant. Halfway to the enemy, he couldn't resist the tickle in his throat. A few seconds before he started to cough, he threw himself to one side and got behind a Hooker machine used for the electrolysis of sodium chloride.

Only twenty-five feet to the east of Camellion, General Skedfu and Rostislav Grusha, who had stopped hacking and were watching the area in front, saw the in-darting figures of Merrit and his two companions and opened fire. Merrit made a dive to his left, a 9mm piece of lead cutting across the front of his right ankle and breaking the flesh. Father Csoki, throwing himself to the right, felt a terrible pain in the left side of his head. Dropping behind a row of filing cabinets, the priest wondered why he wasn't dead, or at least unconscious. Then he rubbed the bloody side of his head and found out why he was still conscious and alive: the bullet had only grazed his temple.

Dr. Frantisek Palfecky had not been as lucky as Father Csoki and Raymond Merrit. Four of Grusha's 9mm Stechkin machine pistol slugs had caught him in the chest, killing him within three seconds. Palfecky lay face down, a ribbon of red twisting its way slowly from underneath him.

Merrit and Father Csoki didn't know what to do. Father Csoki began to pray. Merrit, listening for the least sound and trying not to cough, wished he had remained a narc.

General Skedfu, Lieutenant General Barthory, and the three KGB agents waited and tried to be as quiet, which was impossible because of the thick, drifting smoke. Boris Lysemki, reloading his Kiraly submachine gun, and General Skedfu were suddenly made helpless by fits of coughing.

Only a short distance to the west, the Death Merchant dared a brief look around the end of the Hooker machine, his eyes taking in the total picture. It was four or five seconds before Lieutenant General Barthory spotted him, jerked up his sub-gun, and triggered off a short burst. Camellion, seeing Barthory, darted back, and the blobs of lead burned on by, to glance off screaming from an overturned table.

Richard smiled softly to himself. Weeks ago he had spent hours studying the photographs of every big shot in the Hungarian government, and he had recognized Sigismund Barthory. How about that! If the head of the AVO intelligence service was there, who else might be with him?

Dr. Imre Meleter?

Camellion had also seen enough to know that the equipment that was protecting Lieutenant General Barthory and his group was used in the complex process of manufacturing synthetic ammonia. He had seen an air compressor, a recirculation pump, and tanks filled with—so he assumed—hydrogen and nitrogen. He had recognized the tall ammonia synthesis chamber, around which some of the enemy were crouched. Best of all, by stepping back from the Hooker machine, he could look over the top and see the coils of large copper tubing leading from the ammonia synthesis chamber to the ammonia storage tank.

Now suppose some mean old nasty put a clip full of slugs into that tubing? *What would happen? As if I didn't know!*

The Death Merchant stepped back three feet from the Hooker device, raised the Ingram submachine gun, and raked the copper tubing with eighteen K-cartridge slugs. The high-velocity projectiles tore the tubing from the top cone of the synthesis chamber, and thick, white clouds of ammonia began to hiss out.

Without a gas mask no human being can withstand the torture of breathing ammonia, which is a dangerous caustic in the concentrated state; and the ammonia hissing from the synthesis chamber was concentrated. The five men were as good as dead—and very soon they would be. Jumping to their feet, coughing and gagging as the ammonia enveloped them, they staggered as the gas seared their flesh. And each time they took a breath, it was like breathing in the flame from a blowtorch.

Having reloaded the Ingram, the Death Merchant charged from the west, Ray Merrit and Father Csoki from the north, Merrit determined to jump down the throat and kick in the liver of the man who had iced Dr. Palfecky.

The Death Merchant fired first, a six-round burst that terminated the brutal and bloody career of General Bela

197

Skedfu. Four K-cartridge projectiles, digging ragged holes in the cloth of the olive-green uniform coat, bored into his skinny chest. The fifth 9mm bullet tore out his lower teeth and blew flesh and blood out the back of his neck. The sixth 9mm smacked him in the upper lip, right in the center of his mustache, broke off three upper teeth, and widened the bloody cave in the back of his neck. His eyes wide open, Skedfu fell back against the ammonia synthesis chamber and slid to the floor.

Ray Merrit got his wish. Careful to keep away from the expanding cloud of ammonia, he raked Rostislav Grusha with a perpendicular motion of the snarling Ingram, the swarm of singing lead butchering the Russian from his groin to his astonished fat pug face. The Stechkin machine pistols slid from his hands, and he fell against the side of Lieutenant General Barthory, who, although half-blinded and half-asphyxiated, managed to raise his submachine gun and get off a short blast at Merrit and Father Csoki. At the time, both Merrit and Father Csoki were stepping back to escape the gas cloud; then, seeing the hated leader of the AVO's Section 4-DII raise the sub-gun, they jumped away from the stream of slugs.

Sigismund Barthory had fired only half a dozen rounds when Camellion killed him with a four-burst blast, the high-powered 9mms making him unrecognizable. His face blown off, Barthory pitched forward, his hands locked on the Kiraly sub-gun in a grip of death, his finger still on the trigger, the muzzle still spitting slugs.

It was one of these freak slugs that hit Father Peter Csoki in his left hand, the fingers of which were wrapped around the forehandle of the vz/25 submachine gun. The hot lead cut off his middle finger just above the knuckle, then sliced off part of the handle—both as cleanly as though they had been chopped with an ax.

The priest cried out in pain and surprise, dropped the Czech vz/25, and stumbled off to one side. He grabbed his left arm by the wrist and gaped in horror at the blood pouring from the stump of his middle finger. He was so stunned that it did not even occur to him to pray!

Boris Lysemki was also stupefied. Half-choked by the

198

ammonia, the KGB chief tried to escape the gas by dropping to the floor. The Death Merchant helped him by slug-raking the left side of the tall, red-haired Russian, the terrific impact of the dozen pieces of lead knocking Lysemki all the way to the ammonia storage tank.

At about the same time Merrit turned his attention to a half-fat slob, who was doing his best to stagger from the gas-filled area. The joker had one of the biggest noses Merrit had ever seen, so huge that when he tilted his head back, his nose resembled a two-car garage. Seconds later, Gleb Ezhov didn't have a nose, or a mouth, or a chin. He also lost his eyes and forehead from the dozen nine-millimeter projectiles which Merrit let him have, the slugs literally blowing his head off and plastering the surrounding metal with bits of bloody bone and pieces of brain and blobs of flesh.

Suddenly there was a burst of Kiraly fire from the southwest. Moments later, a loud, terrified voice screamed in Hungarian, "Stop! Stop! W-We give up! We s-surrender!"

The Death Merchant, moving rapidly back from the gas, shoved a fresh magazine into the Ingram and called out to Merrit, who was coughing and helping Father Csoki to his feet, "We'd better get over there. Arpad is all alone."

The three of them heard another long burst from the Kiraly sub-gun as they moved closer to the square metal special chamber. They found Tibor Arpad standing by the east side of the chamber, his Kiraly pointed at a trembling, big-boned man, who looked like he was pregnant. They immediately recognized the man as Dr. Imre Meleter, the inventor of the horrifying NK-hk-4 gas.

"There were four more of them inside, but I figured we needed only this piece of trash," Arpad said gruffly, glaring at Dr. Meleter.

"You figured right," the Death Merchant said. "He's the big fish and we've hooked him."

"Yeah, but if we don't get the hell away from here, we'll never reel him in," Merrit said. For the first time, there was an edge to his voice.

Camellion almost smiled. "Where's your pipe?"

"A bouncing bullet broke it!"

A strong whiff of ammonia drifted to the men as they turned and moved through the smoke-filled, eye-watering, throat-irritating atmosphere, heading northeast, their destination one of the stairways on which the P-T fire had burned out. Camellion and Merrit kept a close watch on the puffing Dr. Meleter. The scientist was so frightened he could hardly move as they pushed him up the fire-blackened steel steps.

Twelve minutes passed. They had reached the Hoplite, which Merrit had set down on the northeast side of the lab roof, lifted off, and the Death Merchant was flying the helicopter toward the pad built over the garage and workshops.

No one spoke; there wasn't anything to say. Camellion swung the craft over the pad and hovered it for a moment in the thick smoke pouring up from below. It was impossible to see the landing pad, and the men knew that Brother Krim was going to land by instinct, from the memory of their earlier, but brief visit.

Main rotor roaring, the Hoplite began to descend. The men, including Camellion, began to cough and gag from the stinking smoke flooding the cabin. Soon the five of them sounded like a chorus of frogs bellowing a pneumonia opera.

The landing gear touched metal. The helicopter settled. The Death Merchant had done it. Shaking from the coughing, nauseated by the smoke, Camellion didn't even bother to switch off the two rotors. He threw open the door to his left, stumbled out of the Hoplite, and began to move toward the south, to the apex of the triangle-shaped landing pad where the big Yak-24 Hound was waiting. Pushing Dr. Meleter ahead of them, the three other men pounded the pad after Camellion.

Six minutes later, the Hound roared upward, Camellion anxious for altitude. High now, they could see only death and destruction below. The entire castle seemed to be burning, the east side and the front a mass of twisting, crawling flames that, nurtured by the strong mountain

200

wind, were struggling to reach the stars. There was a low, distant rumble, a flash of flame, and the laboratory roof fell in amid a colossal shower of sparks. Karolyi Castle was doomed.

The Hound was at two thousand feet and Camellion was about to head on a northwest course when there was a large explosion, a deep volcanic *wwerrrooommmmm*, a tremendous flash of light, and a wave of concussion that buffeted the Hound slightly. The fuel tanks had blown up. Now, where they had been was only a raging fire-storm, a cataclysm of burning death.

The Death Merchant glanced at the compass and put the Hound on a course that would take the helicopter across the Hungarian border, only a short distance away, to the Austrian town of Oberwart Schachen.

Dr. Imre Meleter sat in the rear between Ray Merrit and Tibor Arpad. Father Csoki, holding his wrist, to which a makeshift tourniquet had been hastily applied, was up front in the control seat next to the Death Merchant.

"Tch, tch, how God's seed could fall on such barren ground," the priest said, staring out the window.

Camellion didn't reply. He didn't know exactly what the priest meant and to what, or to whom, he was referring. The Death Merchant had other things on his mind, such as the conversation he had had with a certain Company man in Miami, Florida, five weeks earlier—*so far, we don't have too much to go on. We do know that Castro and his boys refer to the operation as Kronos. That's the code name for the whole deal. And we're positive they intend to blow up the locks of the Panama Canal. There's no doubt about it.*

Father Csoki turned and looked at the Death Merchant in the near-darkness. Only the red, blue, and green lights of the control panel illuminated Camellion and the priest's face.

"Thank God we won," Father Csoki sighed. "Thank the good Lord we're the victors."

"Yes, we're the victors, Father. We won," Camellion said automatically.

Yet there were never any real victors, only emptiness and the stupidity of a reality no one really understood.

Only emptiness and the next job: smashing the Kronos plot.

I'll be in the Caribbean within a month!